The Sword of Torrac

Book One in

The Pruglin Chronicles

D1739184

This book is dedicated to my Dad, the inspiration and motivation for everything I do. Without him, I would never have been born and couldn't have written this story.

Thanks, Dad. I love you.

Abby

CONTENTS

PROLOGUE

He looked up, surveying the bleak, wind-whipped landscape, his eyes burning from the glare of the sun on the sand and particles of dirt that the ruthless, ever-blowing wind had flung into his eyes. The same sight had met his gaze every time, but he knew that at some point this misery had to end. It could only last for so long, and he had already endured two days of it. He understood now why this wasteland was a place people did their best to avoid. No one with a grain of sanity would subject themselves to this torture without a very good reason. His was hardly a very good reason.

This time, though, when he looked up, something *was* different. In the hazy, far-off distance, he saw something, a blemish in the otherwise unbroken, featureless terrain. It was too far away to tell what it was, but there was something different on the horizon.

It didn't really matter, though. He wasn't looking for a flaw in the otherwise never-ending sameness. He was just looking for the end of his trek, the mountains that would signify he had reached Risclan Valley once again. There wasn't much he wouldn't give to see those mountains right now.

When he looked up several minutes later, the blemish in the wasteland had taken the distinct form of some kind of caravan. He knew that some merchants braved this hostile trail to circumvent the longer path around the mountainous terrain east of Etneog City. But after trying out the route for himself, he didn't know why anyone would take it, even if it was a shorter distance when coming from the northwestern corner of the valley.

He plodded forward, small puffs of dust rising from the sunbaked ground beneath his feet. The approaching caravan threw up larger clouds of debris, enough that he pitied those traveling in the convoy. The dust, added to the intense heat, would make an already unpleasant trip absolutely miserable.

As the caravan drew near, individual forms began to emerge from the general mass. Horses and their riders were scattered among wagons carrying supplies and whatever merchandise these particular traders specialized in. At the front of the procession, a man presided, riding on a black mount that was covered in grime and sweat but would have been a majestic animal under different conditions. The leader stopped as he reached the traveler, a warm smile showing from beneath the dirt on his face.

"Hello, traveler!" he said amiably, the smile widening. "It's good to see that someone else is crazy enough to brave this wilderness every once in a while. What brings you to the Syntor?"

The traveler smiled at the man's good humor. "I'm traveling to Pruglin City and was unwise enough to try this shortcut. On a map, it's a tempting way to avoid a week journeying through bogs and mountains, but the reality is slightly different."

The merchant laughed. "You'll get used to it, son. It just takes a few years. I've been traveling these roads since I was fifteen, and each trip gets a little easier. Another thirty years of practice like I've had will make the Syntor feel like home."

"Good to hear!" the traveler replied. "But I don't think I'll be here again. Next time I'll take the bogs and mountains."

The merchant chuckled again. "It's good to meet you, ..."

"Lesric," the traveler said, filling the blank. "And you, too."

"Well, I don't want to stop you, Lesric, but let me wish you a smooth and uneventful remainder of your journey. The pass to Pruglin isn't too much farther away. I think you'll survive."

Lesric laughed again. "I plan on it," he said. "And thanks for the encouragement. It's good to know the end is in sight." He liked the friendly trader with his cheerful personality and constant smile. Even the brief encounter with the man lifted his spirits considerably, and the knowledge that his trek was almost over had completed the motivation. He was ready for the last leg of the journey.

"A safe trip to you," the caravan leader said as he urged his horse forward.

"And you," Lesric said, beginning to walk again. As he passed the merchant, he saw the man look back to someone in the main body of the caravan and nod, probably a signal to start moving again. He veered to one side to pass by the edge of the caravan and kept his head down to keep the dust from entering his nose and eyes. The cloud kicked up by the many animals and vehicles of the caravan made him cough and sputter and blurred his vision, making it impossible to see very far into the moving column of men and beasts.

He was passing the first wagon when it happened. Strong hands gripped his arms and pinned them behind his back while something struck the backs of his knees, making them collapse beneath him. Before he knew what was happening, he was bound hand and foot and being dragged towards the wagons. He struggled, but his assailants, nearly invisible in the cloud of dust that was growing thicker by the moment, kept going, unhindered by his attempts to free himself.

Instinctively, he opened his mouth to shout for help, but closed it immediately as he got a mouthful of sand and dust. He knew it was useless, anyway. There was no one for miles around. He was on his own.

One of the men struck him in the face, and he felt blood trickling from his nose. The warm liquid mixed with the grime on his face, forming a sticky paste. He kicked back and was met with another blow to the face, this one harder than the previous. He tasted blood in his mouth now as well, and decided that resistance was going to get him nowhere. Now was not the time to fight.

The men dragged Lesric into the center of the caravan, then raised him to his feet. Before him stood a long line of prisoners, hands tied together and then to a central rope that ran down the line, connecting the unfortunate captives and destroying any hope of escape.

For the first time, he saw his two attackers clearly. They were both stocky, rough looking men. A grotesque scar stretched from the first man's hairline down to his left jaw. The other was distinguished by a crooked nose that had evidently been broken at least once before. Neither was the kind of man you wanted to mess around with.

The scarred man shoved him into the line while the other cut the rope around his ankles. He resisted the urge to kick the man as soon as his limbs were free. It wouldn't accomplish anything. Before he could think further, he was tied to the rope binding the prisoners together, squeezed in next to a middle-aged man with downcast eyes and a defeated stance.

"Move, you lazy scum!" one of the captors shouted, and from the back of the line, someone cracked a whip.

"What's going on?" Lesric asked, addressing the man beside him. The man refused to acknowledge him, not even looking up from the ground. "What's happening?" he repeated more frantically, instinctively knowing the answer but wanting confirmation.

"Shh!" the man snapped, finally meeting his gaze. "Just keep walking."

"Where are they taking us?" he asked.

"How should I know?" the man muttered, his gaze back on the ground. "You're a slave now. That's all I have to tell you."

"But..."

"But nothing. Stop talking." The man clamped his mouth shut, refusing to divulge any more information. As if in response, another whip cracked, much closer.

"No talking!" a gruff voice bellowed. "Keep moving!"

And realizing that resistance was futile, Lesric started walking and resigned himself to his fate.

CHAPTER 1

Two years later...

*T**hunk!* The arrow whistled through the air and embedded itself in the target, striking dead center. The archer smiled with satisfaction and placed another arrow on the string. An instant later, it was whizzing toward the mark, burying itself in the ripe green fruit and adding to the pincushion look the melon now presented. The missile collided with its target and joined the four-inch group the previous arrows had formed. The archer stepped back.

"Your turn," he said, motioning to the figure behind him. "Beat that."

"All right. I will."

The man, who was twenty with light brown hair and hazel eyes, stepped back, and a woman took his place. She looked the same age, and just a cursory glance revealed their close family resemblance. The sunlight reflected off her copper hair, and her green eyes flashed as she stepped forward to accept his challenge.

In a smooth motion, she pulled an arrow from the quiver on her back and placed it on the string, then pulled it back and took her aim. The arrow slammed into the target, this time a melon just to the right of the first. The corners of her lips twitched slightly, giving the faint impression of a smile, as she released another three arrows in quick succession. As the smile grew clearer, so did the frown on her brother's face, which turned to an all-out glare as the last bolt slammed into the target.

"Lianna, that's not even fair!" he protested as she stepped back and surveyed her handiwork. "You force me to do this and then you cheat on top of it! Unbelievable."

"Force? Cheat?" she exclaimed in mock anger. "I did nothing of the sort. You challenged me, remember? And how do you cheat in archery? I won fair and square."

"Bye," he said, turning towards the towering house twenty yards behind them. "I'll see you later."

"If you don't want me to confiscate your arrows, you might want to think about picking them up," she called over her shoulder as she started forward to retrieve her arrows.

A door slamming was her only reply, and Lianna laughed. It had been quite a while since she had shot with her brother, and she had thoroughly enjoyed the experience.

Ten minutes later, she tossed the arrows and quivers into the closet in her bedroom and turned back down the hall. Kedrin was climbing the stairs at the end of the hall.

"Good shooting, Kedrin," she said as he passed. "I'm going uptown, and I think I'll stop by the council house. Want to come?"

Kedrin shook his head. "I'm heading to the fletcher's to see if he has any bowstrings. Mine is fraying, and I need to replace it before it snaps."

"All right," she said. "If you want to test out your new string when you come back, let me know. I'd be glad to shoot with you again."

"No thanks," Kedrin replied, grinning. "I've been beat enough for one day."

Lianna headed for the front door and hurried down the steps, then started down the tree-lined lane toward the road. From here, it was almost impossible to tell that the house was in the middle of Pruglin City. Taran, her father, had built the manor for his country bride, Rilan, over twenty years ago when they were first married and moved to the city. The trees and vegetation that covered the huge, two-acre city plot made the residence a country paradise. This property was a haven of peace in a sometimes chaotic world, a refuge they could always retreat to.

Lianna turned onto the street and started heading for the city square. On a sunny spring afternoon like today, she knew that the marketplace would be teeming with farmers selling early produce, butchers their finest cuts of meat, and fisherman the day's catch from the Pruglin River, as well as the host of people coming to buy food and all the other miscellaneous items the market had to offer.

But right now, the market wasn't her destination. She was heading for the council house, the building where the eighteen members of the Pruglin Council met. Her father, as one of the councilors, was at a meeting right now, and she knew that the Council was currently having an hour intermission before getting back down to business.

They hadn't seen much of Taran lately, as the Council had been unusually busy sorting out a problem with a group of bandits in the north while simultaneously trying to manage relief efforts for victims of a flood in the west. It had meant late hours and long meetings for the Council, and whenever she did see Taran, his eyes were heavy and bloodshot, and all he wanted was rest. Things had calmed down slightly over the past few days, but she knew her presence would help cheer her father up.

The streets grew more congested as Lianna left the well-to-do residential area where her family lived and came to the business section of the city. As she neared the marketplace where the largest concentration of people was located, she had to push her way through the crowded streets, the cries of merchants advertising their wares ringing in her ears. Though the streets were still busy, she noticed that there were fewer people today than usual. The market was usually packed, making it difficult to get anywhere, especially at three o'clock on a spring afternoon. She wondered where all the people were.

Most of the marketplace was located in the city square, but it spilled out into the surrounding streets as well, and so far she hadn't made it past the outlying booths. As she emerged from River Street into the square, though, the concentration of people increased. The shadow of the bell tower, located on the opposite side of the open area, loomed over the vendors nearest it, and soon it would cover the far side of the square as well. She noticed a congregation of people at its base and wondered what was going on. They were clustered together, trying to get closer to something in the middle, but she couldn't tell what was drawing their attention.

She headed for the entrance to the Council house, located to the right of the people. She glanced over at the crowd once again as she reached the door, still not able to glimpse the object of their attention. Then she slipped inside.

The meeting room was at the end of the hall, the door still closed. The meeting had run late. Lianna stopped outside, but she didn't have to wait long. Less than a minute later, the double oak doors swung outward and a group of councilors exited, looking for a change of scene before the meeting resumed in an hour. They all appeared as exhausted as her father, ready for this mess to be over.

She slipped in and spotted her father at the far end of the table, talking to Mathalin, the head of the Council. At sixty-five with silver hair and a pronounced stoop, Mathalin was the oldest man on the Council. He was nodding in agreement to something Taran was saying.

Then Taran looked up and saw her. Surprise and pleasure mixed with the fatigue on his face. "Lianna! It's good to see you. What are you doing here?"

"Just coming to see you," she said, joining him at the far end of the table. "How are you doing?"

Taran exchanged a glance that she didn't understand with the older councilor. It contained some emotion she couldn't name; exasperation was the closest she could come.

"It's been quite the day," Taran said, shaking his head. "We were about an hour late starting. My horse went lame and the market was busier than I anticipated, so I showed up a little late, but it didn't matter. I got here just before we actually got down to business. Some fool had come in claiming that he had been kidnapped by Lentours in the Syntor Wasteland and that they are building some impregnable fortress on the far side."

He chuckled. "And if that's not crazy enough, he

claimed that Torrac was leading them and is planning an invasion."

"He what?" she asked, not even knowing what to say. "Lentours? Torrac? We're both talking about the Lentour kingdom we wiped out in the war fifty years ago, right? It sounds to me like someone got too interested in their history lesson and went crazy." She stopped. "Lentours?"

"Yes," Taran said, overwhelmed by everything that was going on and the fact that some fool had wasted an hour of their day. "Lentours." He shook himself out of his reverie and focused on the present. "But as crazy as that seems, though, that's not the strangest part."

"What do you mean, that's not the strangest part?" Lianna asked. She didn't know what could be stranger than the fact that someone expected the Pruglin Council to believe that the Lentour Kingdom, a former continent superpower that had been wiped out half a century ago, had been resurrected and was coming to conquer them.

"He was looking for me," Taran said.

"What do you mean, he was looking for you?" she asked, not comprehending.

"I told you I was late to the meeting," Taran said.

"Yes," she said slowly.

Taran looked at Mathalin, and the older man took over the story. "He showed up just as we were about to start. He burst right in here unannounced and said he had an urgent message for someone named Taran, who he had heard was a member of the Council. When he heard that Taran wasn't here, he asked where to find him.

"There was obviously something different about this man; it's not just everyone who barges into the

Pruglin Council meeting and demands to know where one of the councilors is. So I didn't tell him. We didn't even acknowledge Taran's existence. We just politely asked him to leave. Instead, he started raving about the Lentours and Torrac, and when Taran showed up, I don't think he even noticed. He kept insisting every few minutes that he needed to find Taran, but we never said anything. Like your father said, it took us an hour to get him out of here. Before he was through, getting rid of him would literally have taken dragging him out and locking the doors, and even then, I'm not sure we could have kept him out."

"So how did you?" Lianna asked.

"We finally told him that we would think about what he had to say and asked him to leave so we could get on with the meeting," Mathalin said.

"And we thought about it all right," Taran said. "Although maybe not quite the way he was wanting."

"It sounds to me like the crazy story of some lunatic," Lianna said.

But both men shook their heads. "He didn't act like a lunatic," Taran said. "He was desperate for our help."

"He was the sanest lunatic I ever saw," Mathalin agreed. "There was nothing about him to make him seem crazy. He acted like a perfectly sane man with an important message to deliver. The only thing abnormal was the message itself."

"So was he lying?" Lianna asked.

"Why?" Mathalin asked. "What would he gain from it? Telling us that an empire that has been extinct for fifty years is now coming to destroy us isn't going to do anything for him."

"Then what?" Lianna asked. "I don't understand."

"Right now, I don't think any of us do," Taran said. "We were supposed to be working on sending relief to the victims of that flood out west, but it was pretty hard to stay on subject today. Everyone was too focused on what must have been the ravings of a madman to concentrate on the important topic."

"Mathalin!" A relatively new councilor whose name Lianna didn't remember burst through the door.

"Yes?" Mathalin asked, maneuvering around Taran and Lianna to face him.

"I think you need to come see this," the man said. "Taran, you'd better come too." The look on his face said that whatever was going on was urgent.

CHAPTER 2

L ianna followed her father and the councilors out of the building. The man who had come for Mathalin stopped outside the door and pointed towards the same gathering of people she had seen when she entered the building ten minutes ago. The only difference was that in that short time, the crowd had grown by at least fifty percent.

"What's going on?" Taran asked, pushing to the front of the knot of councilors to stand beside Mathalin and the younger man who had brought the message.

"It's Lesric," the councilor said. "The madman. He gave up on the Council and decided to address the people instead."

"This isn't too difficult, gentlemen," Mathalin said. "All we have to do is arrest him under charges of disturbing the peace. It's as simple as that."

But the other councilors didn't seem so sure.

"There are several hundred people listening to him, spellbound, and more are coming all the time," Taran said. "That's not normal. I don't know how he's managed to get that many people to take him seriously, but he did, and they don't look like they're about to let us arrest him."

"I'll handle this." Lianna recognized the speaker as Ildug, a councilor in his mid-forties with a receding hairline and salt-and-pepper goatee. "I can get him away from the crowd to arrest him if I have to."

"Go ahead," Mathalin said. "I don't think anyone has a better idea."

"Mathalin, Taran, would you mind coming with me? I think the presence of three important councilors will ensure that this goes as smoothly as possible," Ildug said.

"What exactly are you planning on doing?" Lianna heard Taran ask as the trio began walking towards the crowd. Then their voices were lost in the confusion of sounds that filled the square.

Lianna edged closer to the crowd, not understanding how the wild story her father had told her could merit this much attention from this many people. There was more to the situation than first met the eye; that much was obvious. She hoped it would prove to be nothing more than some raving madman who had managed to convince a few people that his story could be true. Hopefully Ildug would be able to get the situation under control.

As Lianna mingled with the onlookers on the edge of the crowd, the same story her father had told her drifted back over the heads of the onlookers. From where she stood, she couldn't hear everything that was being said, but she could make out enough to get the general gist of what the man was saying. She strained her neck, trying to see exactly what was going on, but too many heads blocked her vision. She hated being blind to what was happening, and her curiosity took over. She began weaving her way through the crowd, searching for the three councilors and the man who had caused such an uproar in the city today.

Finally, Lianna saw them, three heads moving through the crowd toward a figure in the center. Although she realized that he was the one who was the focus of the crowd, she still couldn't make out anything that was being said. All she could see was a man in his mid-twenties, his hair tousled by the wind, his tunic worn, ragged, and caked with dust. Despite his disheveled appearance, there was something captivating about him. The tone of his voice, the expression on his face, the look in his eyes, all said that he believed what he was saying and everyone else needed to as well.

Lentours, Lianna thought, staring open-mouthed as she heard the word for the first time. *He really does think the Lentours are back.* It was absurd, but frightening at the same time. She had no idea how this man could have gathered an audience this big with his ridiculous story, and it was rather disturbing. This could prove more serious than it had sounded at first.

"Lesric!"

It was Ildug's voice. Lianna craned her neck to see what was going on, not wanting to miss anything. All heads turned to face the councilor, and she felt a chill run down her spine. She didn't know what, but something wasn't quite right.

"Yes?" the man responded, turning to face the three councilors.

"As member of the Council of Pruglin and head of the Pruglin militia, I am taking you into custody for the good of the city," Ildug said, stepping closer.

"You're arresting me?" Lesric asked, his voice carrying through the square. "There's no need for the fancy language, Councilor. I know what you're saying. I'm a crazy man and need to be kept under control. I'm a threat to the city, a disturber of the peace, and need to be disposed of as such."

"You seem to know how this works," Ildug said. "Now I'm going to ask that you kindly step down from that box and come with me."

"And if I say no?" The voice was calm and smooth, flowing like honey.

The crowd was suddenly silent. They stood quietly, waiting, listening, wondering what would happen. The tension, already palpable, intensified with every passing moment.

Lianna wished she could see the councilors' faces more clearly. Ildug's was stony as he looked at the young man who was daring to defy him. Mathalin and Taran were obscured by the crowd, which was becoming increasingly restless and threatening

"If you say no," Ildug said, undeterred, "I'm going to have to use force."

"All right," Lesric said. "No."

"Lesric!" Mathalin exclaimed, joining Ildug. "I'm adding my authority as head of the Pruglin Council and giving you one last chance. Come with us or face the consequences."

Lesric's face made his response obvious. He wasn't backing down. He was determined, and it was going to take more than the threats of the Pruglin Council to make him retreat now.

Ildug glanced back into the crowd and three men stepped forward. "Seize him," he said calmly.

The men stepped toward Lesric, but that was as far as they got. At that point, the control of the councilors vanished and the mob took over. Hundreds of people surged forward, the closest grabbing Ildug's men and pulling them away from Lesric. Angry shouts filled the square as the people protested Ildug's attempt to arrest the lunatic whose story they seemed to believe.

Ildug's voice was lost in the din as he tried in vain to regain control of the situation. He had crossed the line, and now he was paying the consequences.

Then a voice sounded above the clamor. "Stop!" Lesric raised his hands in the air, trying to quiet the mass of angry onlookers.

The sound died away instantly and the crowd fell back, clearing the area around Lesric, Mathalin, Taran, and Ildug. The three soldiers now stood in the front of the crowd, afraid to come any closer to Lesric and the councilors.

With the shifting of the crowd, Lianna's location had changed, and now she had a front row seat.

"I'm not about to be arrested," Lesric said calmly when the noise had died down, addressing the three councilors. "I don't have time for that. My mission is too urgent. I would be happy to talk, though. That is why I'm here."

"Very well," Ildug agreed, shrugging. "Let's talk. Come with us to the Council house and we'll see if we can have a more civilized conversation."

"I'm not going to fall for that," Lesric said. "As soon as those doors close, you're going to try to arrest me again. It's as simple as that."

"Lesric…"

"Listen, I'm not here to cause trouble. I'm here to save lives—yours and those of the thousands of people of Risclan Valley. I know you think I'm crazy, and frankly, I don't blame you. But I do have proof. If you would just help me, I could give all the evidence you need. I have to find someone named Taran. He will tell you that I'm telling the truth."

Lianna laughed as her father snorted in amusement. *A likely story,* she thought as Taran regained control of himself.

He exchanged a glance with Mathalin and stepped forward. "I'm Taran," he said. "But I'm not about to verify your story. I'm going to need just as much convincing as everyone else."

"Will you?" Lesric asked, stepping off the box and taking a few steps towards him. "Does the name *Oslir* mean anything to you?"

Taran took an involuntary half step back. "Where did you hear that name?"

"So you do recognize it?"

"Yes, I recognize it," Taran said. "But he's been dead for twenty years."

"No," Lesric said, "he hasn't. He sent me to you."

"That's impossible," Taran said. "He was lost in the Syntor twenty years ago."

"Exactly," Lesric said, smiling. "Lost. But not dead. Just like I was lost in the Syntor two years ago. Just like thousands of people have disappeared in that wilderness over the last half a century."

Lesric knew he had their attention.

"It's a trap," he continued. "You know the stories; dust storms consuming whole caravans, huge monsters coming up out of the wilderness, wild men appearing from nowhere and slaughtering everyone. 'Stories,' that's the key word. That's all they are. Yes, the Syntor is a dangerous place and a few caravans do fall prey to various natural threats. But not the vast majority."

Lesric stopped, letting the crowd hang on his

words. "Do you want to know what happens to them? Slavers. Torrac's slavers have been patrolling the wasteland for half a century, capturing everyone and sending them back to join his massive force of workers. He's inflated his army of slaves to immense proportions, and at the same time ensured that we don't discover the kingdom he's building just a few hundred miles away."

He let what he had said sink in, then continued.

"No, Taran. Your brother is not dead. He's the organizer of the rebellion at Cortim Castle, and the one who got me out so I could deliver the message. Your brother is alive."

"How do you know Oslir's my brother?" Taran asked. His eyes were wide and piercing, and he studied Lesric carefully, searching for any sign of deceit. It didn't seem like there was any way the man could be telling the truth, but someone had to have told him, and Taran didn't know who it could be. His brother had disappeared in the Syntor Wasteland two decades ago, but Taran didn't ever talk about it. It was something very few people were aware of, and the fact that this stranger was one of them was alarming.

"What's it going to take for me to convince you?" Lesric asked. "He told me, that's how. Do you need me to describe him? He's below average height. Piercing brown eyes. Black hair."

"What about his hand?" Taran asked.

Lesric didn't have to think about it. "He was missing the little finger of his right hand. I assumed it had happened more recently, while he was working for the Lentours, but apparently not. Is that enough, or do you need more?"

Taran looked at him, then nodded slowly. "That's

enough. I believe you, Lesric. I apologize for doubting you."

"Taran, are you crazy?" Ildug interrupted. "This is insane! There are no Lentours! Torrac is dead!"

"No," Taran replied. He had a faraway look in his eyes, and he was shaking his head slowly, trying to take in what he was hearing. "He's telling the truth. There's no other way he could give such a perfect description."

"I believe you," Mathalin said. "If Taran says you're telling the truth, I believe you."

Ildug stared at Taran for several seconds. Then he nodded. "All right, Lesric. I believe you, too."

"Then I would be glad to talk in the Council house," Lesric said. "That's why I'm here—to warn the districts and ensure that this storm doesn't catch us unawares."

"Let's talk," Mathalin said, turning to lead the way to the Council house. Then they were gone, and the crowd, suddenly finding nothing to hold their attention, began to disperse.

Lianna hurried to run her errands and get the groceries back before the cook needed them for dinner.

CHAPTER 3

Lentours.

The war had begun fifty-seven years ago, when Torrac, ruler of the Lentour kingdom to the east, had launched his invasion. His ruthless men had marched through the surrounding lands, slaughtering innocent people by the tens of thousands in their brutal conquest. But although other lands were tempting additions to Torrac's savage realm of power, the real prize he sought, the one that shone brighter than all the others, the finishing jewel to Torrac's glittering crown of conquests, lay further to the west.

Risclan Valley.

At the time, Risclan had been the strongest power on the continent, rivalled only by Torrac and the Lentours themselves. Its natural assets were immense, including fertile ground, vast timber tracts, and extensive mining of coal and precious metals in the north. It was the trophy of trophies, and Torrac was determined to have it.

A standoff had ensued lasting three and a half years, during which Lentour forces hit various areas of Risclan's eastern and southern borders, searching for weak points while doing as much damage as they could in small raids. The districts resisted valiantly, but the hit-and-run approach took a toll. Farms and small villages were no longer safe, and as they were abandoned, food became scarce.

But it wasn't enough. Risclan's people were tough and proud, and even with a shortage of food and the constant threat of invasion, they resisted with everything they had in them. Weakening the valley into surrender wasn't working, so Torrac changed his approach.

The first region hit by the storm was Forsid, the southernmost district. The defenders fought valiantly to guard the southern entrance to the valley, guarding the pass with a barrier of human defenders. But the invading force was too great. Several hundred soldiers broke through and marched up to Pruglin, wreaking havoc as they went. At the same time, half a dozen smaller groups of men braved the wrath of the Syntor Wasteland and managed to enter the valley from the desert side to the east. Pruglin was surrounded and stood on the brink of collapse. Forsid was all but overwhelmed. Brodalith, just north of Pruglin in the center of the valley, had sent all its troops to Pruglin's defense when yet another host succeeded in entering the valley through the Syntor. They besieged the city, and, with its defenders absent, it was mere hours from defeat. Torrac had as good as won.

And then, just before the three besieged districts completely collapsed, help arrived. Armies from Etneog and Qatran had come to the relief of undefended Brodalith, then marched down through the valley towards Pruglin and Forsid. The Lentours caught wind of their approach and abandoned Pruglin, gathering all their troops around Forsid. Risclan followed suit, and the result was the most gruesome bloodbath in Risclan history.

Thirty thousand brave men died that day.

RisclanValley's strength and prestige were crushed. What had once been the undisputed power of the continent was now an inconsequential group of five districts, isolated, crippled, and effectually cut off from the rest of the world. Its might and glory would never return.

But the sacrifice was worth it. Among those who perished in the battle was Torrac, along with legions of his brutal fighters. With the end of the Battle of Forsid, the Lentour kingdom had been vanquished. Though several evil leaders had risen from its ruins and attempted to rally the survivors, it was useless. Risclan hadn't stopped with the death of Torrac, and went on to eradicate every trace of the Lentour kingdom. Ten years after Torrac's death, the Lentours were a legend of the past.

And yet now some stranger had appeared claiming that Torrac was alive, nearly sixty years after the man had first become a force of destruction in the far off Lentour kingdom. Lianna was overwhelmed by it all, and still trying to take it in.

"Lianna!"

Lianna looked around, trying to locate and identify the speaker. It took her several seconds to see him standing across the street. "Kedrin? What are you doing here?" she shouted as she crossed the busy street.

"Were you at the square?" Kedrin asked, getting right to the point.

"Yes. I take it you were too?"

He nodded. "What do you think?"

"I think he's lying," she said. "I don't know how he could know to look for Father, and I really don't know how he knew about Uncle Oslir, but there's just no way his story could be true."

"There's no way it could not be true," Kedrin countered. "I was walking through the square when he pulled me aside and asked if I knew where to find Councilor Taran. He said that he had been told to go to the Council house, but that Father wasn't there."

Lianna interrupted him. "So you saw him before he talked with Father?"

"Yes," Kedrin continued. "I asked what he wanted, and while he told me his story, a crowd began to gather. Then Father showed up and everything came out about Oslir. Just listening to him talk was convincing, even if the story seemed absurd, but now that there's a good reason to believe him, I'm pretty sure he's telling the truth."

"So you're telling me that you think Torrac and the Lentours are coming to annihilate us?"

"Father believes him."

"That doesn't make it true."

"How else do you want to explain it?" her brother asked. "Did you actually listen to Lesric? Talking to him alone nearly convinced me, and Father took away the rest of my doubts. Yes, it seems unbelievable, but what other explanation is there?"

"If you want to believe that there's an army coming to destroy us, go ahead," she replied. "But it's going to take more than some stranger saying so to convince me."

"That's fine," Kedrin said. "But when the Lentours show up, don't say I didn't tell you."

"I won't," she grinned. "But when nothing comes of this, just remember who was right."

"I'm going home," Kedrin said. "The fletcher didn't have any bowstrings and said to come back tomorrow, so I have nothing else to do. Are you coming or not?"

"I have to pick up some meat for supper, but you're welcome to come along if you want," Lianna said. "It will only take a few minutes."

"Oh, all right. I guess I can come to keep you in line," Kedrin said. "You need a lot of looking after."

The wooden door creaked as Lianna entered the butcher's shop, and the meat seller looked up.

"Kedrin and Lianna! It's good to see you!" the butcher said, a broad grin on his face. "What can I get for you today?"

Five minutes later, they were heading back down the cobblestone street in the direction of home, Kedrin carrying the package of beef under his arm. As they entered the square, Lianna noticed a small knot of men leaving the Council house.

"Looks like the meeting's over," Kedrin said. "I see Father. Let's go see if he wants to come home with us."

"All right," Lianna said, following her brother toward the group of councilors.

Of the seven men in front of the building, she was able to identify Taran, Mathalin, Ildug, and, of course, Lesric, the man whose story, in a single afternoon, had become the topic of excited and alarmed conversation of a city of thousands. She still didn't buy his story, but the demeanor of the six councilors suggested that the Pruglin Council did. They had chosen to believe Lesric's story, and they would reap the consequences, whether good or bad.

"Tomorrow morning at eight?" Taran asked as they approached.

Mathalin nodded. "We'll see you then."

"Kedrin, Lianna!" Taran exclaimed, seeing them approaching. "What are you doing back here?"

"We're heading home," Kedrin said. "We saw you out here and wanted to know if you were done and wanted to come with us."

"I'm glad you stopped. I was just leaving."

He looked at his colleagues. "I'll see you tomorrow," he said to the councilors. He began to walk away, then remembered something and turned around. "Lesric, do you have anywhere to stay?"

Lesric shook his head. "I'll find somewhere," he said. "I'm sure there's an inexpensive inn nearby where I can stay for tonight at least. I'll try to find a more long-term place, maybe a boarding house, tomorrow."

"No," Taran said. "Come with us. We have plenty of room, and we would be happy to have you."

"No, I..." he began.

Taran didn't let him finish. "Don't argue with me. Please join us, at least for tonight. You can repay me by telling me everything you know about my brother. I want to hear it all."

Lesric studied him briefly, then nodded. "Thank you," he said. "I would be glad to accept your invitation."

Taran smiled. "Good! By the way, this is my son and daughter, Kedrin and Lianna. And this is Lesric," he said, addressing the two of them.

"Good to meet you," Lesric said cheerfully. His warm smile was infectious, and Lianna could already understand the effect his open, friendly demeanor had had on the crowd. Though she still didn't believe his story, she could see why so many others did.

As they walked, Taran plied Lesric with questions about his time at Cortim Castle. Lianna listened silently, and the more time elapsed, the more her conviction that Lesric was either wrong or lying began to dissolve. The picture Lesric painted was too full, too detailed, and too consistent to be either a lie or the ravings of a madman. Either he was the best liar she had ever seen, or he was telling the truth.

By the time they neared home, a vague fear, born of the realization that the story she had heard was indeed true, was creeping into Lianna's heart. She didn't know how it could be true, but after listening to Lesric, she didn't know how it could be anything else. Relief swept over her as they turned onto the familiar tree-lined lane that led up to the brightly lit, inviting home. Here she felt secure, safe from any Lentour raiders roaming the Syntor Wilderness in search of slaves to do their dark lord's will.

Lesric gasped at the sight of the house and the wealth it represented. A stately building, it was smaller and less elaborate than the homes of most of the councilors, but still impressive. He obviously wasn't used to this kind of wealth, and had probably never dreamed of actually staying at a house like this. His capture by slave traders while crossing the Syntor Wasteland told Lianna that he was probably from the mountains of Etneog, a fact that explained why city life and wealth were a completely new experience for him.

Rilan rounded the corner just as they stepped into the entryway of the house. "Taran!" she exclaimed. "It's good to see you. The meeting went long."

Taran nodded toward their guest. "Rilan, this is Lesric. Lesric, this is Rilan, my wife."

"It's good to meet you," Rilan smiled. "Welcome to our home."

"Lesric is the reason the meeting went late," Taran continued, the grin on his face showing that he was teasing, "but I think when you hear why, you'll agree it was worth it."

"Oh?" Rilan queried.

"Try not to laugh at me too hard," Lesric said, also smiling.

* * * * *

"So you really mean the Lentours are building an empire across the Syntor," Rilan concluded, shaking her head, as they sat down in the living room after a hearty meal. "Who would have thought that day would come?"

"How long has it been since you left Cortim?" Taran asked.

"Two months," Lesric said. "It took me that long just to get out of Milsad Forest and cross the Syntor again. I had to hide from everyone I saw, and scavenged for food on the way."

"This fortress," Taran continued. "Cortim Castle. What exactly is it?"

"Cortim Castle," Lesric began slowly, as if repulsed even by the memory, "is the strongest, most fortified stronghold imaginable, as close to impregnable as it gets. Massive towers, bulwarks—you name it. It was built on an island in the middle of the lake, and the island itself is a fortress. The castle is on a plateau surrounded by a steep precipice. The only access is a road winding up the face of the cliff, and it's designed so that anyone coming up can easily be picked off by archers from the fortress walls." His voice trailed off as he remembered.

"The gate is also uphill, making it even harder to approach," he continued, "and the walls are thick and tall. And they're getting thicker and taller by the day under the labor of hundreds of slaves—like Oslir. It's the culmination of decades of labor and a work of strategic genius."

Quiet filled the room as his listeners processed the information.

"So it's impregnable?" Kedrin asked, breaking the silence.

"Nothing's impregnable," Lesric said.

"Then there is a weakness?" Taran queried.

"Somewhere," Lesric said, nodding in agreement. "Everything has a weakness, somewhere. Some weaknesses are just less consequential than others."

"You don't sound very hopeful about capturing this fortress," Taran observed.

"The fortress isn't the problem," Lesric explained. "Not at this point, at least. It's the men in the fortress that are the problem. The fortress isn't going to come and slaughter us if we don't watch our backs."

He thought for a moment, then continued, "We're hardly ready for an offensive move at this point in the game. Risclan Valley has grown lax and unprepared. The war robbed us of our strength, and we've been fading for the last half a century. We're not ready for another conflict. That's why so many men risked their lives to get me out of Lentour domain. They knew that our people wouldn't stand a chance if they weren't warned, and someone had to get out."

He stared into the distance, not speaking for several seconds. "At least three of them gave their lives. I'm sure more were discovered later, but three were dead before I was even off the island."

"I've heard enough stories to know what the Lentours did to rebels in the past, and from what I've heard this afternoon, they haven't changed," Taran said. "I know what you risked by escaping, and on behalf of everyone in Risclan Valley, I want to thank you."

"Anyone would have done it," Lesric said.

And something about the way he said it convinced Lianna that what he had said, all of it, was the truth.

CHAPTER 4

T hree days after Lesric's arrival, Pruglin was not the same city it had been. Hundreds of men had already volunteered for the army that the Council was scrambling to organize. Messengers had been sent to the other districts to warn them of the looming danger. The city was a buzz of activity as people who had known peace for half a century prepared for war.

As preparations moved forward, Taran helped Lesric assemble a special reconnaissance unit to travel to Cortim Castle, the only Lentour base whose exact location was known. Kedrin immediately volunteered to join the expedition, and was accepted nearly as fast. He eagerly trained with the other few members that had been chosen so far.

In all the bustle and commotion, Lianna remained unnoticed at home. The chaos that held most of the city in its grip hadn't affected her. Her life was all but unchanged.

This afternoon, the sunshine and warm weather outside was irresistible, and Lianna was unable to stay indoors.

Archery had been her favorite hobby for many years. On her tenth birthday, her father had given her a small, delicately fashioned recurve bow. Though lightweight, the sturdy maple weapon was no toy, but a tool that, combined with her unusual aptitude, enabled her to develop the skill of archery to a level astonishing for one her age. That small bow had long since been replaced by a heavier but no less graceful and beautiful bow, and with it, she honed her skills to perfection.

It was natural that target practice was the first thing that came to her mind, so now she stood behind the house shooting. Her target was series of rings, painted on a piece of canvas and tacked to a box. The bullseye and the ring encircling it had taken on the appearance of a pincushion early on in the session, and now bristled with arrows.

She placed her last arrow on the string with the ease of many years' practice, took her aim, and released the projectile to hurtle through the air, only to come to an abrupt stop as it slammed through the canvas and stuck there, quivering. She surveyed the overall result, then nodded in satisfaction and stepped forward to retrieve her arrows.

Someone started clapping from behind her. "Lianna!" her father called. "I've been so busy lately that I haven't had a chance to see your skills in action for a long time. That was outstanding!"

Lianna turned toward the voice. Taran, Rilan, Kedrin, and Lesric stood watching on the back porch, and from what she saw, Lianna guessed that they had been there for several minutes.

"Thank you, Father," she replied, smiling, and turned again to recover the arrows.

"Now you see why I refuse to shoot with her anymore," Kedrin muttered to the others, shaking his head. "I tried the other day, but I'm done! It's not even fair."

"Aha! You finally admit it!" Lianna said triumphantly over her shoulder. "You've been denying that for two years, Brother."

"I didn't mean..." Kedrin began, but it was too late. The sibling rivalry that existed between them was strong, and he had just given her a weapon that she was going to be able to use against him for a long time.

"Don't even try, Kedrin. We all heard it." Lianna grinned impishly as she removed the arrows from the shredded piece of fruit. It would take Kedrin a long time to live this down.

She pulled the last arrow out, stood up, and headed back to the house, slinging the quiver over her shoulder as she walked. Kedrin shot an angry scowl in her direction, and she smiled sweetly back at him.

"She has you this time, Kedrin," Taran laughed. "There's no denying it. Just accept the inevitable."

Kedrin's reply was cut off as Lianna slipped inside and hurried upstairs to stow her bow and arrows in her bedroom closet.

As she made her way back down the stairs, Taran and Lesric passed, heading for the front door. She guessed they were on their way to yet another meeting at the Council house. It seemed like those were always going on now, whenever the councilors weren't busy working to pull Pruglin's military from the weak state that had been the consequence of five decades of neglect and disuse. Half a century of peace had resulted in everything related to the military falling into complete disarray, and they were, in effect, starting over from scratch. The Council was kept very busy.

"They off to another meeting?" she asked as her mother rounded the corner.

Rilan nodded. "It seems like it never ends. When

you consider that this time three days ago, Lesric was under arrest for disturbing the peace, it's a little over-whelming to think that because of his warning, we are now preparing for war with a kingdom we thought was vanquished fifty years ago."

Lianna had to agree.

That night, Taran, Lesric, and Kedrin gathered around a map, discussing the reconnaissance mission that was to depart shortly. Lianna knew that, like every other map in Risclan Valley, this piece of paper showed just a vague depiction of the western edge of the Syntor Wasteland and beyond that, an empty void. No one in Risclan knew exactly what was on the other side of the Syntor, not since the end of the war. After ensuring, or at least, doing their best to ensure, that the Lentour king-dom would never be able to rise again, Risclan had re-treated into a shell, and no one knew exactly what now lay beyond the Syntor's fierce domain.

No one, that is, except Lesric, the first one in decades to cross the desert and come back alive. He pointed to it now, touching various places past the sec-tion marked 'Uncharted' and commenting on what he had learned on his journey. Taran nodded as he spoke, inter-jecting remarks every now and then, but mostly listen-ing attentively to what the younger man was saying.

It had become obvious over the past three days that Taran took Lesric's opinions very seriously, and he had seen to it that Lesric played an integral part in the decision making of the Council. Lianna had heard him tell Rilan, "That man has wisdom beyond his years. Not everyone has the ingenuity and the courage to do what he did." Lianna knew that it wasn't just anyone who could earn her father's esteem like Lesric had, and she respected that.

"So how many more do you need?" Taran asked, loudly enough that for the first time in the conversation Lianna was able to hear from across the room.

Lesric pursed his lips and stared into the distance in concentration. Then he spoke. "At least two," he said. "At least. We have to be able to defend ourselves, and four people isn't enough. I would like an archer or two as well. That's a skill that will come in very useful."

"Hey, Lianna, want to come to Cortim Castle?" Kedrin asked. "We all know you know how to shoot."

Lianna glared at him. "No. I don't."

"Don't know how to shoot?" Kedrin asked in feigned shock. "Don't lie to me!"

"You know what I'm talking about," Lianna said, rolling her eyes. "And you know how to shoot, too, remember? According to you, you would beat me every time we competed if I didn't cheat."

She smiled, knowing that Kedrin had just been cornered. He was persistent, but she had put him in a position where he had to either back down or press his point by admitting she was better than him. She knew the second alternative wouldn't even cross his mind, which meant that he was going to have to back down.

"Two is better than one," Kedrin said, sidestepping her point in a way she hadn't anticipated.

"Kedrin, I'm not going to Cortim Castle. That's all there is to it, so you might as well forget it."

"If you change your mind," Lesric said, "you would be a welcome addition to the team. I've never seen anyone who can shoot as well as you."

"I appreciate the compliment, but I'm still not going on a dangerous mission beyond the ends of the known world," Lianna said. "Danger and me, we don't mix. I'll stay home and do anything I can from here. I'm just not going to Cortim Castle."

"I think I'll keep working on you. I rather like this idea," Kedrin said. "You really should think about it, Lianna."

"You know that's not going to work," Lianna replied firmly. "You seem to have forgotten how very stubborn I can be when I want to, and this is one of those times. You're not going to change my mind."

Kedrin gave her a *'we shall see'* look, but she just smiled. *Yes,* she thought. *We will.*

* * * * *

The day before the departure of the expedition, a flurry of preparations were underway. Kedrin and Lesric were busy all morning, taking care that every detail was in place for the next day. Not wanting to be a hindrance, Lianna kept out of the way as much as possible, and when Alssa, her cousin and best friend, stopped by, they stayed outside.

Like Lianna, Alssa was an avid archer, and it didn't take long for them to pull out their bows for a friendly competition in the backyard. Lianna won, as always, but they were just shooting for fun, and Alssa didn't care.

Alssa was about to leave when Kedrin appeared on the back porch. "Lianna! I was looking for you!"

"What is it?" Lianna asked as Kedrin hurried down the steps.

"I have a favor to ask," Kedrin said slowly.

"Yes?" Lianna prompted when he didn't continue.

"We have a problem," he began, choosing his words with caution. "Lesric..."

"What about Lesric?" Lianna prodded when he

trailed off yet again.

"He's still short on people and doesn't have any archers for the mission. He asked me if I knew of anyone else to ask and I..."

"No," she interrupted. "Don't even go any farther. I'm not going."

"But, Lianna! You have to! They're considering calling off the mission! There are only four of us, including Lesric. None of them are archers."

"I thought you were the accomplished archer whose skills far surpass mine," Lianna said sarcastically. "You're plenty."

"Lianna, I'm being serious. You know your skills far surpass mine. I'm not an archer, not one worthy of the name. Lesric is in the house right now talking to Father and Mathalin about calling off the mission. We can't let that happen. We need that information, but it's not worth jeopardizing lives and the success of the mission by going without the necessary manpower. You have to come."

"Kedrin, I told you a week ago, and I'm telling you now. I'm not going."

Then Alssa broke in. "What if I go, too?"

CHAPTER 5

"I can't believe I'm doing this right now," Lianna said as she trudged along River Street toward the gate that opened by the Pruglin River. The gray pre-dawn light illuminated the frames of the buildings lining either side of the street, but that was all. A slight fog blanketing the city further obscured her already limited vision.

"I told you you were going to come," Kedrin said. "You shouldn't have doubted me. You know I'm always right."

"Always right?" Lianna asked, letting out a snort of amusement. "Is that so?"

"I was this time," Kedrin said.

Walking in front of them, Lesric laughed. "You two are mean."

"Would you let your sister sass you around like that?" Kedrin asked.

"No," Lesric said. "If I had a sister, I probably wouldn't. But being that I don't, there's really no telling for sure."

"No sister?" Kedrin asked. "Lucky."

Lianna turned on her brother. "You're evil!" she exclaimed, slapping him on the arm.

Then they reached the gate, the rendezvous that the team had agreed upon. They were the first ones there.

Lianna shivered, looking up at the murky sky and wondering why she had ever agreed to do this. Misgivings had plagued her ever since she said goodbye to her parents and stepped out the front door twenty minutes ago, and the more time passed, the more certain she became that this had been a very bad decision.

Less than a minute later, a figure emerged from the fog. Alssa greeted them cheerfully as she reached them. Within the next few minutes, Leumas and Elyk, two of Kedrin's acquaintances who made up the remainder of the group, had arrived. As they stood around, looking at Lesric and waiting for him to lead the way, Lianna felt all her reservations about this expedition welling up inside of her and threatening to overwhelm her. She looked at the looming gate before them and what lay beyond, thought of the miles of danger they were about to face, and wondered what had ever possessed her to agree to do this. Suddenly, she didn't know if she could.

Lesric looked them over, doing a mental head-count to double check that everyone was there. Then he nodded. "All right, then. Let's go."

As the sun's first rays peeked over the mountains, Lesric led them through the gateway and into the vast world beyond the confines of Pruglin City. Lianna had to take a deep breath as she took the first step that plunged her into a mission she had never wanted to be a part of. She forced herself to put one foot in front of the other. She was committed now. There was no turning back.

The road kept to the Pruglin River at first, and as they walked along its banks and drank in the sights and sounds, the birds in the trees and on the water, the deer in the forest, and the rabbits that scampered away as they approached, Lianna wondered if this was all just some crazy dream. Everything was so peaceful, so quiet. To think that after all these decades war might be coming was a thought almost too hard to believe.

After a mile, the road left the river and wound through the trees. They walked until midday, when Lesric called a halt for lunch. Except for the birds chirping nearby and the breeze that rustled through the boughs of the trees above and the dead leaves on the ground, all was silent. No one spoke until Lesric stood up and slung his pack over his shoulder once again.

"Let's keep moving," he said, looking up at the sky to judge the time. "We can get in another six hours before the sun goes down."

They camped that night by a small stream. Lianna shot two rabbits, which, when roasted over the fire and supplemented by the biscuits each had packed, made an excellent supper. No one felt like staying up long after the meal was over. They would have to leave by first light, and there was no point in staying awake when they could be getting needed rest. Lianna went to sleep to the sound of the brook and the occasional hoot of an owl.

For the next few days, they continued to trek east towards the Syntor Wasteland. Early mornings, late nights, and long miles drained Lianna's strength faster than she had expected. She wasn't looking forward to reaching the infamous wasteland.

It was several days later, when the trees began to thin out and the air became hot and dry, that the party had their first taste of danger. Lianna knew they were getting close to the Syntor, and she also knew that the desert was the real beginning of the perils they would face. But she hadn't expected danger yet, and she hadn't expected it to appear in the form that it did.

It was mid morning, and they were plodding through the forest when Kedrin suddenly stopped. "What was that?" he asked, facing a thicket on their left. His hand hovered near his sword, and his body was tense as he looked for whatever it was that had caused the alarm.

"What was what?" Lesric asked, whipping around from his position at the front of the column and staring at the thicket where Kedrin's attention was focused. His hand gripped the hilt of his sword, ready to yank the weapon out at an instant's notice.

Lianna shrugged her bow off her shoulder and, sliding an arrow from her quiver, readied herself to shoot if needed. She heard it now, a grunting sound coming from the thicket. At the sound of steel on leather, she glanced over to see Lesric slipping his sword out of its scabbard and slowly edging closer to the thicket.

Without warning, a massive beast unlike anything Lianna had ever seen hurtled out of the underbrush. It barrelled toward Lesric, the closest to it, a low growl emanating from its throat. Lesric raised his sword at the last possible instant, and the creature sprang, only to impale itself on the weapon. It jerked backward with a roar of fury and then collapsed on the ground several yards away, the sword still in its chest, and lay still.

Lesric backed up to where the rest of the group stood staring. "Shoot it!" he exclaimed, not taking his eyes off the creature. "Shoot it!"

"But it's de..." Alssa began. She stopped as one of the beast's eyelids flicked open to reveal a staring, yellow orb. At the same instant, a blood-curdling roar sounded behind them. Lianna spun around to see an identical creature rushing toward them from the opposite side of the road. As the new enemy neared, the first brute growled and sprang to his feet, unimpeded by the blade still embedded in its throat. Lianna turned on the first monster and released the arrow that was still on her string. The bolt struck the creature just before it reached them, and it skidded to a halt mere feet from where Lianna stood. This time there was no sign of life, and Lianna was satisfied that the arrow had done its job. But the danger wasn't past.

The second brute now had Elyk pinned to the ground with a massive claw. It glared at the horrified onlookers, daring them to attack, and let out a snarl of glee. Panic gripped Lianna, and she found herself paralyzed. She knew that she needed to shoot, but, seemingly weighed down by some invisible force, she was unable to move.

"Shoot!" Kedrin screamed as the beast raised its head. Huge yellow fangs gleamed in the morning light as it prepared to close the crushing jaws on its helpless victim.

An instant before the beast would have ended Elyk's life, Alssa's arrow plunged into its neck. The creature reared its head and roared in agony as another arrow, this one from Lianna's bow, struck it in the chest. The claw that had been pinning Elyk to the ground batted at the two bolts, trying in vain to stop the burning pain. Elyk scrambled back, wasting no time putting as much distance between himself and the beast as possible.

As the beast convulsed in death throes, Lianna drew another arrow from her quiver and placed in on the string, waiting to see if a further shot was necessary. It didn't appear to be. With a final bellow, the creature collapsed to the ground and lay still.

"Again!" Lesric exclaimed. "Shoot it again! You saw the other one play dead."

This time, no one questioned him. Two shafts buried themselves in the creature as Lianna and Alssa released their bolts simultaneously. The monster didn't move.

For several seconds, silence reigned. Lesric was the one who finally broke it. "Siladis," he said, staring at the corpses of the two brutes. "Who would have thought that there would be two siladis in Risclan Valley?"

"Siladis?" Leumas asked. "The mythical creature that supposedly lives in the Syntor Wasteland and attacks caravans?"

"Exactly," Lesric said. "And 'destroys' caravans would be a more accurate description."

Lianna looked at the massive creatures on the ground and believed him. The closest description she could come up with for the beast she was looking at was some kind of cross between a boar and a bear. As big as a horse, some of the features were reminiscent of a hog, including a boar's snout, ears, and savage tusks. But shaggy fur and sharp claws that promised a quick but painful death looked more like a bear than any kind of pig Lianna had ever seen. As disturbing as the rest of it was, the creature's most frightening feature was the gleaming yellow eyes that had seemed to see right through her. This was unlike any creature she had ever seen before.

"And when, before today, have you seen one of these things?" Elyk asked.

"Two years ago," Lesric said simply. "I've been in the Syntor before, deeper into the Syntor than anyone else in Risclan Valley. Let's just say that there's a reason slavers in the Syntor Wasteland travel in large groups with many more fighting men than you would think it would take to keep a few slaves under control."

"And we're going out there only six strong?" Lianna asked, incredulous. "If these things destroy whole caravans with scores of men-at-arms to protect them, what chance do we stand?"

"I crossed it alone," Lesric said. "If I didn't think we could get across the Syntor Wasteland without being killed by the siladis, I wouldn't have started this mission."

And this, Lianna thought, staring at the monsters, *is exactly why I didn't want to come on this mission in the first place.* She was coming face to face with dangers that most of the inhabitants of Risclan Valley regarded as mere legend. She had grown up believing that siladis were as nonexistent as Lentours, and now she was finding that the so-called facts she had never doubted weren't necessarily true. It was almost too much to handle.

No one wanted to stay at the site of the near disaster any longer than they had to. By wordless consent, they started moving again. The only thing changed by the encounter was that the whole group was alert and on edge. The slightest cracking of a twig made Lianna snap her head around, searching for the source of the disturbance, and everyone else seemed equally tense.

Less than an hour later, they emerged, without warning, onto the brink of a precipice. The ground fell away suddenly, dropping a hundred feet to the sandy desert floor below. Lianna caught her breath as she surveyed the breathtaking panorama. It stretched away as far as she could see, a vast, unbroken wasteland. Barren, desolate, and forbidding, it was everything she'd expected times ten.

"We have to cross that?" Alssa asked faintly, disbelief in her voice.

"Cheer up. It's only ten days," Lesric said, smiling. He remained his usual cheerful self, the only one who seemed unaffected by the prospect before them.

"That's very encouraging," Kedrin said dryly.

"The road begins just over here," Lesric said.

"You're sure there's not a way around?" Elyk asked.

"Oh, there is," Lesric said. "The Syntor doesn't stretch on forever. I'm sure you could go all the way south to the sea, and then Milsad Forest from the coast. But that could take months, if we even found the castle, and we don't have that much time. The Syntor is our only option."

"All right," Kedrin said. "Let's stop procrastinating and get it over with. The sooner we get started, the sooner we'll be done." He started off in the direction Lesric had indicated. Lesric followed, but the others hesitated. "Meet you at Cortim Castle," Kedrin called over his shoulder.

Lianna took a deep breath and hurried to catch up.

CHAPTER 6

A t the bottom of the precipice, intense heat radiated from the ground. It was early afternoon, nearing the hottest part of the day, and the air was sweltering. For at least the hundredth time, Lianna wondered what had possessed her to agree to come on this mission. So far, the Syntor Wasteland lived up to even the most exaggerated stories she had heard.

"We make camp here," Lesric announced, stopping at the base of the precipice.

"But we still have five hours of daylight left," Kedrin protested.

"Exactly. We sleep for those five hours, then leave after dark. It's too hot to travel now."

Following his instructions, they set up a quick camp, wanting all the rest they could get before dark fell and it was time to go again. Lianna slept soundly until someone shook her several hours later. "Lianna! It's time to get up," Alssa said.

Lianna inwardly groaned, certain there was no way she could walk all night without more rest. She forced herself to climb to her feet and help strike the camp. They hadn't unpacked much, and far too soon they were ready to go.

Following a seldom used trail, they walked through the night. Lianna was painfully aware that each step brought them closer and closer to Cortim Castle. And danger.

They'd been plodding along in wordless silence for about six hours when Lianna was sure that she saw a light ahead. When she looked again, she saw not one, but several lights, beacons in the blackness.

"What is that?" someone whispered, addressing Lesric.

Lesric's voice echoed the fear he felt at encountering an old enemy and he spat out the word. "Slavers."

Lianna froze, staring at the glowing lights. They reminded her of eyes, watching from the darkness, daring them to come closer. She shivered at the sight.

"There's no possible way they could have seen us yet," Kedrin said optimistically. "We just need to circle around until we're ahead of them, and then put as much distance between us and them as possible."

"But if we leave the trail, we might never find it again," Lianna protested. She knew how easy it would be to get lost in the vast expanse of the Syntor. Without the trail, they could wander until they died of starvation. She didn't want to be captured by the slavers, but she didn't want to die in this wilderness, either.

"We don't have a choice," Lesric said. "If we keep the lights in sight and swing around in a wide arc, we won't lose the trail."

That decided, they carefully and quietly circled around the camp. It was larger than it looked, and it took them nearly an hour to get back on the trail. Dawn was only a few hours away, and they had to be well hidden by the time it arrived, so they quickened their pace.

As the horizon ahead of them turned from black to gray, Lianna began nervously glancing behind them.

When the sky began to grow pink, Lesric led them off the trail for a good half mile. Now that they were in the territory of the slave catchers, they weren't going to risk letting a caravan stumble across them while they slept.

As exhausted as she was, Lianna couldn't sleep. Still tense from the near encounter with the slavers, she was worried about the possibility of running into more. The sun had climbed well over the horizon before she was finally able to doze off in a fitful slumber.

At mid afternoon something suddenly woke her. She sat up, but dropped to the ground instantly as she glanced to her left, towards the road.

A caravan was winding its way along the trail. The huge clouds of dust billowing from beneath the hooves of horses and heat waves shimmering above the sand clouded Lianna's vision, but she could still see the row of supply wagons and the horses pulling them. Faint shouts and calls echoed across the sand as men on horseback rode up and down the length of the column. And she could imagine the slaves marching in its center, heading towards whatever evil fate was in store for them.

Most of the others were also awake, silently watching the procession. They instinctively knew they were safe as long as they kept low, but everyone also seemed to feel that silence wasn't an unjustified precaution, and no words were exchanged.

They watched tensely for the next twenty minutes as the long caravan crawled past. Though Lianna knew there was no way they could see her, she stayed low to the ground and remained on edge until the last cloud of dust finally vanished into the distance. Lianna breathed a sigh of relief and went back to sleep.

* * * * *

That night they made even better progress, eating up mile after weary mile before streaks of light on the eastern horizon signalled them to stop for a well-earned rest. They camped well off the road again, but it proved unnecessary. For one day, at least, no other human beings crossed their path.

They continued to camp in the same way, hoping to avoid other caravans or the robbers and bandits, outcasts of society, who were also drawn to these desolate regions and preyed on the few travelers foolish enough to pass this way. But for the next five days, they encountered no signs of human life.

On the sixth day, though, another caravan passed their camp. Not as big as the previous one, it was still impressive and dangerous, and they were careful to avoid notice. The long line of men and wagons wound its way down the lonely road and disappeared into the vast unexplored regions of the Syntor, paying no heed to the six travelers watching warily from a safe distance.

Lesric was the one who found the tracks. It was near midnight on the seventh day, and they had been walking for several hours when he knelt down and examined something on the ground. It didn't take long to learn what it was.

"Siladis," Leumas said.

"I don't like to mention this, but those tracks are massive compared to the siladis in the forest," Kedrin said.

"The siladis in the forest were small," Lesric said. "Very small. Did you think that an animal that size could wipe out a whole caravan? While they are deadly, they're not that strong and lethal. The tracks we're looking at now, unfortunately, belong to an average size siladis."

"Nice," Alssa said sarcastically. "You wouldn't by any chance have an idea of how old these tracks are, would you?"

"Not very old," Kedrin said from where he knelt beside Lesric, studying the imprints in the moonlight. "Not very old at all."

Lianna shivered. "Let's keep going."

For the rest of the night they were on edge, turning around at the slightest sound or a shadow flitting past in the peripheral vision. But as dawn drew near, nothing else had made them suspect that a siladis was in the area.

Lianna thought she would be too tense to sleep, but exhaustion finally overcame her and she drifted off. She didn't wake up again until, late in the afternoon, Alssa shook her and held a finger to her lips to signal silence. Lianna slowly rose to a sitting position and saw the rest of the group staring at something to the west. Tension filled the air, and she grabbed her bow and arrows as she silently joined them to see what caused their alarm. Alssa pointed wordlessly to a silhouette on a sand dune, framed by the setting sun. Lianna didn't need to be told what it was.

"How long has it been there?" she asked quietly.

"Two or three minutes," Elyk answered without taking his eyes off the form of the siladis. "It's a monster," he added, staring in awe.

"A little bigger than the two in the forest," Kedrin agreed nervously. "What do you think we should do, Lesric?"

"We can't just leave it alone and hope it doesn't come after us," Lesric said. "In the desert, they're usually nocturnal. They don't depend on sight like we do, and rely more on smell and hearing. They move silently, and when you're least expecting, they strike. Once the sun sets, all the odds are against us. They're built for stalking their prey at night, and we won't stand a chance if we don't do something within the next few minutes," he concluded.

"So what do you suggest?" Alssa asked.

Lesric glanced over at the rapidly sinking sun and bit his lip, thinking quickly. "We don't have enough time to fight it, assuming we could even catch it. It knows that once darkness falls, the tables turn in its favor. If it can, it will keep out of our way now and strike when all the advantages are on its side."

"So what do we do?" Leumas asked, growing impatient.

"Lianna," Lesric said. "What's your maximum range with your bow? And when I say maximum, I mean the farthest you can be and still get a lethal shot. It has to drop with the first arrow."

"That thing is three, four hundred yards out," Lianna said. "I can't do that."

"I don't expect you to," Lesric said. "I'm just wondering how close we have to get."

Lianna thought fast, her heart racing as she realized exactly what he had in mind. "That dune," she said, pointing to a rise that would significantly shorten the shot.

Lesric nodded and spoke quickly. "Let's go. Kedrin, you come too. Alssa, Elyk, Leumas, head that way, to its other side." He indicated a position to the left.

"We're going to flank it in case it runs. Alssa, shoot after Lianna. Everyone else, be ready to finish it off if necessary. Any questions?" He paused to let them reply, and when no one did, he nodded in satisfaction.

"Good. Now let's do this. We don't have long."

Lianna keenly felt the weight of responsibility she was carrying. She knew that she was the only one capable of making the shot Lesric was requesting, but that didn't lessen the apprehension she felt.

Still, Lesric had proven himself a more than capable leader, and Lianna knew that if there was a better course of action to follow, he would have found it. Since this was the only option available to them, she didn't have a choice but to do her best.

Lianna glanced at the rapidly sinking sun and knew that they only had a few minutes to get in position and make their move. She slipped an arrow from her quiver and then slung the quiver over her shoulder, keeping her bow and the arrow at the ready. Then she hurried after Lesric.

They moved quickly and kept low, heading toward the rise Lianna had specified and keeping an eye on the beast that still sat unmoving on the ridge a quarter of a mile away. To their left, the rest of the group headed toward another rise two hundred yards south of the one she'd chosen. Lesric's brow furrowed as he glanced back at the sun.

He didn't say anything, but he upped his pace. Lianna and Kedrin matched it, and Lianna's breath began to come in quicker gasps. Her heart pounded in her chest, but not from the exertion. Knowing what she had to do, and what would happen if she failed, became more and more frightening with every passing moment. If she missed this shot, at worst they would die. At the least, they would face a brutal attack in the dark by a beast that was built for night stalking.

They stopped on the back side of the knoll she had

chosen, out of sight of the siladis. Lianna took a deep breath and knelt. She quickly jabbed three arrows in the ground in front of her, just in case. If necessary, she could fire the extra arrows within a matter of seconds. She hoped it didn't come to that, but she was going to be prepared.

Lianna placed another arrow on the string and paused, taking deep breaths to calm her pounding heart and prepare herself for the shot. She funnelled all her concentration into the moment. She couldn't see Alssa, but she knew that her cousin was watching, ready to fire as soon as she did.

"Stay calm," Kedrin said softly from behind her. "You can do it. You know you can do it."

Coming from Kedrin, the brother who loved to tease, the words meant more than anything else could at that moment. Still, it wasn't enough to take away the fear she felt. *Shooting at a fixed target in my back yard is completely different from shooting at a beast that is going to kill me if I miss,* Lianna thought wryly. At home, there weren't lives depending on her ability to hit the target.

Knowing she was as ready as she was ever going to be and that she was losing light, Lianna drew back the string halfway in preparation for the shot. Then, slowly, steadily, Lianna rose to her feet, pulling the string back to full draw as she did. She sighted down the shaft and took her aim.

The siladis sat there unmoving, daring her to shoot. Its confidence was somehow unsettling, and she struggled to ignore it.

She focused on the target, and only the target. She ignored the sand glowing orange with the reflection of the setting sun, ignored her brother and Lesric standing behind her, and even ignored the siladis itself, except for the bullseye—the center of the creature's chest. She took a deep breath then let it out slowly. And then, when she knew that there was no better time than the moment, she released the arrow.

She had the next one on the string in an instant and let fly as a bellow of agony split the air. The siladis was hit.

But it wasn't dead.

It collapsed to the ground an instant before Alssa's arrow landed in its side, and Lianna sent her third arrow hurtling in its direction as the monster raised its head and let out a long, doleful wail. As the first cry died away, the siladis let out another one. Something didn't seem right about it.

"What's it doing?" Kedrin asked, confused. The creature was mortally hit, but it didn't seem to comprehend the fact.

"It's calling for help," Lianna murmured, finally grasping what was going on. She let another arrow fly in its direction, but the siladis was thrashing, and she couldn't get a steady shot. Its cries grew more intense, but that was all that changed.

The siladis jerked in response to another arrow from Alssa's bow, and its frantic thrashing slowed. Lianna took advantage of the slackened motion to shoot again, and the siladis finally lay still.

As soon as the thrashing stopped, Lesric and Kedrin darted forward. They weren't worried about keeping low anymore. Now their only concern was in crossing the ground to the apparently dead beast as quickly as possible. They had to confirm that it was indeed dead, and they didn't want it running off before they got there.

Lianna sprinted after them and from the corner of her eye caught a glimpse of the other three doing the same. They all arrived at the fallen siladis as the sun dipped halfway below the horizon. Wasting no time, Lesric plunged his sword into the chest of the siladis.

The creature didn't move.

They stood there silently, panting and staring at the monster for several moments. Then Lesric looked up. "Let's get out of here. I don't know what that creature was trying to do, but just in case, I don't want to stick around."

"You don't have to say that twice," Elyk said. "Let's go."

CHAPTER 7

O n the tenth day, they reached the forest and made camp just inside the trees. While the rest of the team scattered to gather wood and set snares to catch some fresh meat, Lesric studied a chart to determine where they were in relation to the general area where he estimated Cortim Castle to be. The fact that he'd never seen it on a map made the task harder, but Lesric was confident he could steer them in the right direction without much difficulty.

"We're farther south than I'd hoped," he concluded as they met back at the campsite thirty minutes later. "We're making good progress, though. If we keep this pace, we'll reach the castle in the next few days. We can also travel by day now, since heat's not going to be a problem like it was in the desert."

The next day they encountered another human being, the first, besides the slave traders, that they'd seen since leaving Pruglin City. As the group made their way through the forest, they came across a narrow trail winding its way through the trees. A man trudged slowly along the road, walking alongside an ox pulling a cart. The cart was laden with as much lumber as the beast could possibly manage, and the creature strained under the burden.

The man kept his eyes on the ground in front of

him as he drew near, refusing to meet their gaze.

"Good morning, sir," Lesric said cheerfully as they drew level with the man. "That's a mighty large load you have."

"For the castle," the man replied. "Just like everything else we do. A man doesn't even have time to tend his own crops and support his own family, with all the work Torrac's requiring from us. He drafted me right out of my field to cut timber for his castle." The man eyed them curiously. "What are six young people doing walking through Milsad without a care in the world? You haven't been drafted? Or are you just neglecting your work?"

"We're travelers," Lesric said. "Just arrived in Milsad. We didn't know all this was going on."

"Then, my advice to you would be to leave before it's too late. I'd flee myself, but with my wife and children, it just isn't possible. We'd be caught and probably killed before we'd been gone a day. But I don't mean to complain to you. Just take my advice and leave while you still can." Then the man was gone.

"I think we'd better get off the road before we're captured or drafted too," Kedrin stated. The others agreed wholeheartedly, and they quickly headed away from the trail.

For the rest of the day, they saw no more people. The next day, though, was a different story.

The closer they came to the castle, the more on edge Lianna felt. She jumped when a stick cracked, and when a bird flew up in front of her, she stepped back in alarm.

But this was different. She heard something else, not a normal forest sound. She supposed it was only her imagination until she heard it again. She stopped, listening. This time she was sure of it. First a shout ahead of them, then an ax thudding against wood. And finally, the crash of a falling tree.

"Listen," she said, standing still.

The others stopped walking. More shouts rang out, accompanied by dull thuds of iron on wood. Everyone looked at Lesric.

"Let's approach slowly, keeping low, with weapons at the ready. I want to know what's going on," Lesric said. "Milsad Forest has changed a lot in the past couple of months."

With an arrow on the string, Lianna brought up the rear. Moving cautiously, they took care not to make any noise. Although they knew the racket ahead would probably cover sounds of their footsteps, instinct told them to stay quiet, that silence was crucial to avoiding detection.

Without warning, Kedrin dropped to the ground, motioning for the others to do the same. He pointed through the trees, and Lianna followed his finger to a small clearing where dozens of men toiled. Some labored to fell trees, while others busied themselves with something she couldn't quite make out. One thing she could see, though, was that the trees were being felled in a line.

On hands and knees, the six of them continued their approach. When they were as near as they dared, they stopped for a better look.

They could see now that the men who weren't felling trees were working to remove the stumps left behind. Fallen leaves and debris had been raked to the side, and teams of horses pulled weights that packed down the dirt, hardening it.

Alssa's whispered voice broke the silence. "Are they making a road?"

"That's what it looks like," Leumas replied in a low voice. "I wonder why."

"Cortim Castle is on the other side of this construction area," Lesric said softly, once again consulting his map. "We need to get around it, and from what that farmer said, we need to do it unobserved. I don't particularly fancy being drafted."

They crawled back until it felt safe to stand up, then walked north until they were around the construction zone. Once on the other side, they continued in a southwesterly direction towards the castle.

After two more days of cautiously circling around the many similar work sites and staying off roads, they reached Milsad Lake.

In the center of the lake rose an island, and in the middle of that, a plateau jutted into the air. Half-finished battlements towered at the top of the cliff.

The castle was more impressive than Lianna had ever imagined. Even though construction obviously wasn't finished, completion wasn't too far off. The fortress was everything Lesric had described and then some. Towers evenly spaced along the wall gave sentries a perfect view of the surrounding area and eliminated any chance of approaching unseen. Even from this distance, Lianna could see that the bulwarks were designed to allow archers to pick off anyone attempting to approach the walls. Flags emblazoned with Torrac's crest fluttered above the battlements.

Despite her initial reluctance to come on this mission and the trepidation she still felt, as she stared at the castle, Lianna realized that something had changed. Aside from those who had been taken here as slaves, she was among the first from Risclan Valley to lay eyes on this magnificent sight. She had the privilege of walking where no free native of Risclan had set foot in half a century. The fear was by no means gone, but it was now tempered by awe.

"How do we get there?" Elyk asked, looking around. No boats were in sight.

"There's a ferry on the southern side," Lesric explained, "But we're not going to take it this afternoon. Let's make camp first and figure out our next course of action from there."

Later that night, as they sat around the campfire eating dinner, a twig snapped. Before anyone had a chance to react, a man stepped into the circle of light. He held up his empty hands as he saw weapons sliding out of their scabbards.

"Stay your blades!" he shouted. "Lesric, I'm glad to see you made it back safely! It's been too long."

Lesric sheathed his sword, relief on his face. "It is good to see you," he said, laughing. "I've been worried for the past three months that they caught you after I escaped." He turned to address the rest of the group. "Let me introduce you to an old friend. This is Oslir."

As soon as she heard the name, Lianna could see the resemblance between her father and his brother. Her uncle was a close copy of Taran, an older, more worn version, but still bearing a strong resemblance.

Lesric introduced them each to Oslir. When he explained who Lianna and Kedrin were, shock crossed the older man's face. He hadn't been prepared for this. "Taran's children?" he asked with astonishment, "It's good to meet you, Kedrin, Lianna."

"How did you know we were here?" Lesric asked as the greetings concluded.

Oslir smiled. "I have my sources," he said. "Once I heard there was a group of strangers in the forest, it wasn't hard to figure out it was you."

"Were we that obvious?" Lesric asked, and Oslir laughed.

"No," he said. "You just happened to run into one of my men."

"You're just the person we need," Lesric told him. "I'm looking for a way to get up to the keep unobserved, and my mind is blank. Any ideas?"

"If you don't mind waiting around for a little while, I can get you right inside the castle. It might take a day or two to get all the bits and pieces we'll need together, but it can be done."

"You can have a week if you want," Lesric said. "We travelled hundreds of miles to get here. We're not going to turn around and go home now just because it's going to take a day or two to get the information we need."

"Then I'll arrange everything," Oslir said. "Right now, I need to go before I'm missed, but I'll be back tomorrow night, or the night after that if I'm delayed. Until then, stay out of sight. Also, you might want to avoid a fire. Rules have gotten a lot stricter over the past month or two, and the Lentours just decided that work crews aren't allowed to build them. And around here, most everyone's on a work crew."

The next day, they stayed close to camp. Oslir didn't come that night, and finally, after waiting up for several hours, they concluded that he wasn't coming and went to sleep.

The following day passed slowly. In the morning, they scavenged for roots and berries to supplement the small supply of jerky from Pruglin that was still left. They sat around for most of the afternoon, and toward evening, they once again started to watch for Oslir. Late into the night they waited.

Oslir didn't come.

"He must have been delayed again," Lesric said after they'd been waiting for hours. "We'd better get some rest. He'll be here tomorrow."

But no one wanted to sleep. Near midnight, they reluctantly went to bed, but Lianna lay awake for a long time, her mind full of questions. *What could have happened to him? Was he discovered because of us?* After what seemed like hours, Lianna fell into a fitful sleep.

The next morning, everyone was on edge. Oslir's failure to come had disturbed them all. Fear filled Lianna's heart as she pondered what might have happened. The slightest forest sound made her jump to her feet and grab her bow. The others, too, were uneasy. The waiting was becoming increasingly difficult to stand, and Lianna was more glad than ever for Alssa's companionship. Her cousin's presence was the only thing that kept her from going crazy as they once again waited in vain for Oslir's arrival.

They stayed in camp all day. That night, they waited hopefully for Oslir.

He didn't come.

When Lesric finally spoke, it was with more confidence than Lianna, or anyone else, for that matter, felt. "Something must have happened," he said lightly. "Maybe he just had trouble finding everything he needed, or getting out unobserved. There's nothing we can do about it now, though, so I think we should get some sleep and decide what to do in the morning." As he turned, though, a worried frown betrayed his confident tone.

The next morning they gathered around to decide on a course of action. "It's not impossible that Oslir was just delayed," Lesric admitted. "But I think we all know that he's probably not coming. We need to find our own way into the castle."

They spent the next hour in cycles of suggesting, discussing, and discarding ideas. Every plan had some flaw that was simply too large to be overlooked. With each passing minute, it became increasingly apparent that they needed Oslir. If he didn't show up, Lianna wasn't sure what they were going to do.

"We need to find a disguise that will get us in unnoticed," Lesric said finally. "But I don't have any ideas. Things seem to have changed a lot since I left Cortim."

"I think we should find out what happened to Oslir before we do anything," Kedrin asserted. "If they found out we're here and know we're coming, we're going to have to approach the situation completely differently than if we had surprise on our side. We don't want them to be expecting us."

"We'll give Oslir one more night," Lesric decided. "But if he doesn't show, we don't have any choice but to find our own way into the keep."

He turned to Kedrin. "I know you want to find your uncle, and I'm sorry, but we don't have a choice."

It was nearly dark, and pinpricks of light appeared in the eastern the sky. Crickets chirped and insects danced through the trees. Conversation died away as it grew later, and aside from the peaceful sounds of the forest, all was still.

Until a voice spoke from the deeper shadows on the edge of the clearing.

"Lesric?"

Lianna spun around to see who the speaker was. *Oslir?* she thought excitedly. But when she looked again, even in the fading light, she could tell it wasn't Oslir.

CHAPTER 8

"Lesric?" the man asked again. "Is that you?"

"Who's asking?" Lesric asked, not answering the man's question.

"My name is Coen. Oslir sent me. You are Lesric, aren't you?"

Lesric nodded.

"Oslir is being watched. Torrac has men waiting for him to lead them to you. He said to tell you that he's sorry he wasn't able to come before, but since he can't, he asked me to give you a message. He isn't quite ready yet, but he wanted you to know he's still working on it. I'll try to be here about this time tomorrow night, provided nothing goes wrong, with everything you need. If I can't come, I'll try to send someone else. Torrac has severely tightened security, and it's become extremely difficult to get on and off the island unnoticed. You'll have to be patient."

"How are you going to get us into the castle? And more importantly, how are you going to get us out?" Lesric asked.

"Oslir has a plan, but he hasn't told me all the specifics yet. I do know it involves disguises, though I don't know how he plans to get them. He has a source."

Coen glanced around at the group, as if judging

how much it was safe to reveal. "Oslir heads the resistance here. He protects the rest of us by only giving us the information we need to know when we need to know it. He alone knows the identities of other members of the rebellion, so I can't say who he's enlisted to help. I'm sorry there's not more I can tell you right now. Oslir just wanted you to know that help is on the way."

"All right," Lesric said. "What would you say is a reasonable amount of time for us to wait, and if you don't return in that time, what should we do?"

"I should be back, but if one of us doesn't come to meet you within three days or so, we've been caught, and you're on your own."

Coen glanced up at the sky. The dusk was quickly deepening, and more stars seemed to be appearing with each passing moment. "I need to go before anyone notices that I'm gone," he said. "I'm sorry I don't have more for you."

"Thanks for coming. We'll be here when you return," Lesric said.

Coen disappeared into the night.

* * * * *

Agitated knocking rattled the front door. A maid poked her head out, wondering who was so frantic, and why.

"Is Councilor Taran here?" a red-faced, sweat-soaked man gasped. "I have an urgent message for him."

Moments later, Taran appeared. "Yes?" he asked, wondering what kind of emergency had brought this man to his door.

"Sir, Councilor Mathalin summoned you. It's urgent. You need to meet him in the Council house as soon as possible."

A short time later, Taran reached the Council house and raced down the corridor to the Council room. Mathalin was there, a disturbed look on his face. Most of the other members of the Council were present as well.

"Taran, you're here. Good." Mathalin waited for him to take his seat, then addressed the group. "I know that you were all summoned unexpectedly, and I'm sorry for that, but I just received serious news. I'll be as brief as possible.

"When we began our preparations for war, one of the first things we did was send messengers to each of the districts to warn them of the danger."

Men nodded, wondering where this was going. This wasn't new to any of them. They had already received responses from most of the districts, pledging support in the upcoming war.

Mathalin took a deep breath and continued. "The messenger we sent to Forsid just returned with news. Bad news."

"They don't believe us?" a councilor asked.

"No, and it's worse than that. Forsid City is gone."

* * * * *

The next evening, Coen arrived right on time. Another man who introduced himself as Edridge accompanied him. Both were laden with heavy packs.

"We've brought your disguises," Coen said, tossing his pack down on the ground. "Oslir wasn't able to come tonight, since he's still being watched, but during the day he hauls timber in the woods. His normal route passes through this area, so he'll meet you here tomorrow morning. I'm not sure exactly what the rest of the plan is, so I'll let Oslir explain it all to you tomorrow."

"Thank you for your help, Coen," Lesric said. "Will

we see you again?"

"Oslir doesn't want the same people involved too often. He wants to avoid rousing any suspicions. This will probably be the last time he'll let me help you."

"Then thank you for all you've done," Lesric said. "We know that you took huge risks, and we're grateful. Thank you."

Coen acknowledged the thanks with a nod. "You were in even more danger by escaping. And I'll be repaid in full by knowing that you were able to deliver information to Pruglin, information that you can use to defeat Torrac once and for all."

"We'll do our best."

Then Coen and Edridge slipped off into the forest.

The next morning, everyone was awake early. They didn't know what to do with the contents of the packs, so they left them alone until Oslir came. He arrived an hour later.

"Hello!" he said cheerily. "I hope you're all ready to invade a castle."

"It depends. Do you have a good plan for going about it?" Lesric grinned.

"I don't know whether it's good or not, but it's a plan," Oslir laughed. "I'm sorry I wasn't able to come before. I sent Coen as soon as I could. But down to business. I was able to find Lentour uniforms for everyone. With these, you should be able to get just about anywhere you need to. I have an inside man who provided us with all the passwords you would be expected to have. He's going to meet us inside the town and give us the grand tour."

"Thank you," Lesric said. "This is a different land than it was a few months ago. It was bad when I was here, but I never expected the regulations to become this much stricter in just a matter of months. It's astounding."

Oslir nodded. "It's gotten far worse. The last month has been brutal for most of the people. I've escaped the worst of it because I've been here for so long that no one expects me to cause any trouble. I'm watched, like everyone else, but people just don't expect a fifty-year-old man who's been here for nearly half his life to cause trouble now, so they're not as hard on me. All that to say, we got you out just in time. Attempting something like that now would be near impossible."

"Well," Lesric said, surveying the group, "There's no reason to sit around here any longer. Shall we head out?"

When they reached the ferry, the ferryman looked nervously at the regiment of seven soldiers marching toward him. Fear and suspicion were a part of his life, and he wasn't sure if they were just coming to cross the lake or if they had another, more sinister motive. Oslir made a sign, and the ferryman relaxed. "Oslir?" he asked in a low voice.

"It's me," Oslir said from beneath the visor of his helmet. "We need a ferry to the castle."

The man smiled. "I happen to know the man for the job. Get in, before someone else comes."

They clambered onto the ferry and were soon moving steadily across the lake towards the castle in the center.

Coming from this angle, Lianna saw that the cliffs on which the castle was built extended all the way into the water on the east side of the island. On that side of the lake, more cliffs that appeared to be the same height and width rose from the water and extended into the forest. Then the sides gradually sloped away, forming a plateau.

"Is the...the island didn't use to be a peninsula, did it?" Lianna asked.

"You're observant, just like your father," Oslir said. "Yes, it did."

"What happened?" she questioned.

"Torrac mined the cliff away."

"That's not possible!" Kedrin broke in. "How could anyone do that?"

"I don't know. It was done long before I got here. They quarried the rock and used it for the castle. Torrac has some uncanny ways of accomplishing seemingly impossible projects. No one knows exactly how."

"Where did all of the rock go?" Lianna questioned, staring at the massive gap of missing stone that Torrac had somehow disposed of. "Even if they used some of it for the castle, that's not a fraction of what was there."

"Once we arrive in the village, you'll notice that most of the houses are built of stone. And some of it was transported to Torrac's other strongholds."

"Other strongholds," Lesric said. "I was going to ask you about that. Do you know where they are? I've been upset at myself for not looking into that more while I was here."

"No," Oslir said. "It's common knowledge that they exist, and I could probably point you in the right direction, but that's the kind of information slaves just aren't privy to."

As the ferry reached the shore, they jumped off and marched up through the village toward the menacing form of Cortim Castle. After a few minutes, Oslir veered off the main road and led them to a little-used side street, the rendezvous point where Oslir's friend, the soldier who had supplied them with the armor and passwords, was supposed to be waiting.

He was there a few minutes later. "Lesric! How good to see you again!"

Lesric grinned. "I'm surprised you remember me. After all, you're a lofty sentry, while I'm only a humble rock carrier."

The man laughed. "Well, I do. It would be hard not to. I'm Neldon," he addressed the rest of them. "There's no time for further introductions, though. We need to hurry if you want to have enough time to see the whole castle today. I can probably get you in tomorrow, but I'd rather not unless we have to."

It's not that big, is it? Lianna thought. From down below, the castle was intimidating, but it didn't appear large enough to take longer than half a day to explore it completely.

But she didn't have time to reflect any further. Neldon hurried them along at a brisk march. She barely had time to take in the sights and sounds of the village.

The houses were close together and crowded, and as Oslir had said, most of them were made of stone quarried from the cliffs. The buildings thinned out as they neared the bottom of the plateau, and they followed a winding road up to the top of the cliff. It was steep, but not so steep that it couldn't be traversed by wagons and carts laden with supplies for the castle.

Neldon led them on, and in a matter of minutes, they were at the top of the plateau. A wide moat surrounded the fortress. The drawbridge was down, but two men stood guard at the near side, and two more at the far side.

"State your business," the first guard barked gruffly.

"Reporting in for duty," Neldon replied.

"On your way."

And they started forward into Cortim Castle.

CHAPTER 9

A s they walked over the drawbridge and then passed under the portcullis, Lianna looked up at the metal grate suspended high above. Beyond the first portcullis was a second one, the walls on either side riddled with slits from which defenders could shoot intruders at a distance or pour boiling oil on those who were unfortunate enough to draw close.

Then they stepped into an open courtyard and surveyed the inside of Cortim Castle. While the outer wall of the castle was nearly done, work on the inner wall was still far from completion. Nevertheless, the fortress was formidable. Gazing at the walls that towered above them, Lianna knew that a good archer could pick off enemies in the open courtyard with ease. She shivered at the thought.

Neldon led them through another passage with a third raised portcullis. In the inner courtyard, slaves toiled to lift stones into place.

"Oslir, where do we want to go first?" Neldon asked.

Oslir looked questioningly at Lesric. "What do you want to see?"

"Everything of strategic importance. Towers, battlements, anything that could be used against Torrac."

At that moment, a tall man clad in armor matching their own stepped into sight.

"What's going on here?" he barked.

No one moved. The same unspoken question was going through every head: *Did he hear what Lesric said?*

"Excuse me, sir?" Oslir asked innocently. "Is something the matter?"

"Are you on duty?"

"Yes, sir." Neldon replied.

"What garrison are you in?"

"Seventh, sir."

"You're in the way of my work crews. Report to your commander immediately. He'll be hearing from me about this." He looked at them suspiciously. "Go!" he commanded.

Neldon led them at a rapid pace away from the man. At a safe distance he whispered, "That was close."

Lianna let out her breath, realizing as she did that she'd been unconsciously holding it.

Around the corner, they stopped.

"Oslir, I think we should split up," Neldon said. "A group this large just attracts too much attention."

"Good idea," Oslir agreed. "I can take half of the group on a tour of the battlements."

"Good. I'll take the other half inside the towers and the keep. We'll meet back here at noon."

"Lianna, Alssa, you're the archers, so you'd probably benefit most from seeing the battlements. Come with me."

Lianna stepped into line behind her uncle and followed him toward the wall. She pulled out a piece of parchment and a charcoal pencil to take notes. They walked along the battlement where slaves labored on the walls of the castle, pretending to be inspecting the work, but in reality mapping out the battlements. She made sure to mark any areas that offered attackers more cover or were safer to approach from.

After a circuit of the inner walls, Oslir took them to the outer ramparts. Very few slaves still worked here, since this section was nearly complete. Lianna continued to take careful notes, scribbling furiously on her sheets of parchment.

They all met at the appointed meeting place at noon. After discussing what they had seen and what was left to cover, they split again. By the end of the afternoon, Oslir had given Lianna and Alssa a thorough tour of the battlements, and Lianna felt that they had learned everything they could. Though they had only scratched the surface, it wasn't worth the risk it would take to go into any more detail.

She stuffed the notes deep into her pack and followed the group back out of Cortim Castle.

* * * * *

"What do you mean, it's gone? That's impossible!" one man shouted incredulously. "Forsid can't have simply disappeared. It's a city!"

Mathalin looked helpless. "I'm just stating the facts. We've sent a team to investigate, but until they return, we won't know anything further."

"The messenger didn't say anything else? Is the city still standing, or is it just the people who are missing? Are the surrounding towns and villages unscathed? Was there some sort of disease that killed everyone, or was the city attacked? What else do we know?" Ildug voiced the questions.

"All I was told is that it was gone," Mathalin explained. "The messenger was shaking so hard he could barely stand, and he had a high fever. He went into a coma not long after arriving here. We won't know whether he's ill or just shocked by what he saw until the doctor is able to give a report. Until we can question him or the reconnaissance team returns, we have to accept that we will get no help from Forsid."

Taran spoke up. "I need to know as soon as that man revives. Ildug and I have the job of overseeing the militia, and if Torrac has an army on the move, we need to be ready."

"I understand, Taran, and I'll notify you as soon as I find out more. Right now we just need to hope that he recovers, because if he doesn't, we won't learn any more until the unit we sent returns, and their information will be days old. This man was there right after whatever it was that happened took place and will probably be able to tell us more.

"That's all I have for now, so you may go home, but expect to be summoned again for further updates. As I am sure you understand, this information is strictly confidential," he warned. "Enough chaos was created when the people learned that Torrac was building an army. If they know that it is possibly already in use, I can't imagine what will happen."

Taran left the building and crossed the square towards his home, shaking his head as he did so. Two months ago, he would never have believed his ears if someone had told him that this would be happening, and yet here he was in the middle of it all. He was completely overwhelmed.

CHAPTER 10

B ack at the camp that night, the six discussed what they'd learned and what they would do the next day. All had charts of various sections of the castle, and they had been sure to look for any weaknesses they could exploit. Still, the fortress was a formidable opponent, and the weaknesses were few and far between.

The next morning, Oslir was back at the camp to show them the remainder of the island and all of the defenses Torrac had put in place.

"Well, is everyone ready for the rest of the grand tour of this section of Torrac's domain?" he asked cheerfully when he arrived.

At the ferry, the same man took them across, once again without pay and as if nothing were out of the ordinary. They reached the village and proceeded according to plan.

After Oslir had showed them all the points of interest on the island, they returned to the forest to explore the country in the immediate vicinity of Milsad Lake. Various roads under construction branched off in different directions, and men built barracks to house the many regiments of soldiers.

For the next two days they studied all the details they had gathered and continued to learn more. When the time came to decide what to do next, the conversation turned into a heated discussion. The main disagreement erupted over whether to go home or to push deeper into Lentour territory.

"If we go home now," Lesric said, "we lose our opportunity to get a better idea of the extent of Torrac's domain and strength. But every day we stay increases our chance of being caught and is another day that the leaders in Pruglin who need our information will have to wait. Eventually, they will have to form their plans without the intelligence we've gathered, and that could potentially spell disaster. The results of making the wrong decision could be catastrophic."

"We have an advantage right now that we may not have again," Kedrin said. "Here we are, already in the middle of enemy territory, where we can gain information vital for victory. Any little bit extra we learn could be the detail we need to win this war. I say that we take advantage of the opportunity to learn all we possibly can."

"But what if we take one chance too many and are caught?" Leumas spoke. "Then, not only will our army lose the information we might gain by staying, they also lose what we have now. If you are right and we succeed, Pruglin will gain much. If you are wrong, or even if you're right and we fail, Pruglin will lose even more. The odds are too great. We need to go back while we still can."

"There's another possibility that no one has brought up yet," Alssa offered. "We could split up. Some of us could return to Pruglin and deliver the information while the rest continue on and learn anything else they can. Then Pruglin will get all the intelligence possible, and we won't endanger the mission."

The discussion continued for nearly an hour.

There were three possibilities: split up, go home, or continue further into enemy territory. The group was evenly divided among the three options, and strong advantages and disadvantages came with each one.

In the end, Oslir turned the tide. His advice was to follow Alssa's suggested course of action and split up. He presented a persuasive argument, the most convincing aspect being that he would lead the group heading farther into Lentour territory.

Once Oslir offered his advice, it didn't take them long to make up their minds. Half of the team would leave for Pruglin at first light the next morning. The other half would follow Oslir deeper into Torrac's domain.

The only question left to settle was who would go and who would stay.

Obviously, Lesric would go with Oslir, and Kedrin volunteered as soon as the decision was made. That left one spot to fill.

Lianna knew what was coming, and she wasn't surprised when Kedrin turned to her. "No," she said before he had a chance to speak. "Absolutely not. I'm going home."

"But, Lianna..."

"No."

"Just listen to me!"

"No! I'm not staying!" she exclaimed. "I'm sorry, but that's just not happening. I'm going home."

"We need an archer," Oslir said quietly.

"Why does everyone always use that excuse? I don't know why I ever picked up a bow," Lianna said, half joking but partly serious. "Just look at all the trouble it's gotten me into."

"So you're coming?" Kedrin asked. "Great."

Lianna glared at him. "I just told you I wasn't."

"Not what I heard," he grinned.

* * * * *

The next morning, Alssa, Leumas, and Elyk left for Pruglin. Lesric, Kedrin, and Lianna stayed behind.

Once the returning party had left, there was nothing to do except wait for Oslir to show up. He was once again assigned to haul timber in the forest, giving him an excuse to head in their direction, and he just wasn't going to show up for work. His men would cover for him, spreading false rumors as to his last known location and claiming to have seen him heading west, the direction everyone would expect, anyways. It was daring, but no one would expect a man who had been working at Cortim for twenty years with no records of insubordination to run away now, and they would never expect him to head east, deeper into Torrac's realm. That just wasn't what runaway slaves did.

Lianna had no doubt that they would escape Oslir's pursuers, so that wasn't what bothered her now. She was just dismayed by the fact that she wasn't heading home. She hadn't volunteered to be on this mission in the first place, and she definitely wasn't supposed to be heading deeper into the Lentour kingdom when half the group was heading back. She was willing to help in the war that she knew was coming, but she wasn't a hero, wasn't made for the constant excitement and danger. Working behind the scenes from home was her ideal method of fighting the Lentours, not participating in dangerous spying missions, possibly even fighting. And yet, here she was, waiting for her uncle to show up so they could begin the next leg of this expedition.

"Well," Lesric said as Alssa, Leumas, and Elyk disappeared into the trees, "It looks like now we get to wait. Anyone have anything to say to pass the time?"

"You haven't told us much about yourself," Kedrin said. "How did you end up crossing the Wasteland in the first place? That's not exactly a route people usually take."

"The story's not that exciting," Lesric said.

"I'll tell you to stop if it gets too boring,"

"Well," Lesric began, "I was born in Etneog. When I was seven, we moved to a small town in the mountains, on a pass between the Syntor and Risclan.

"At twenty, I decided that I didn't want to be a farmer like my father. I wanted to learn a trade. I hadn't made any progress until my father's friend, who lived in a town just outside of Pruglin, wrote to me, saying that he needed an extra hand and wondered if I was interested. But he ran a blacksmith shop, and I wasn't sure I was interested in that.

"After looking around for another year, I thought about him again and wrote to him, asking if he would still be willing to hire me. He was, so I started out for Pruglin. I was impatient, though, and decided to take the shortcut: crossing an arm of the Syntor Wasteland. That ended up being the best decision I ever made. If I had taken the usual route, we might not have found out about the Lentour invasion until it was too late."

"It's more exciting than anything I've done," Kedrin said. "Our life is pretty boring. We were born in Pruglin City, and we've lived there ever since. That's about it."

"And we had to ruin that beautifully boring life by coming on a crazy mission to the Lentour kingdom," Lianna said. "I don't know what it is about you that craves excitement so much, Brother, but you don't seem to be able to live without it."

"There has to be some excitement just to keep me going," Kedrin said. "You can't expect me to survive on nothing."

"You did fine for two decades," Lianna retorted.

"The more I'm around you two, the more I think you thrive on arguing, not adventure," Lesric grinned.

"I'm telling you!" Kedrin said. "You were very lucky to not get stuck with a sister."

At that moment, Oslir entered the clearing. "All packed and ready to go?" he asked, then continued without waiting for a response. "Good. No one will miss me at the timber site for a while, but I'd still like to put as much distance as possible between us and the castle before nightfall. We need to hurry up."

Oslir took a roundabout way, avoiding farms and people. By the end of the day, Lianna was ready to collapse, but their pace didn't slow until the sun was a giant molten orb on the horizon, just showing through the leafy boughs overhead. Finally Oslir stopped, alert and listening.

Kedrin started to speak, but Oslir quickly put a finger to his lips. Lianna looked around but was unable to identify the cause of his alarm. Nothing was out of the ordinary. A bird chirped from a nearby tree, and something scurried through the dead leaves and pine needles on the ground. But other than that...

Then she heard it. The steady marching of feet in perfect coordination. Oslir dropped onto his belly, and she, Kedrin, and Lesric followed his example.

Through the trees she caught a glimpse of armor

flashing as it caught the last rays of light. Ranks of soldiers were marching, heading southeast, in the same direction they had been travelling.

They waited for what seemed like forever while the soldiers marched past. Then came new sounds, the snort of a horse and the thumping of hooves on the road. Saddles and tack clinked together as the foot soldiers were followed by cavalry. For several more minutes, they waited as the horsemen thundered past. And then all was still.

"What was that?" Kedrin asked as they stood up.

"If you ask me," Oslir said, "those were the majority of the soldiers from Cortim Castle. I believe our friend Torrac is on the move at last, although I can't imagine what he's doing with an army like that. Based on what I saw, I think we only caught the tail end of it, and they'd been marching past here for some time before we arrived."

"The only thing in that direction is the sea," Lianna said. "What would they be doing there?"

"I really couldn't answer you," Oslir said. "But I doubt that we'll encounter any more soldiers for some time after a host like that."

"I sincerely hope you're right," Lianna said. Inwardly she groaned. *Why did I agree to come on this trip in the first place? And not only that, I had to let them convince me to go farther into enemy territory!*

"The good news is that now we know which direction the army is headed, and thus, where the next city is likely located," Lesric said. "All we have to do now is follow the road. It shouldn't be that hard."

Glancing up at the sun, Oslir seemed to make up his mind. "Let's get a bit farther away from this road and then make camp," he said.

Two hundred yards from the road they set up camp. It wasn't much, since they couldn't light a fire to break the blackness that was going to follow the setting of the sun. But Lianna was too tired to care.

* * * * *

"Taran!" A man's shout was accompanied by a loud pounding on the door. "Let me in!"

"I'm coming, I'm coming!" Taran hurried to the door, blinking sleep from his eyes. *What is wrong?* He had been taking a brief nap, trying to catch up on the rest he had been deprived of for many nights in a row. The maid who was supposed to answer the door had gone to the market for groceries, but it didn't seem like it mattered. Whoever was here obviously wanted to talk to him.

"Yes?" He finally reached the door and opened it. "Mathalin? What on earth is the matter?"

"It's the messenger. If you want to see him alive, you need to come now."

"I'm coming."

Together, the two made their way to the doctor's home. "What happened?" Taran asked on the way.

"I don't rightly know. All I know is that Dr. Jedur sent a message saying that the man is conscious but he doesn't have much time left. Something strange is going on, and he said that it's crucial we come now."

They finally reached the doctor's house on the other side of the city. Jedur, a short, stocky man, opened the door. "Mathalin, Taran, come in. You're here just in time. He has an extremely high fever, and he's been hallucinating for the past hour or so. He doesn't have long left."

Jedur led them into a small room. The messenger

lay on a cot in the corner where he tossed and turned feverishly, beads of sweat running down his face. He was muttering unintelligible phrases.

"What's he saying?" Taran struggled to catch the man's words.

"He's been talking about fire and monsters for almost an hour," the doctor replied. "I've done everything I can to break the fever, but it just keeps rising."

"What happened to him?"

"I really can't say. He developed some serious illness, but I've never seen anything like it before. This is more than a typical virus or infection."

Suddenly the man's voice rose in volume. Taran leaned closer to listen. "Fire!" he screamed in a raspy voice. "They'll all be burned. They don't know what's coming. No one knows what's coming." His voice rose in pitch and weak hands clawed at the air in terror as he tried to ward off whatever it was that so terrified him. "They're coming for me!" His voice became frantic. "Monsters, huge, terrible monsters! They're going to kill us all!"

"He's been talking like this for an hour?" Taran asked.

The doctor nodded.

Suddenly the man raised his head and looked straight at Taran. "You don't know what's coming." He paused. "You will all die. There is no stopping them." He sank back on the pillow. "Death, destruction, fire they will bring upon us!"

Taran shook his head. "You don't have any idea what happened to him, Doctor?"

"All I know is that he had a terrible fright in Forsid. That's not what's causing his fever though, so something else must have happened. I tried to find out what he saw, but I was too late. By the time he woke up from his coma, he was rapidly going downhill, and his fever was already quite high. I've done all I can for him."

"Our squad should be back within the week, provided the same thing doesn't happen to them. Hopefully they'll be able to give us some more clues. Until then, we just have to wait," Mathalin said.

"They'd better be back soon with answers," Taran said. "Kedrin and Lianna are still out there, and they have no idea that this is going on. They are in danger, and the sooner I know exactly what's going on out there so I can do something about it, the better I'll feel."

They left the house and were stepping onto the road when Jedur called after them. "Wait! Come back! There's something I forgot to tell you!"

"Yes?" Mathalin asked.

"He did have a scratch on his arm. I wouldn't think anything of it, except that it is, well, come and look."

He led them back to the sick room to where the ill man lay moaning. The hysteria was gone, but beads of sweat ran down his face. Jedur rolled up his patient's sleeve and undid a bandage to expose a shallow scratch three inches long. It was hard to tell how deep it was, but Taran thought it had barely broken the skin. It wasn't the kind of injury usually classified as life threatening. Except for one aspect, that is.

"Quite unnerving, isn't it?"

A bluish liquid oozing from the wound had dried around the edges of the gash, forming a crusty blue perimeter around the injury. Taran shivered. Something sinister was going on here. "That squad had better return with answers."

CHAPTER 11

T he first rays of dawn pierced the leafy foliage overhead, and Lianna's eyes flickered open. She rolled over and looked around at her unfamiliar surroundings, taking a second to register where she was. Then she remembered that they had left their old camp-site and were on the trail of a massive group of soldiers that was probably heading for one of Torrac's major out-posts.

She sat up. Oslir and Lesric were still asleep, but Kedrin was already up, searching for something in his pack. He finally pulled out his water skin and stood up. "Lianna, want to come along?" he asked as he spotted her awake. "I thought since no one else was up yet, I'd try to find some water."

She climbed to her feet. "Sure." Grabbing her water skin, she followed him to the edge of the camp, then into the forest beyond.

They walked in silence for several minutes. Kedrin was the one who broke the quiet. "Do you find it as strange as I do that the Lentours have been able to hide their existence from us for so long? The more I learn, the more I'm amazed that we didn't catch any of this years ago."

Lianna agreed. "They're just across a desert from us, and we didn't even know it for half a century."

"All of the districts closed up to the outside world after the war," Kedrin mused thoughtfully. "Not many people leave Risclan Valley anymore, and the ones that do usually don't come back. And almost no one comes into the valley. I think that we've aided Torrac by remaining so isolated."

"There's a reason no one enters the valley," Lianna pointed out. "More than Risclan being too weakened by the war to care about what goes on beyond our borders. Maybe that's the purpose of the slave traders: to keep people from coming in and out as much as possible, and get laborers for Torrac in the process. Legend has spread of monsters lurking in the Syntor Wasteland, of bandits who slaughter whole caravans, and of dust storms that come up so fast you can't escape, which people think explains why so many who enter the desert never come back. Yes, siladis do exist, but even they are nothing like the creatures described in the stories we grew up hearing, and most of the rest of the tales have nothing to them. But other than the siladis and the slavers, we never faced any real danger."

"Do you hear that?" Kedrin stopped moving.

Lianna heard it too; the sound of water trickling over stones. They followed the sound to its source and filled the water skins, then turned and made their way back to the camp.

A short time later, the four were back on the move. They traveled parallel to the Lentour road, far enough that it was easy to hide when anyone passed. There wasn't much traffic, and for the next two days they continued, skirting around farms when necessary, but otherwise moving unhindered.

On the third day after leaving Cortim, though, this

changed. The number of people on the road tripled, and they found themselves having to avoid farms altogether too often. Finally, there was no choice but to take the road and just try to blend in with the other passersby. Their plan succeeded, although Lianna inwardly cringed each time they passed a Lentour soldier. Outwardly she remained calm, but she wasn't able to conquer the constant nagging fear that they were going to be discovered.

By mid-afternoon, the number of people they passed had tripled again. The road had grown wider, and a steady stream of people was now traveling in both directions. She could see figures silhouetted against the blue sky at the crest of the hill they were climbing, passing over the summit of the ridge either coming towards or heading away from them.

As they reached the top of the hill, everyone gasped, astounded by the unexpected sight.

The Syntor Wasteland had been huge, but it had prepared them only slightly for this sight. This was completely different from the Syntor. A vast body of water lay before them, stretching away as far as the eye could see until finally blending with the blue sky on the horizon. The sapphire water sparkled in the sunlight, unlike anything Lianna had ever seen.

"I've heard the ocean was large, but I never expected that," Kedrin said in awe.

Only Oslir didn't seem surprised. "I didn't realize we were this close," he said, "although I should have known by the number of people on the road. My guess is that our quest is nearly over. If you ask me, the stronghold we've been looking for is an ocean port. We'll probably reach it today."

Lianna was amazed. The largest body of water she

had seen was Milsad Lake. This was so much bigger and so open that she was overwhelmed. As they descended the hill, the ocean became hidden behind the trees. But another hour of walking proved Oslir's prediction true.

It took them only a short time to reach Medfe, a thriving port city with a strong Lentour presence. Unlike Cortim Castle and the area around it, the citizens of Medfe seemed to be just that: citizens. No forced laborers, no sign of the oppression that had settled over the inhabitants of Cortim like a thick cloud, were present here. The people of Medfe were, more or less, free.

But evidence of Torrac was everywhere. His soldiers guarded the gate, and she spotted them throughout the city. They might not have enslaved the citizens, but they were there, ready to quell the slightest hint of a rebellion. The soldiers were passive, but they were present.

The four slowly crossed the sprawling city to the harbor on the opposite side. It was massive, with huge ships of various designs anchored in its extensive docks. While some appeared to be built for transporting soldiers from place to place, others were clearly designed for sea battles, and a third group of peculiar-looking ships seemed to have some unique purpose Lianna couldn't imagine. They resembled cargo barges intended for the open sea, but something was different. The hatch in the center of the deck was huge and solidly built, designed for something more than covering the hole that led below decks. Everything about it was made to withstand incredible force, but she had no idea why.

"What's that?" Lesric asked, pointing to the far corner of the harbor.

A large, sturdy pier enclosed by a strong fence a

good eight feet high extended far out into the water. Once on land, the fence rose to ten feet and was reinforced by more massive logs to form a pathway to a structure that bore a striking resemblance to a massive barn.

"One of those bizarre looking ships is pulling up to the pier," Kedrin observed. "The ship and building are both built for the same purpose."

"But what's the purpose?" Lianna asked.

"Let's find an inn where we can spend the night," Oslir said, glancing up at the sinking sun. "We can explore more in the morning."

* * * * *

The next morning they left the inn to further scout out the city. Not knowing where else to start, they began at the harbor.

The only thing they discovered that day was the location of the barracks, a sprawling collection of buildings capable of housing hundreds of soldiers. It was situated just off the harbor, a location that made transporting soldiers by boat and getting supplies to the garrison easy.

"I don't understand how Torrac could have hidden something this massive from us for this long. A castle in the middle of the forest, maybe. But a whole operation like this? How could we remain so blind to the rest of the world?" Lesric asked back at the inn that night.

"Lianna and I had the same conversation a few days ago," Kedrin said. "The districts closed up from the outside world so much after the war that we became completely blind to everything going on outside of our small sphere of influence."

Oslir nodded his agreement.

"I think Torrac helped us stay ignorant by planting slavers in the Syntor and making travel difficult and dangerous," Kedrin continued. "The five districts even pulled apart from each other, and while I agree that this scheme should have been discovered decades ago, I think our biggest problem now is stopping it."

"I think you're right," Oslir agreed. "Tomorrow, we will do some careful questioning and try to find out what's going on here. Where are the soldiers coming from and how many are there? And how widespread is Torrac's domain?"

"I think we also need to learn the purpose of that strange barn-like contraption at the harbor," Lianna said. "It could just be some kind of warehouse. But that dock looked much too sturdy for unloading normal cargo. Something doesn't feel right about it."

Medfe bothered Lianna, the whole city. It just wasn't right that something this large had remained hidden just a few hundred miles from Risclan Valley. She didn't like it. She hoped that the next day brought some answers.

CHAPTER 12

A nother steady knocking at the front door interrupted Taran's train of thought. Ever since visiting Dr. Jedur, he hadn't been able to shake the specter of the messenger from his mind, and it was the object of his concentration now. That, and the hope that the squad sent to Forsid would return quickly with answers. He knew it was too soon to expect them back, but still, he was anxious for their report.

He was also becoming increasingly apprehensive about Lianna and Kedrin. The reconnaissance team sent to Cortim should be back, but they weren't, and with everything that was going on, he wouldn't feel better until they were back in the safety of Pruglin's walls.

"There's someone here to see you, sir." The maid stuck her head through the door of his office.

"Bring him in," Taran said, glancing up from his desk.

A minute later, a man entered the room. "Sir, Councilor Mathalin sent me to tell you that the messenger to Forsid died."

Taran sighed. He had expected as much.

"He also said to tell you that Dr. Jedur is still trying to learn what the mysterious illness was. He's conducting tests now, and he will let you know if he learns anything."

"Thank you for the message. Is that all?"

"Yes, sir."

"Tell Mathalin that I'll be over to see him some-time today," Taran said.

"Yes, sir."

"You may go."

After the messenger left, Taran decided to pay Dr. Jedur another visit. Setting off at a brisk pace, he made his way to the doctor's house.

The doctor answered the door at his knock. "Why, Taran, it's good to see you. Come in! You got the message?"

Taran nodded. "I came to see if you had any more information."

"You came at precisely the right moment. I believe I might have found the problem," Jedur said. "I investigated the blue substance oozing from that scratch. It comes from some kind of poison I've never seen before." He paused. "I don't think the messenger just stumbled across a group of Lentours and was shot as he fled. He didn't just manage to escape."

"What are you trying to say?" Taran asked.

"They didn't want him to die," Jedur said. "Not yet, at least. Based on the wound and what I believe I've learned about the poison, he was captured and administered a very small amount of the poison through that scratch. Not enough to prevent him from getting back, but enough to have an effect. Then he was allowed to escape."

"They wanted us to see this. They wanted us to know what they're capable of."

Jedur nodded.

* * * * *

It was Lesric's idea to divide and explore the city separately. Dividing the city into quarters, they each took one and split up, agreeing to meet back at the inn at noon to compare notes and decide what to do next.

Lianna was given the quarter of the city containing the harbor. Since she was still curious about the fortified unloading dock they'd seen the day before, she was pleased to be able to investigate further.

She made her way down to the harbor and looked around. The sheer size of it overwhelmed her, and she pondered where to start. Deciding on the section of the harbor near the barracks, she made her way there.

As she neared the dock, she noticed a child of around five playing with a toy, and she had an idea. A small child was the perfect person to ask about the ships, someone who perhaps could tell her what she needed to know without wondering why she wanted to know it.

As she approached the child, she saw that the toy was a small boat. It appeared to be a homemade miniature imitation of the large ships that lay in the harbor. Her decision had been better than she realized.

"That's a nice boat you have," she said as she reached him and crouched down to his level.

He looked up and smiled. "Thank you."

"It looks a lot like the big ones out there."

He nodded. "I love to watch the big ships sailing. Someday I'm going to have my own, just like my daddy."

"Does he have a ship like those?" Lianna asked.

He nodded emphatically. "A great big one with lots of funny animals."

"Funny animals?" Lianna asked. "What kind of funny animals?"

"Oh, they're so big, and they take them over there

102

and put them in that big barn."

"Do you see a lot of these funny animals?"

He looked sad. "No, not very often. And once they're inside the big building, I don't see them anymore." His face brightened. "I saw some yesterday, though."

"Are they still in the barn?"

He shrugged. "I never see anyone take them out of the big barn. It must be terribly full, 'cause they take lots of animals in there, but they never come out. Those poor animals probably want to go outside and play, not get stuck in that dark barn."

Lianna smiled. "Thank you for talking to me. I like your boat," she said, standing up. He waved as she walked off. *Well, I solved one mystery,* she thought as she left. *Funny animals. Now what could he mean by that?*

Lianna knew the stories of strange creatures that once roamed the land. But if they still existed, she hadn't heard of them. Supposedly huge lizards that could eat an ox in a single bite had inhabited the area, as well as the lendaros, cat-like animals as tall as a horse. Had Torrac managed to find some of these, and was he now transporting them to where he could use them as weapons of war?

She made her way over to the building where the boy had said the animals were kept. Towering thirty feet above her, it was at least a hundred yards long and was surrounded by an imposing ten foot high fence to discourage any curious passersby. She tried to find a way in, but two intimidating sentries guarded the only two entry gates. A threatening glance from them warned her off.

When it was time to rejoin the others, she had

learned nothing further. She shared what the boy had told her, and the rest were as surprised at the revelation of strange beasts as she had been.

"Look what I found," Kedrin said, holding up a piece of parchment. Oslir's face stared out at them from the center of the page, and the text below provided a detailed description and what he was wanted for. "You might want to think about a disguise," he said, and Oslir nodded.

"The last thing I want is to get caught and hauled off to Cortim now," he said. "Freedom has tasted pretty nice. I should have tried this a while ago. But frankly, I'm surprised that I was able to get this far with no sign of pursuit. I think the very boldness of the plan enabled us to get this far."

"I don't think we are making much headway here," Kedrin said. "We've searched and searched, but we barely have any information, especially considering how long we've been here. I say we keep looking for the rest of today and tomorrow, and unless something else happens, leave the next day. Maybe we can find some leads to follow, maybe not." The others nodded in agreement.

"This seems to be a central location that Torrac sends his supplies through," he continued. "We need to find where he gets those supplies."

"Let's switch the areas we're looking in," Lesric suggested. "Someone else may be able to see something we missed."

They decided to follow his advice. This time Lianna was assigned the section of the city by the gate they'd entered through. She learned nothing. But at the inn that night, Lesric, who had searched the harbor, had some news.

"Almost all of the ships are coming from some island five days' sail off the coast. The impression I got was that Torrac has troops training there. I believe it is also where the animals that Lianna learned about come from."

"How do we get there?" Kedrin asked.

"That's the problem. We don't. People don't go there. It took a lot of digging to learn this much, and I don't think many people are supposed to know about this place."

"So we need a boat, and a good enough excuse to get into a highly restricted area," Oslir said.

"Except for the fact that there's another problem," Lesric said, taking a deep breath. "A second port city lies farther west and just south of Risclan. Apparently, a lot of soldiers are being transported here overland, and then by ship to the city. I think Pruglin needs to be warned."

"So we need to decide whether to go and warn Pruglin, or take our chances and catch a ride to the island. We can't split up like we did last time. There wouldn't be enough of us to hold our own in a fight." Kedrin said.

"Right."

"How imminent does this attack sound?" Lianna asked.

"I don't know," Lesric said. "There are just too many unknowns."

"I think the risk is too great. We need to warn them while we still can," Oslir said.

"I agree," Lianna concurred.

"I hate to give up a chance that we might never have again," Kedrin said, "but I think we need to warn Pruglin and the other districts."

"I happen to agree with all of you, so it's unanimous," Lesric said. "I say we stay for one more day to do a little more exploring and then head home."

CHAPTER 13

A fter two weeks of uneventful travel out of Medfe, they reached Forsid, the capital of the southernmost district and the city that marked their return to Risclan Valley.

At least, where Forsid should be.

As they emerged from the dense forest onto a hill that overlooked the city, Lianna's jaw dropped in horror.

Instead of a busy city, bustling with people and activity, charred remains of wrecked beams and blackened stones lay strewn around the site. The walls of the city, which had once towered proudly into the sky, were crumbled in some places, ripped apart in others, and stood in a scant few locations as broken reminders of former grandeur. Forsid City was no more.

Kedrin inhaled sharply, and Oslir gasped.

"We're too late," Lesric said dully, staring at the scene of destruction. "They were already here."

Numbly, they started forward, drawing nearer to the desolation and struggling to comprehend what they were looking at. As they neared the city, Lianna realized with shock that this devastation was not the work of men. This was something bigger.

"Look!" Lesric pointed.

Lianna followed his finger to a large indentation in the ground.

"What is that?" she asked.

They walked over to inspect it up close.

"That's impossible." She refused to believe her eyes.

But there was no denying what they saw.

* * * * *

Taran was worried. The squad he'd sent to Forsid should have been back three days ago, but it wasn't. And then there had been the arrival of Leumas, Alssa, and Elyk—without Kedrin and Lianna. They had given him maps and charts of Cortim Castle, and the news that his son, daughter, and brother, Oslir, who had been lost for twenty years, had gone farther into Torrac's domain with Lesric.

It sounded absurd, yes, and two months ago he wouldn't have believed it. But he was getting used to incredible news now, and even though it made him angry and concerned, he had no choice but to accept it.

He pondered sending another team to Forsid, but thought better of it. If nothing happened in a few more days, he would go himself. It sickened him to think that he might have sent those men to their deaths, and he wasn't going to do that again.

Right now, another Council meeting was about to begin, and as he sat at the table, councilors trickled into the room. Once everyone had assembled, Mathalin stood up from the head of the table and quiet fell. He took a deep breath and began to speak.

"I'm about to tell you something that you're probably not going to believe, but bear with me and remember that I'm just passing along the information I was told. I'll begin with this: the team we sent to Forsid is back. And this is what happened."

* * * * *

"It can't be!" Oslir gasped.

They stared in awe at the spectacle. It was a footprint, a reptilian footprint, bigger by far than anything Lianna had ever seen. Though the ground was fairly dry and it hadn't rained for days, the print had sunk a good three inches into the ground. Whatever creature this belonged to was bigger than anything she had imagined in her wildest dreams.

Lianna staggered back, lightheaded. *There are no animals that big.* Yet here was clear, undeniable evidence that there were. *It's not possible. I'm dreaming; I'll wake up.* But she was not dreaming, and no matter how many times she told herself she was imagining things, the footprint didn't go away.

Looking behind her, Lianna could see a clear path through the trees where massive pines that had stood for decades, in some cases longer, had snapped like twigs. Large trees had been splintered by some creature that was even larger.

"I think we know what type of animals Torrac is transporting," Kedrin said.

"That's impossible! You can't transport something that big on a ship." Lianna was still in shock.

"My guess is that he moves them to where he'll need them when they're young," Lesric said. "There's no way something this massive could be moved on a boat."

As they drew nearer to the ruins of the city, Lianna saw that the buildings were ripped apart, splintered by something of colossal size. Apparently not satisfied with the destruction wrought by the beast, the invaders had then set the demolished city ablaze.

Lianna felt sick. "Pruglin is next."

"We need to get there as fast as we can and warn them of what's coming!" Kedrin said with anger in his voice.

Oslir looked up from where he was sifting through the remains of a building. "This was probably done a week ago. If that army's next target was Pruglin, it's already destroyed. And even if it's not and we can still make it in time, what can we do against something like this? Look here. This beam was snapped as easily as you would break a stick. We can't fight something like that."

"I agree," Lesric said. "Our army is weak after fifty years of inaction. Most of the veterans from the last war have died, and the ones that haven't are old and feeble, not capable of fighting a war. We have an army, and we are going to do everything we can, but no one knows how to fight a battle, not against an enemy like this."

"But we can't just stand by and watch as they are killed! We have to at least make an effort," protested Lianna. Even if there was no chance of winning, they had to fight.

"That's not what I'm saying," Oslir said. "I won't stand by idly while someone orders a massacre of helpless people. I'm all for fighting. I'm just saying that I don't know how we're going to do Pruglin any good."

"I say we see what else we can learn here, and then get to Pruglin as fast as we can." Lesric said.

They spread out and searched quickly through the rubble for any more clues about what had happened. Scattered throughout the ruins were human corpses, some burnt, some crushed by the beast or by falling buildings, and a few killed by swords. It became obvious that the monster had been the cause of nearly all the casualties, while the soldiers had played a minimal part.

The beast's tracks trailed around the ruins, showing where it had stalked through Forsid and left destruction in its wake. There was very little to indicate that an army had accompanied the beast, though. While they found the remains of a small campsite to one side of the city, no more than a hundred or so men could have stayed there, nowhere near enough to destroy something like Forsid.

Lianna was horrified by what she saw. *Torrac must have trusted that thing to do his dirty work for him. He knew an army wasn't necessary.*

They made camp in the forest on the edges of the city and prepared for the next day's journey.

* * * * *

"Forsid was attacked by a giant beast," Mathalin said. "The team we sent found huge beams snapped like sticks and houses flattened by some monster bigger than anything you can imagine. When the creature had finished its work, Lentour soldiers burned the remains."

His announcement was met with heated denial.

"There are no animals that big," one man shouted.

"That's impossible! The city was burned, sure, but no creature is that large," another added.

Mathalin nodded to a man who wasn't a councilor and whom Taran hadn't noticed before, and he stood up. "I was there."

"You're lying!" someone shouted.

"I'm from Werlsog, a small village a few miles out of Forsid City," he began slowly. "I'm a logger, not someone who makes a living talking to city councils. But I know that if I don't do that now, every person in Pruglin City is going to be slaughtered, just like at Forsid, so listen to what I saw and decide if it's a threat worthy of your

111

attention."

He took a deep breath and began his tale. "Two weeks ago, I was cutting timber in the forest a mile or so from the city when I heard a sound more hideous than anything I've heard in my life. It wasn't human, but it wasn't any ordinary beast, either. It was the most terrifying thing I've ever heard.

"I wanted to run, but I couldn't. That sound drew me, it pulled me in. I lost track of how far I'd gone, when above sounds of crashing and roaring, I could make out screams. This time, though, they were from people."

The man stopped and looked down at the ground, the horror of what he had seen and heard still fresh in his mind. "I slowed my headlong pace and started creeping closer, trying not to be seen. At the edge of the trees, I stopped.

"It was a lizard, a lizard as tall as the trees. It stalked right through the city, crushing houses with its feet or swiping them away with its tail. This thing was a city destroyer. Forsid was on fire, and I saw the animal for only a moment before it vanished into the smoke, but that was more than I needed or wanted. I got out of there as fast as I could."

He looked up, making eye contact with them for the first time. "I know what that monster did to Forsid, and I know that if you don't believe me, thousands of people are going to die." He looked at them, pleading in his eyes.

"Is there any doubt that he's speaking the truth?" Mathalin asked.

"I can see that he thinks he does," one man spoke, "but he could still be delusional."

"Am I delusional too?" Taran recognized the

speaker as the leader of the reconnaissance team to Forsid. "I didn't see the beast itself, but I saw its tracks. So did the ten men with me. Maybe we're all delusional?" He spoke scornfully.

"Gentlemen," Mathalin said, "we can deny it all we want, but it's not going to change anything. We need to stop arguing about whether such a creature really exists and start worrying about how to fight something like this."

Which, Taran thought grimly, *is far easier said than done.*

CHAPTER 14

T he look of relief on Rilan's face when they stepped through the front door five days after leaving Forsid was priceless, and the twenty minutes following their arrival home were the best twenty minutes Lianna had spent in over a month. She was exhausted, but she was home, and her part in this war was over.

Then Taran turned back to business, wanting to know everything they had to tell about Medfe and the other sections of Torrac's realm. Mathalin arrived soon after, and he grilled them on every aspect of the mission. For the next two hours they answered questions until Mathalin was finally satisfied that he had heard everything. He scheduled a Council meeting for the next day to give a report to the rest of the councilors.

As they sat down to a feast that night, Lianna was almost able to forget that they were at war and that the monster that obliterated Forsid could exterminate them whenever Torrac saw fit.

Almost.

* * * * *

They were sitting down to breakfast the next morning when the courier arrived. Agitated and out of breath, he panted his message in between ragged gasps.

"Councilor," he said, "three of the scouting parties patrolling the Pruglin border didn't report back to the city last night. Councilor Ildug is leaving to investigate, and asked you to meet him at the South Gate in twenty minutes."

"They never came back?" Taran asked. "Three parties? Out of how many?"

"Six," the man responded, his breathing becoming more controlled. "Three out of six."

"Those parties had fifteen men each! How could three of them just disappear?" Taran stood up, anger mixed with fear on his face. There was only one explanation, but Lentours in Risclan this close to Pruglin City, disposing of three scouting parties consisting of fifteen men each, boded nothing less than disaster. The evil kingdom that had stayed hidden for the past half a century was finally on the move, and its first actions had been very bold. "How many men is Ildug taking with him?" he asked.

"Fifteen."

Taran stared at him. "Fifteen? If the Lentours are out there, they killed forty-five men last night. Go tell Ildug I'm on my way, and tell him not to even think about going out there with only fifteen men. That would be suicide."

"I can be ready in five minutes," Kedrin said, jumping to his feet as the messenger left for the South Gate.

"So can I," Lesric said, and Oslir agreed almost simultaneously.

"Five minutes it is," Taran said.

Kedrin started out of the room on the heels of Lesric and Oslir, then thought of something and turned around. "Father, what about Lianna? She could help us out a lot with her bow. Do you know what a well-placed volley of arrows out of nowhere would do to their morale?"

No! I don't want to get involved in this again! Lianna wanted to be done with this fight, and she opened her mouth to say so. But something stopped her.

"He does have a point," Taran said thoughtfully. "Lianna, your skill could be an immense asset. Your talent is unnatural. I think it's a good idea."

"Come on, Lianna. It's not that much different than the mission we just got back from." Kedrin pleaded.

"We didn't go to Cortim Castle to fight," Lianna protested. "We went to spy. It's completely different." She looked at Kedrin and saw that he wasn't giving up. She thought back to the siladis in the Syntor, remembered how her archery had more than likely saved the team, and realized that he was right. She had an unnatural talent, and she couldn't let her aversion for fighting keep her from using that ability to save lives. She took a deep breath and let it out slowly. "All right. I'll come."

Kedrin smiled with relief but couldn't resist one last comment. "I'm getting pretty good at this."

"You're on dangerous ground," Lianna replied. "You'd better be careful or your victory is going to be very short lived." But she smiled.

"Kedrin," Taran said, "here's a friendly word of advice: go get ready and leave your sister alone. You're setting yourself up for trouble."

Kedrin grinned and disappeared through the door.

Thirty minutes later, they were moving out of Pruglin at a brisk pace, heading towards the site where one of the patrols had disappeared. The group was only twenty-five strong, and it had taken a heated debate between Taran and Ildug to even decide whether or not to risk the mission. Ildug believed that with strategy and stealth they could overcome any Lentours lurking in the forest, while Taran still held that venturing out of the safety of the city with such a small group was madness. It was only after the arrival of five more men swelled the group's numbers to its current status that Taran finally relented and let Ildug have his way. The look on his face still said that marching out was against his better judgment, and he brought up the rear of the procession warily, searching the forest for any sign of danger.

They moved stealthily along the route that the first squad had taken, making as little noise as possible, while searching for clues. But they saw nothing to show what had happened to the missing patrol. When an hour of searching had passed, Lianna started to wonder if the scouts had just fallen behind schedule and hadn't made it back to the city when they were expected.

The scream dispelled all doubts that the threat was real.

It was a woman's scream, and it came from some-where east of them. As heads snapped around in the dir-ection of the sound, Lianna saw her father catch Ildug's eye. She knew what the message was. Taran was remind-ing Ildug of their agreement: stealth and strategy before brute force. They had no idea how many Lentours were out there. All they knew was that forty-five men had disappeared last night, and the chances were small that any of those men were coming back. Confronting the Lentours head-on before they knew more was a very bad idea.

"Spread out and move in quietly," Ildug whis-pered. "We're going to find out what's going on and act from there. Don't do anything without my signal."

In just minutes, they had spread out around the

perimeter of a farm, staying low to the ground and out of sight. The farmer, his wife, and three young children huddled together just outside the open door while Lentour soldiers swarmed around them, ransacking the house and destroying everything they didn't steal.

Satisfied that they had everything they could use, one of the Lentours put a torch to the house. Another man set the barn on fire, and within minutes the two structures were engulfed by flames. The wind fanned the inferno and blew smoke in Lianna's eyes. Above the roaring of the flames, she could make out the bawling of frantic livestock as they tried in vain to free themselves from the blazing prison.

Ildug and Taran held a quick consultation, arrived at a plan, and softly gave orders. The half dozen members of the team who carried bows spread out around the perimeter of the farm. Half of those remaining circled around to the far side of the clearing, and everyone else stayed where they were to wait for Ildug's signal.

At least twenty Lentours milled around the terrified farmer and his family. Lianna scrutinized the situation as she moved into position and realized that the victims presented the biggest problem. Unprotected, they would be the first to fall when the fight started. The job of the archers, once the footmen broke cover, was to ensure that didn't happen.

At Ildug's shout, twenty men burst out of the forest. The Lentours reacted more quickly than Lianna thought possible, drawing swords and moving swiftly into position to deflect the onslaught. At the same time, three Lentours branched off from the main body to deal with the farmer's family. Lianna knew what she needed to do, but didn't know if she could do it. She froze with the arrow pulled back and ready to release, unable to let it go.

Suddenly the youngest child, a toddler, let out a piercing scream and clung to his mother as he stared in horror at the Lentours that were nearly upon them. That was enough for Lianna. She released the arrow and closed her eyes as it hurtled toward its target. She opened her eyes a second later and grabbed another arrow, trying not to look at the man on the ground with a feathered shaft protruding from his chest. The next Lentour collapsed with an arrow from another archer as she drew back the string a second time, and the third man fell with her arrow embedded in his neck.

The family stood there for an instant, trying to understand what had happened. Then the man quickly picked up the toddler and pushed his wife and the other two children towards the trees where Lianna was concealed. They didn't know what was going on, but they still intended to take full advantage of the diversion. They weren't going to give the Lentours another chance to end their lives.

The middle child, a six-year-old girl, pulled ahead of her family, running straight towards Lianna. Seeming to understand what was at stake, she put as much distance as possible between herself and the men who had burned her home and tried to kill her. She didn't stop until she was within ten feet of Lianna, then realized that her path was taking her straight towards another stranger armed with a bow. She stopped short, sure that she had run right into another Lentour.

Lianna dropped the bow and smiled reassuringly. "I'm not going to hurt you," she said. "We're here to help."

The farmer stopped behind his daughter, staring

at Lianna. "You're from Pruglin?" he asked, and she nodded. Relief flooded his face. "Thank you," he said. "You saved our lives."

"Come on," Lianna said, picking up her bow and turning away from the skirmish. "We need to get further away from the fighting."

The farmer led the way into the forest, guiding them with the ease that came with years of living in these woods. Stopping in a thicket a hundred yards from the clearing, they waited as the sounds of conflict gradually subsided. Everyone stayed still and quiet, all senses tuned for the slightest warning that they weren't alone.

As more time passed and they heard nothing, the six-year-old curled up beside Lianna, the gentle rise and fall of her breathing having a calming effect on Lianna's agitated mind. She couldn't shake the image of the two bodies on the ground from her brain. She couldn't rid herself of the knowledge that she had killed two men.

Did they have families? she wondered, seeing the men in her mind's eye and still unable to believe that she had killed them. *Killed them.* The words rang through her mind, and she shivered.

"Lianna!" Kedrin's voice jerked her back to reality. She stood up and stepped out of the thicket, scanning the area for her brother.

"Kedrin!" she called, finally spotting him a short distance away.

He spun around toward the sound of her voice and smiled, relieved. The next instant, the relief turned to fear. "Behind you!" he shouted, breaking into a run. Lianna spun around. A man stood mere feet behind the farmer and his family, his sword drawn and raised for the fatal strike. Lianna knew she had only seconds to act.

The six-year-old screamed as she saw the Lentour, and again, a child's desperate danger gave Lianna the determination she needed. She wasn't going to let him slaughter these innocent, helpless children.

As the sword began its deadly descent, the girl cowered on the ground and held her arm over her face in a futile attempt to ward off the blow.

Lianna acted from pure instinct. She knew the range was much too close for her bow, but she grabbed an arrow anyway. Drawing back her arm, she hurled it at the man like a dart. It met his chest with a sickening *thunk*, and he collapsed to the ground. One look told her he was dead.

The girl retreated to her mother's grateful arms, sobs racking her frame. The past hour had been something no child should have to endure, but this had sent her over the edge. Lianna was amazed that she hadn't completely collapsed much earlier than this.

Then Kedrin bounded up beside her. "Are you all right?" he asked.

She nodded. "I'm fine." Inwardly, she didn't really feel fine. Now she had killed three, and the last one had been from ten feet away, looking into his eyes as he fell to the ground. Guilt weighed her down.

Kedrin's eyes met hers, and she knew he felt the same way.

As they headed back to Pruglin, Lianna realized that something had changed in her. She hated killing, but after seeing what atrocities Torrac's men were capable of first hand, she harbored a fierce determination to do all she could to stop them. Kedrin wasn't going to have to beg her to come along next time. She was going to do everything in her power to stop the Lentours. She was going to fight.

CHAPTER 15

T he next day, Lianna began learning the art of the sword. Taran, a master at the craft, was also an excellent trainer. Within a few days, the blade no longer felt large and unwieldy in her hands, and Lianna began to understand the strategy involved.

Lesric and Kedrin dueled in the backyard daily, and Lianna was still amazed at the speed with which their swords flew. They attacked with such agility and force that she was astonished they didn't kill each other. The two of them had become inseparable. Their trip to Cortim Castle and beyond had forged in them an identical single desire: to see Torrac overthrown, and the friendship their common goal had produced was a strong one.

Practice in horseback riding also became a regular occurrence. Lianna had learned to ride at a young age, but now, the skill had gone from a recreational talent to something that could save her life. Kedrin often joined her, and occasionally, when he had time, Lesric did as well.

On the fourth day after the fight at the farmhouse, two members of the Brodalith Council arrived. Two more from Qatran reached Pruglin the following day, and a representative from Etneog was on his way as well.

Whenever Lianna was in the streets, she saw fear

in the faces of nearly everyone she met. After hearing about the destruction of Forsid, the people were in a state of near panic, knowing that at any time they could be slaughtered like ants. The missing scouting parties had never been found, and although the scouts now took more precautions than ever, the disappearance of several more patrols over the next few weeks didn't help to raise the people's morale. Their lives were in the hand of the evil and brutal Torrac, and when he gave the inevitable order, they would all be killed, just like the citizens of Forsid. The Council hadn't told them about the mammoth beast, but somehow word had leaked out that some type of monster had accompanied Torrac's army, and the news magnified their fear to absolute terror.

Soon refugees began to arrive from Forsid district. They all brought the same story: parties of soldiers had appeared without warning, raiding farms or even whole villages, slaughtering the inhabitants, and burning the buildings to the ground. Their stories added fuel to the smoldering fire of fear, and soon the councilors had difficulty restraining the terrified populace.

Taran came home from a meeting exhausted. "We need to find a way to calm the people, to give them confidence that we still have a chance of defeating Torrac. We need to remind them that we are not just sitting idle waiting for the army to arrive bringing our doom." His face was gaunt and pale, and Lianna realized for the first time just how much of a strain the situation had put on his health. He was completely worn out.

Lesric leaned forward from the corner where he sat. "You need to appoint a leader, someone who officially is in command whom they can trust. Show them the soldiers that you have trained, and remind them that there is a force standing in between them and Torrac. We're not helpless, and we will fight when the time comes."

"I think I'll tell the Council about that idea." Taran nodded, considering Lesric's words. "I like it."

Three days later, Ildug was formally declared head of the Pruglin army, and he marched through the streets at the head of a contingent of the best of the soldiers who had been training for the past few months. The parade helped for a few days, but it didn't last.

News continued to trickle in from the southern end of the valley. More farms were burned, villages obliterated, people massacred. Lianna watched helplessly as chaos built over the following weeks. She was powerless to stop it, and she knew that it was destroying the city. If they weren't able to get the people under control, when Torrac did show up, he was going to massacre them as easily as he had slaughtered the citizens of Forsid. They would all die.

One sunny day two months from the fight with the scouts at the farm, a messenger arrived at the house, summoning Taran to a meeting immediately.

"You'd better hurry, sir," he said. "Mathalin said that it is crucial that you are there as soon as possible. And sir, he looked as scared as I've ever seen him."

Taran had hurried out the door, and Lianna watched in breathless suspense. She didn't know what was going on, but she knew it was bad. Very bad.

Thirty minutes later, another messenger arrived, out of breath and anxious. "Councilor Taran told me to ask for Lesric, Kedrin, and Lianna, and to tell them to come immediately."

"Lesric, Kedrin, and Lianna?" Kedrin asked when

he heard the message. "That's a little bit random. Lesric, yes. He's a local hero. But why do they want us?"

"That is a very good question," Lianna said, just as puzzled as her brother.

Five minutes later, they were jogging toward the city square. A cold knot of dread tightened in Lianna's stomach as she ran. The suspense was too great, and though she wanted to be aware of what was going on, at the same time, she was afraid to know.

They finally reached the door of the Council chamber. Breathless, the three of them stopped, panting, and stood there for a moment. Then Lesric reached for the double oak doors and swung them open.

Taran, Mathalin, and several of the other more influential Council members paced the floor, extremely agitated. Mathalin looked up as they entered.

"Thank goodness," he said. "You're here. We have an urgent mission for you. A farmer from Forsid District just arrived in town. He said…" Mathalin trailed off, staring into the distance. "He said the Lentours are marching. They're burning Forsid District as they go, sacking towns and leaving a wake of destruction. And he heard that same sound the man who witnessed the destruction of Forsid City described. We need you to perform reconnaissance and determine whether this is a real threat, and if so, how imminent."

"Why us?" Kedrin asked. "Lesric I understand. But Lianna and I? We went to Cortim Castle. But so did three other people, and I don't see how that qualifies us more than anyone else. We're just two nobodies."

"You went on from Cortim to Medfe," Mathalin said. "And your father has vouched for you. He believes you have what's needed. You've already worked with

Lesric on multiple occasions. And the most convincing argument is that we don't have time to find anyone else. Whoever we send needs to leave within the hour, so if you have any objections, voice them now."

"I won't speak for all three of us," Lesric said, "but I will happily go if it's how I can best help in the defense of the city."

"I'll go," Kedrin said. The expression on his face said more than his words. There was a fierce determination, a fiery resolve that Lianna hadn't seen before. He was utterly committed to seeing this mission through.

Only two months ago, Lianna would have refused such a mission. But after the fight at the farm, something inside of her had changed. Whenever she remembered the terror on the faces of the children facing a cruel death, she felt rage boil up inside of her. She would do everything she could to help protect the helpless, and if that meant going to find the army that destroyed Forsid, she wouldn't hesitate. "I'll go."

"Good. We'll have the farmer give you directions. We tried to convince him to take you, but he says he won't go a step farther south than the South Gate of Pruglin. He's even considering fleeing on to Brodalith to be farther away from the threat. You'll just have to make do with oral directions."

"That's fine," Lesric said. "Finding a creature big enough to trample a city shouldn't be that hard."

A few moments later, a man, who appeared nearly petrified with fear, entered the room. "Y-yes, s-sir," he stammered.

"I need you to give directions to the group I'm sending to investigate the threat. That is, if you haven't changed your mind about accompanying them."

"No, sir! Not for all the money in the world. I'm not going near that thing." His stammer disappeared as he firmly voiced his decision, and Lianna could see that there was no changing his mind. He was truly terrified.

"Directions to the farm?" Ildug prodded.

The farmer spoke quickly, his eyes darting around the room and over his shoulder as if he were afraid Lentours would appear around the corners or through the windows at any moment. Lianna was used to the fear she saw in the citizens of Pruglin, but this took the word "terror" to a much higher level.

When they were satisfied that they knew where they were going, Ildug briefed them on the specifics of what information he needed. Lesric nodded his understanding, and Kedrin seemed to be taking it all in, but Lianna felt so overwhelmed that she found it hard to focus on all the details as she tried to process what was going on.

The briefing concluded and they left the Council house and jogged back home. After a few minutes spent gathering provisions and weapons it was time to leave. Rilan stood on the front steps and watched as they headed down the lane, the same look on her face that Lianna had seen when they left for Cortim Castle.

"Be safe!" she called after them. "Please try to come back in one piece." Her voice quivered.

Lianna had heard this speech time and again, and she smiled She recalled hearing versions of it when she went on picnics with her friends as a ten-year-old, or went with her father to the river. She turned and waved for the last time just before they turned the corner and Rilan disappeared from view.

"We need to move fast if we're going to get information back in time to benefit the city," Kedrin said.

"Agreed," Lesric said. "I wish we could have brought horses, but it's just too hard to stay hidden with them. If one of them snorts or stomps a hoof at the wrong time, we could be done for. This way is slower, but there's a better chance of making it back alive, which is my biggest priority."

"But can we make it in time without them?" Kedrin asked. The question was rhetorical, but it remained at the forefront of everyone's mind.

They quickly traversed the fastest route to the South Gate, then without a backward glance, Lianna stepped outside of the town, marking the beginning of the third expedition against the Lentours she had been a part of in the last few months. The road that emerged from the South Gate would take them nearly all the way to the farmer's house in the forests of Forsid, but Lesric worried that in following it they would be more likely to encounter Lentours scouting ahead of the main army, so they turned off the road soon after departing the city.

The farm was a two days' travel from Pruglin following the road at a normal pace, but the farmer had told them that he was able to make the trip in a little over a day by cutting through the forest and running most of the way. Since it was imperative that they return as quickly as possible, they would follow the journey he had taken.

Lianna was glad when Lesric finally called a halt for lunch. They all ate quickly, knowing that they needed to be on the road again as soon as possible.

"We can't maintain the breakneck pace we've been traveling at," Lesric said as they finished their food. "Let's start out again slowly and try alternating bursts of speed with a more maintainable rate."

Kedrin and Lianna agreed with his reasoning, and when they set out again, it was at a slow, steady speed. By the time they sped up to a brisk walk, Lianna felt rested and was able to keep up fairly easily for some time.

They kept going into the night, not stopping until two hours after the last rays of sunlight had disappeared behind the trees. Lianna was thoroughly worn out, and was asleep almost as soon as she hit the ground.

The next morning followed the same pattern as the day before. Birds sang in the trees, and rabbits scampered away as she passed. Nothing hinted at the destruction that was steadily approaching.

It was close to noon when Lianna thought that she smelled smoke. It was faint, and she wasn't sure if she was just imagining it until Kedrin stopped dead in his tracks a few minutes later.

"I smell smoke," he said.

"Now that you mention it, I do too," Lesric agreed.

"Listen," Lianna said.

"To what?" her brother replied after a moment of silence. "I don't hear anything."

"Exactly. When we started out, there were birds and other forest creatures all around. Now, we seem to be the only living things for miles."

"I think we're nearing our destination," Lesric said. "Let's slow down and be more careful. I don't want to run right into the army."

An hour later, Lesric spoke. "Someone's coming."

"Should we hide?" Kedrin asked.

But it was too late. As soon as the words were out of his mouth, a man turned the corner. He looked like a bear was chasing him. He stopped, startled, when he saw them, then appeared to be satisfied that they were friends, not foes. "You're going the wrong direction!" he exclaimed. "Haven't you heard? Torrac is coming!"

"Did you see him?" Lesric asked calmly. "Can you tell us what you saw?"

"Yes," he panted. "I was in my field harvesting my wheat when I heard a blood curdling screech, frightening enough to let the stupidest person in the land know that their life was in danger. I did what any sane person would do. I ran."

He glanced over his shoulder, as if ensuring he hadn't been followed, then continued.

"I stopped at the far side of the field and turned around, and then saw something flash through trees. I'm sure it was armor. Then I heard the screech again, and I didn't wait to see any more." He looked at them. "Why are you interrogating me? You don't believe I'm telling the truth?"

"Actually, Torrac is the reason we're coming this way," Lesric replied. "We're a reconnaissance party from Pruglin City."

"That so? Well, let me give you some advice. Turn around and go back. It's the only way to save your lives, and if Torrac catches you, you won't help Pruglin at all."

He gave a brittle laugh. "Not that you can help them anyway. There is no stopping him. I know what happened to Forsid. Mark my words, Pruglin is doomed to the same fate. Flee while you still have the chance. And don't flee to Pruglin either. I'm going on to Etneog, as far from Torrac and that beast of his as I can get. You'd do well to follow my example."

Without another word, he turned and ran.

The three of them exchanged a glance, then set off

again, towards the south, from which so many stories of terror had come.

CHAPTER 16

T wo hours after they had met the refugee fleeing for his life, the thing Lianna had been expecting and dreading happened.

A horrible screech split the air.

She froze, and for a fraction of a second, her heart
seemed to cease beating. Her blood ran cold. She held
her breath.

The sound faded away, and she let out her pent-
up breath. The relief was premature. Another shriek
sounded, louder than the first, and she resisted the urge
to clap her hands over her ears. It was the most hideous
sound she had ever heard, a sound that froze the blood in
her veins and locked her muscles in place.

Lianna's first instinct was to turn around and run.
But she couldn't move. All she could do was grip the hilt
of her sword until her knuckles turned white and wait
until the sound died away.

When it was finally over, she looked at her brother
and Lesric. They, too, were frozen in place, staring toward the south from which the sound had come.

"Did you hear that?" Her voice was shaky. "There
are two of them."

They stood there for a long time, but the sound
was not repeated. "Do we go on?" Kedrin finally asked.

"We've come this far," Lesric said. "You're welcome to go back, but I'm going to find this army and those creatures, if it's the last thing I do. Don't feel compelled to go with me, though."

"No, I'll go with you." Kedrin glanced back at Lianna. "That is, as long as you're fine, Lianna."

"I'm all right," she said weakly, and tried to force a smile, but she felt the expression come out as more of a grimace.

"Are you sure you want to do this, Lianna?" Lesric asked. "All three of us don't need to go. I can finish the mission alone if you want to go back."

"No. I agreed to come, and I'm going to see this through, whether it ends when we return to Pruglin or when we die at the jaws of those monsters."

After a few more seconds, Kedrin started walking. "Well, we don't want to wait around for them to find us. Let's go."

A mile later, the screech again tore the air, sending another bone-chilling wave through Lianna. She stiffened. *Maybe this wasn't the best idea after all,* she thought. Maybe she should have stayed home.

"We need to be careful," Lesric said as the sound died away. "We're getting very close. It would be easy to walk right into a trap."

At that moment, a man appeared out of the forest for the second time that day.

"What are you doing?" he asked. "Don't you know that Torrac is coming?"

The three of them exchanged a glance, and no one spoke. The man glanced from one to the other, understanding dawning on his face.

"You're spies?" he asked.

"Are you a refugee?" Lesric replied, not answering

the question.

"Yes," the man said, shuddering. "I heard that beast of his and took off running. I'm making for Brodalith. Pruglin is too close to that monster for me."

Lianna didn't detect the same terror in him that had been in the other man.

Lesric spoke again. "Where? Where did you see them?"

"Back that way." The man cast a nervous glance over his shoulder.

"How far? Exactly what way?" Lesric demanded, growing impatient.

"Look, I don't like Torrac any more than you do, and I want to save innocent lives in Pruglin just as much as you. If you think it will help, let me take you to where my best guess is that they'll be."

"Lead the way."

The stranger turned and led them back the way he'd come. As he moved, his tunic shifted slightly, and Lianna thought she caught a glimpse of the tip of something long; it almost resembled the pommel of a sword. She fingered the hilt of her sword warily and kept all senses alert for any sign of danger.

They had been walking for ten minutes when, as they neared a dense copse of trees, Lianna could have sworn she heard a horse snort. If she had had suspicions before, now they were doubled. She quickened her speed until she'd caught up with Kedrin and tapped him on the shoulder.

Her brother turned and looked at her questioningly.

Lianna jerked her head towards their guide and then towards the cluster of trees.

Kedrin caught her message. His hand hovered near his sword, and he stared at the stranger suspiciously.

Lesric, always cautious, was walking ahead of them beside the refugee, and although she couldn't see his face, his body language led Lianna to guess he suspected the supposed refugee as well.

A moment later, she heard the muffled clink of armor and another horse whinny impatiently. Silently, she slid her sword out of the scabbard a fraction of an inch, ready for anything.

Kedrin caught up to Lesric and made eye contact with his friend, then glanced toward the stranger. Lesric nodded.

"Say," Lesric said, stopping, "We haven't heard that creature for a long time. You sure we're on the right path?"

"Of course I'm sure, you..." the man seemed about to launch into an angry discourse, but suddenly checked himself, as if remembering something. His smile was warm, but his eyes seemed cold. "I'm taking you toward my farm, where I first heard that hideous shriek," he explained. "So yes, we are on the right path."

"I think we should be veering more to the right," Lesric said.

Lianna knew what he was doing. The grove of trees was on their left.

"Do you want me as your guide or not?"

"Of course. Just making sure."

The man's eyes flicked nervously from person to person. Suddenly, without a word, he threw aside the farmer's attire to reveal soldier's armor, a sword at his hip, and a drawn dagger. Before Lianna could react, he lunged at her, knocking her down. She felt cold steel at her throat.

Her face was pressed to the ground, but she could hear Lesric and Kedrin draw their swords. It was too late.

"Drop your weapons," he growled, "or she dies."

The sound of galloping horses from the direction of the grove of trees served to emphasize his point. Within seconds, the riders had surrounded them. Horses nickered and hooves stamped as the Lentours pulled their mounts to a halt.

"Commander Wirpen, three spies from Pruglin came to see our little army," the Lentour said, his words dripping honey as he addressed someone Lianna couldn't see.

"Good work, Sergeant. I'm impressed."

The stranger who had tricked them dragged Lianna to her feet. He took her sword, bow, and arrows while the other men surrounded Kedrin and Lesric and confiscated their weapons.

Lianna fell into line behind Lesric as they were marched towards the enemy camp. They had planned on seeing the army, but not like this. She decided that she preferred observing from a distance over a front-row seat.

"Hurry up! We've already been gone too long, and General Calsym is not going to be happy with us," Wirpen ordered.

"The sight of three enemy spies will appease him," one of the soldiers replied with a chuckle.

"Keep moving!" the commander barked.

A short time later, they emerged from the forest into a large clearing. Lianna blinked as they moved from the shadows into the bright light. A large army camp was spread before them. Several large tents dominated the center, probably those of the commanders of the army. Soldiers milled around the area, occupied in the various tasks involved in setting up camp for an army.

They were marched to the large pavilion in the center, where Commander Wirpen paused at the opening. Two guards barred the doorway with swords.

"What do you want?"

"I have three prisoners for General Calsym."

One of the guards disappeared into the tent, reappearing a moment later and announcing, "General Calsym will see you and the prisoners immediately."

The commander ducked into the pavilion, and the guards escorting Lianna, Kedrin, and Lesric pushed them in after the commander.

A man with graying hair and cold blue eyes paced back and forth on the far side of the tent. "Yes, Commander?" he asked, the condescending tone all too evident.

Wirpen's eyes seethed, but his tone didn't show it. "I, by my outstanding cunning and cleverness, was able to capture these three prisoners from the district of Pruglin," he began. "We all know the skill it takes to capture alive not one but thr..."

"Enough, Wirpen! Stop flattering yourself and tell me why you want to talk to me. You know what we do with prisoners. The gonadaws will be happy tonight. I don't have time for this."

"You don't seem to understand, General. These are not just common peasants from Pruglin. They're spies, and they're more important than you seem to think."

"Very well. Put them under guard and prepare my gonadaw. I will see to them later. You'd better not be wasting my time."

"Yes, sir."

The guards pushed the three prisoners out of the pavilion and roughly escorted them to a row of wooden pens constructed of sturdy posts close together. Most of the pens held half a dozen people, but they were thrown into an empty one and the door was latched securely behind them. Remembering what the general had said about prisoners, Lianna guessed that the other captives were unfortunate peasants awaiting the same fate as them. She didn't know what a gonadaw was, but based on what she'd heard, she didn't think she wanted to meet one.

"Well, we got to see the enemy camp up close," Kedrin said wryly as the soldiers disappeared into the distance.

"As close as you can get," Lianna agreed.

Lesric pulled out a piece of parchment. "Might as well take some notes while we're here. There's always the unlikely possibility that we'll make it out alive." He began scribbling words Lianna couldn't read from where she sat.

After an hour, they heard the clanking of armor and tramp of boots as several men approached. It was clear that the soldiers were heading straight toward them.

"If an opportunity presents itself, I'm going to try to overpower one of them and get a weapon." Lesric spoke quickly and quietly. "Once I make the move, we all need to grab a weapon and make a break for it. We only get one chance, so let's make it count."

The door swung open and a man poked his head through. "Come on. General Calsym is waiting for you."

Remembering the giant beasts that they knew were accompanying the army, Lianna looked furtively around as they wound their way through the camp, but not only did she not see any animals, aside from horses, she didn't see a beaten path through the forest like the one at Forsid. *Were we wrong about the creatures from Forsid being here? But if so, then what was it that we heard?*

She purposefully stumbled as if she were too tired to go on much farther. A few minutes later she again tripped and caught herself wearily, attempting to put the soldiers off their guard. She waited for Lesric to make his move.

As they reached the southern edge of the camp, Lesric glanced at his guard and Lianna knew he was readying himself for the attempt at escape. She got ready to make a break for it.

But then the soldiers stopped, waiting. A regiment of twenty men was making its way towards them. She glanced at Lesric and saw that he was watching the approaching soldiers. It would be impossible to fight their way unarmed through this many men. They would have to wait for a better chance.

The twenty soldiers joined the group, and they continued their path to the edge of the forest. To Lianna's surprise, they continued into the trees until they were a good quarter mile from the camp, and then emerged into another, significantly smaller clearing.

In the clearing stood a stout wooden cage, made of thick stakes ten feet tall. It was a rectangular shape about twelve feet wide and twenty long. She couldn't see between the poles, but she already had a horrible guess as to what was inside. General Calsym, along with a dozen soldiers, was waiting for them. His evil smile gave her a sickening feeling that she didn't want to know any more about whatever lurked inside the enclosure.

Why are there so many soldiers here? What are they so nervous about? There are three of us, and we're unarmed. We're not that dangerous. Close to fifty soldiers were in the clearing, far more than were needed to guard them.

The soldiers led them halfway to the pen, then stopped and backed off. General Calsym stood between them and the pen.

A screech identical to the one they'd heard earlier that day split the air from behind the wooden fence.

"Well, my young friends," Calsym said, a cruel smile twitching at his lips, "shall we get started?"

CHAPTER 17

A shiver ran down Lianna's spine, and she moved closer to her brother.

Calsym looked behind them at the soldiers and nodded. Fifty swords slid out of their sheaths. A man brandishing a naked blade stepped forward slowly. He walked past them towards the fence, a terrified look on his face. He was nearly paralyzed with fear, and Lianna could see it was all he could do to walk forward.

What's in there? What could be so bad that a trained, well-armed soldier is so scared?

The man took a deep breath and grasped a crossbeam that held the door shut. He lifted it out of its restings and tossed it to the side. Then he swung the massive door open.

Through the opening Lianna caught glimpses of scaly, reptilian skin moving eagerly in anticipation. As the creature inside shifted, she saw fangs glisten in the sunlight and a cruel, bloodthirsty orb flick closed and then back open. A foul stench, like a rotting carcass, filled the air.

His job done, the man scurried back to the main group of soldiers. Only Calsym seemed unmoved by the monster in the pen. He stood between them and the beast, but Lianna could still see it clearly.

A massive head was set on a thick, stout neck,

with a yellow, lizard-like frill surrounding the joint where the head and neck met. It stood on its two back legs and its feet boasted cruel claws designed for ripping and tearing flesh. Its two front legs were small in comparison, but still shared the razor-sharp talons of the back legs and promised the same incredible strength. Sharp spikes began just below the frill and ran down the length of the spine.

It was the most terrifying creature Lianna had ever seen.

Suddenly, the creature lifted its head and shrieked again, the loud screech splitting the air.

Lianna couldn't resist the urge, and she clapped her hands over her ears. The sound faded away into silence, and she cautiously lowered her hands.

Calsym laughed a cruel, menacing sound of evil glee. "This, my dear young friends, is a gonadaw. It delights in the taste of human flesh. This particular beast hasn't eaten for several days, so it's hungry, and will be only too ready for a meal if I provide one. But don't be mistaken, it won't kill you quickly. It would much rather play a game of cat and mouse than end the fun immediately."

He looked at them shrewdly.

"Of course," he continued, "there is an alternative to filling the gonadaw's stomach. I need information about Pruglin, and should you provide it, I will be glad to let you go your own way."

He smiled. "As you have no doubt figured out, this gonadaw is a smaller relative of the creature that trampled Forsid. Torrac didn't feel our small mission merited the larger beast, or kingalor, as it is properly called, because it is quite costly to transport such an enormous creature. He sent several of these instead, to use in the battle as well as to interrogate prisoners such as your-selves."

He stopped a moment, smiling, as the beast turned its hideous eyes on the captives.

"So think long and hard before you make your decision. This gonadaw obeys my every order, but it is longing for your flesh, and once I give it permission, it will strike. You will die, slowly but surely. There will be no escape."

As if to emphasize his point, the creature let out another ear-piercing shriek. Lianna shivered. They had to betray the city or be killed by that monster? She looked at Kedrin and Lesric. Kedrin's mouth was a thin line, and his face was grim. Lesric didn't show fear, but she knew that he was carefully considering their options.

"Let's get this straight," Kedrin said. "If we tell you what you want to know, you won't allow your gonadaw, or whatever it's called, to eat us. Otherwise, it kills us."

"You seem to understand how this works," Calsym said.

"That hardly seems fair. You get a lot, but we don't get anything in return. How exactly is that an equal trade?"

Calsym laughed. "You are my captives, and I name the terms. I get the information, you get your lives. It's as simple as that. You're not getting anything more."

"And if we say no?"

"I don't think you do understand," Calsym said. His focus moved to the semicircle of men. "Commander!"

"Yes, sir!" Wirpen turned and gave an order to one of his men, who hurried back the way they had come.

Five minutes later, the soldier returned, leading a man in ragged clothing who stumbled along, terrified. The soldier prodded him with a drawn sword, past Lianna, and even past Calsym. Fifteen feet in front of the gonadaw, the soldier stopped. Leaving the prisoner there, he hurried back to the rest of the soldiers.

"Since you don't seem to fully appreciate the strength and power of a gonadaw, I have provided a demonstration for you. Don't worry, I'm sure that it will still be hungry, should you persist in refusing my generous terms. And even if it's not, it will be more than willing to kill you for the mere fun of it. Now, have you changed your mind, or shall I give the order?"

Calsym hesitated for an instant, then raised his hand in the air and opened his mouth to give the command.

"Wait!" Lesric shouted.

The general lowered his hand. "Do you want to talk?"

"You don't seem to understand," Lesric said with a patronizing smile. "You see, it doesn't matter what you do. You can order this beast to eat your whole army, but we won't tell you what you want to know. Not unless you accept *my* terms, that is. We'll answer your questions, if you answer ours. And we leave with our lives."

"That's not going to work on me." Calsym raised his hand again and began to shout once more, but his voice was cut short, and his order turned to a shocked and agonized scream. An arrow protruded from his chest. Another arrow whizzed past Lianna's head. She dropped to the ground, not wanting to become the next target.

"Hurry!" Kedrin said. He started to crawl towards

the forest, away from where the arrows were coming.

Chaos erupted around them. At Calsym's fall, the gonadaw, no longer restrained, charged out of the pen. Lianna turned her head away from the brutality, unable to bear the sight.

When she reached the treeline, Lianna rose to her feet and ran, doubled over, farther from the clearing. Twice she turned and looked back, but no one appeared to be in pursuit. Finally they stopped, panting for breath and trying to figure out what they had just seen.

"What just happened?" Lesric asked.

"I have no idea," Kedrin replied, shaking his head.

"We have to get out of here," Lianna said. "We have no weapons, and I don't want to share Calsym's fate."

Lesric laughed. "We got a much closer look at the army than we would have if we hadn't been captured. Maybe that's what we should do from now on."

"It worked this time, but I'd rather not try it again," Kedrin said wryly. "Let's get out of here."

A branch snapped in the distance.

"We need to leave," Lesric agreed.

But it was too late. An arrow whizzed through the air, landing in the ground a yard in front of him.

"Put your hands in the air!" A voice called seemingly from nowhere.

The trio hesitated.

"We have arrows on all of you. You have three seconds before we shoot." Five men emerged from the trees on all sides of them, bows in hand and arrows on the string.

CHAPTER 18

"On second thought, maybe it's better to avoid being captured," Lesric muttered under his breath, raising his hands above his head.

Lianna and Kedrin reluctantly followed his example.

The man who appeared to be the leader addressed the three. "We know you aren't Lentours, and we aren't either. We are wholeheartedly against the Lentour kingdom, but until we know who you are, we can't let you go. I apologize for the necessity of making you our prisoners, but you have to understand our position."

"If you aren't Lentours, who are you?" Kedrin asked.

"First answer my questions, and if I'm satisfied, I'll consider answering yours. Fair enough?"

"Since we're your prisoners, we don't really have much of a choice," Kedrin laughed.

"Captain, we need to get away from here. With all that commotion, our little attack back there has likely been discovered, and they'll be looking for us."

"You're right. We should get back to the others. Tie their hands and let's be off. The commander can question them."

After two hours of marching up into the mountains, they reached a camp where several dozen soldiers waited. The man whom one of the soldiers had addressed as captain took them to a large pavilion where a man named Commander Faldug questioned them.

The commander went right to the point. "Where are you from?" They didn't answer, and after several seconds, Commander Faldug repeated his question.

When they remained silent, Faldug spoke again. This time, however, he addressed one of the guards. "Release them."

It was a relief for Lianna to feel the rope slip off her hands. The rough cord had dug into her wrists and cut off the circulation. She rubbed her wrists together to get the blood flowing again.

"Now," Faldug said, "Do you trust me? I'm not your enemy. I'm just understandably curious about why the three of you were being interrogated by gonadaws. So where are you from?"

"Pruglin," Lesric said. Lianna couldn't tell whether he was giving in because of Faldug's show of trust, or had simply decided that this was a piece of information there was no point in withholding.

Faldug exchanged a surprised look with the captain. "You mean the same Pruglin that Torrac defeated in the war fifty years ago?"

Kedrin shook his head slowly. "We defeated Torrac at the end of that war."

It was Faldug's turn to look confused. "What do you mean, you defeated Torrac? Pruglin was burned to the ground and the people annihilated at the end of the war. Enough damage had been done to their forces that the Lentours retreated for several decades, but they won the fight."

"It was still standing and full of people yesterday

morning," Lesric said.

"Regardless of how the fight ended, we are talking about the same Pruglin that warred with the Lentours half a century ago?" Faldug asked.

"Yes."

"So was the city rebuilt after the war?"

"It was never destroyed," Lianna said.

"We've been led to believe otherwise for fifty years," Faldug mused, more to himself than to them. "What were you doing so near the Lentour army?" That was a piece of information that could potentially get them hung, but their silence didn't keep him from coming to the conclusion by himself. "You're spies," he said. It was a statement, not a question, but no one made any move to either affirm or deny the accusation.

"We are against the Lentours just as much as anyone else might be, and we didn't rescue you from them just to kill you ourselves. We share a common enemy, and that makes us allies," Faldug said.

"Who are you?" Lesric asked. "We haven't had any contact with the world outside Risclan for half a century. We're bordered by wilderness on three sides out of four, and our only neighbors are the Lentours to the south. So where are you from? And what are you doing in Pruglin District?"

"I realize you're in a hurry and we've delayed you considerably, so what can we get ready for you while we talk?" Faldug asked. "What weapons do you want, and can we give you horses and food?"

"Three swords and a bow," Lesric said. "And horses and supplies would be wonderful if you have any to spare."

"Go get them," Faldug said to the guard standing

by the entrance to the pavilion. "Is there anything else we can get for you?"

When they responded in the negative, he began. "We're from Glinsier."

"Glinsier?" Kedrin asked. "I thought it was defeated by Torrac in the war."

"I'm getting the feeling that history has been tampered with all around," Faldug said. "We weren't conquered. Our strength was gone and we were further weakened by a civil war involving a fight for the throne, but we weren't conquered. We've been at war with the Lentours for half a century. Not full-out war," he amended. "Torrac would crush us instantly. But we harass any small parties of soldiers foolish enough to venture into our domain, and do all we can to weaken the Lentours. We're here now because our scouts learned that an army was preparing to move, and we were sent to learn its purpose." He paused to think, then continued.

"We all know the history behind Risclan Valley. After all, before the war, the kingdom was the most powerful on the continent. But we've been told that it was completely and permanently obliterated. Until today, we thought the five districts of Risclan Valley were nothing more than history, but apparently that's not the truth.

"We found south of here the relatively fresh ruins of a city which appeared to have been destroyed by a kingalor. Based on what you've told us, I'm going to guess that that was the ancient city and capital of the district of the same name: Forsid. Am I correct?"

"You are," Lesric said.

"I'm sorry we don't have time to talk further on this subject," Faldug said. "We've obviously both been severely misinformed, and I wish we had time to get history straight."

At that moment, a horse snorted and stomped its foot from just outside the door. A man ducked into the pavilion with an armful of weapons and sacks of food.

"Excuse me, Commander, but the horses and other things you requested are ready."

"Thank you. We will be outside directly. You may go."

The man deposited his burden in a pile in the center of the tent, then turned and left.

"I assume you wish to leave immediately?" Faldug spoke.

"Yes, sir," Lesric said. "We need to beat the Lentours back to Pruglin, and we're running out of time."

"Then don't let us stop you," Faldug said. "The horses are hardy and can keep up a good pace for hours. If you hurry, you'll beat the Lentours with enough time left to deliver your intelligence and make the necessary preparations for their arrival."

"Thank you for your help," Kedrin said, and Lianna and Lesric nodded in agreement. "We owe you our lives."

"I'm sorry it had to be this way," Faldug said. "Next time it will have to be under different circumstances."

Lianna gathered up her share of the weapons and food and swung into the saddle. Lesric glanced back to ensure that she and Kedrin were ready and flicked his reins on the back of his horse to urge it forward and down the mountain—and towards Pruglin.

CHAPTER 19

As they made their way down a ridge overlooking the valley, Lianna didn't really see
the magnificent view. She was too concerned with beating the Lentour army to Pruglin to notice the scenery. At
the bottom of the ridge, they entered a meadow. Wild-
flowers blanketed the clearing in a spectacular display,
but Lianna could only think about what was going on
back in Pruglin right now. She just wanted to get home,
wanted this nightmare to be over, wanted her life to go
back to how it was less than six months ago, when the
word *Lentour* was just a legend from the past.

For the next three hours, they rode in silence.
Then the sun began to go down, disappearing behind the
crest of the mountains far too soon. Kedrin, in the lead,
reined in his horse.

"Let's take a break to eat and stretch our legs. We
can't make camp if we want to reach the city in time, but
we can at least stop for supper."

"I'm not going to argue," Lesric said, sliding out of
the saddle, and Lianna voiced her agreement as well.

"I've never been so hungry in my life," Kedrin said,
sinking his teeth into a piece of dried meat.

Lianna laughed. "You've said that pretty much
every meal of every day I've known you, brother, which
is quite a long time. I'll let it pass right now, considering

you haven't eaten since breakfast, but if you really want me to take your word for it, you may want to add some variety to your pre-meal vocabulary."

"Well, it's true," Kedrin said. "I could eat a horse."

"That's the other sentence you always say," Lianna grinned. "Come on, Kedrin."

Kedrin glared at her, and Lesric looked from one to the other. "Your poor mother, settling arguments between the two of you when you were growing up. I don't even want to know what your fights looked like when you were ten if this is how you behave a decade later. I can imagine some of them got nasty."

"I'll say!" Lianna exclaimed. "He knocked out my tooth when I was nine."

"You started it, and the tooth was loose to begin with," Kedrin retorted.

"I may have to play the role of peacemaker anyway," Lesric joked.

Twenty minutes later, they were riding again. It was nearly dark, but they had found the road leading to Pruglin and had no trouble following it, even in the deepening dusk.

By the time they had ridden another five hours, Lianna didn't think she could keep her eyes open any longer. She nearly fell asleep riding several times, and finally spoke.

"Can we stop for a few hours and get some sleep? I can't stay awake for another ten minutes."

"I was hoping someone would say that soon," Kedrin said.

They halted by the side of the road, tied up their horses, and unrolled their blankets. Lianna was asleep nearly as soon as she lay down.

When she woke up the next morning, she knew they'd overslept. The sun shone through the trees, and birds chirped. She jerked into a sitting position and looked around. The horses were contentedly munching grass, and Lesric and Kedrin were still asleep. But she knew that this was urgent, and there was no time for relaxing.

So much for a few hours' rest, she thought. It had to be seven in the morning, and she guessed that they had slept for at least six hours.

"Kedrin! Kedrin, wake up!" She shook her brother until he moaned and rolled over.

"Ten more minutes."

"We don't have ten more minutes! It's broad daylight! We slept for at least six hours."

"What?" He sat up so fast that he nearly knocked her over. He crawled over to where Lesric slept and started shaking him. "Lesric, we slept in! Wake up!"

Lianna hurriedly rolled up her blanket and tied it in a bundle that could be tied to the saddle of her horse. She began to saddle the horses while Kedrin and Lesric hurriedly packed the rest of their supplies.

They scrambled onto the horses and set off at a reckless pace, trying to make up for lost time. The situation wasn't hopeless, but it wasn't good, either. No one said anything, and a grim look was on every face.

An hour later, they came across a beaten path through the woods. Many men had obviously passed this way, and from the looks of it, not very long ago. Lesric slipped off his horse and examined the trail.

"Fresh," he said. "But not as fresh as I'd like. We'd better hurry."

"Do you think we'd better leave the road now?" Lianna asked. "We don't want to run into that army again."

"I think that that might be wise," Lesric replied. "The road winds a lot at this point, and we can probably make better time by leaving it, anyway."

For the rest of the day they rode, alternating a steady trot with short stretches of galloping. Faldug had been right, and the horses didn't wear out quickly. They seemed fully capable of maintaining the swift pace set for them. Finally, after the sun had passed its highest point and was beginning to sink, the river came into sight. The Pruglin River wound its way through the valley, and they would follow it all the way to the city.

Lianna knew they were nearing Pruglin, and apprehension grew inside her. Even though she knew they had made much better time than the army and that her fears were unreasonable, she was worried that all they would find when they reached the city was smoking rubble and charred timbers.

She breathed a sigh of relief as they reached the final bend in the river and turned the corner. The city sat just as it had been when they left.

"Maybe all that trouble we went to was worth it," Kedrin said.

"Don't get your hopes up," Lesric warned him. "I don't want you to be disappointed if we're being baked alive in a burning city by this time tomorrow. We still have an inferior army, and even with the information we learned, we'll still be lucky to survive."

"Thank you for your encouraging remarks," Kedrin said. "I was suffering from depression over the fact that I was possibly going to survive this attack, until you relieved my worries by informing me that I will likely be burnt to a crisp within the next twenty-four hours."

"You're welcome," Lesric replied.

Lianna laughed. It was hard to believe that a few short months ago their family had come to the conclusion that Lesric was crazy.

"Should we go home or to the meeting house?" she asked as they entered the city.

"Straight to the meeting house," Kedrin said. "If the councilors aren't in session, we can send messengers to gather them, and if they are, we won't have to do anything."

It proved to be the right decision. Word of their arrival had spread, and Taran was waiting outside when they reached the meeting house.

"You're back!" he exclaimed. "We were worried. When you were a day late, we were afraid you had been captured."

"We were," Kedrin said. "Twice."

"Come inside and we'll hear it. The Council is already assembled," Taran said.

They tied their horses to a hitching post and followed him to the meeting room. Once there, they gave a detailed account of what they had learned, including the seeming resurrection of Glinsier, a kingdom north of Milsad Forest that was supposed to be as dead as the Lentours.

After they'd been questioned for close to two hours, Mathalin interceded, stopping the endless flow of questions the councilors had come up with. "I believe that nothing more will be gained by this discussion," he said. "The Lentour army will be here soon, and we need to get ready."

The councilors left the room in twos and threes, talking as they went, and soon Mathalin, Taran, and Ildug were the only members left. Ildug, in charge of military operations, questioned them for several more minutes on different aspects of the army before thanking them and following the other councilors down the hallway.

Mathalin smiled. "You must be exhausted. Why don't you head home and get some rest. Taran, I'll be over this evening to make some final plans with you."

"I'll be there," Taran said.

"Let's go home," Kedrin said. "I'm spent, and someone woke me up bright and early this morning and made me get back on a horse and keep riding."

"If I hadn't, you would still be riding," Lianna said.

"Whatever," he said, rolling his eyes.

CHAPTER 20

T he next morning, Lianna woke up in her own room for the first time in several days. Light poured in through the windows, and she knew that for the second morning in a row, she'd slept in later than normal. *The army! Has it reached the city yet?*

"Is the house on fire, Lianna?" Kedrin asked as she burst into the living room where the rest of the family was seated.

"Not as far as I know. What about the city?"

"That's what we were just discussing," Taran said. "The army hasn't shown up yet. In fact, our scouts say that it appears to be detouring around the city."

"Then Pruglin isn't the destination?"

"It could be a ploy, but that's how it appears." Taran pointed to a map. "They're on the road towards Brodalith."

"Does Brodalith know?"

"We sent a messenger pigeon to the city to warn them. We're hoping their scouts will spot the danger before the pigeon even arrives, but we can't be too careful. They're expecting any Lentour threats to be aimed at us, not them. We all are."

For the rest of the morning, they waited tensely for further news. When it finally came, no one was sure whether to be relieved or disturbed.

"The army has passed Pruglin," the messenger reported. "They are still heading towards Brodalith. Councilor Ildug has called a meeting at noon. He asked for Lesric, Kedrin, and Lianna to come as well."

An hour later, as they neared the square, a bone-chilling shriek split the air.

All movement stopped. A woman standing near Lianna dropped the basket of groceries she was holding. Children screamed and buried their faces in their mothers' skirts. Men's faces filled with fear.

"What was that?" Taran asked, although Lianna guessed he had a pretty good idea.

"That," Lesric said, "would be a gonadaw."

* * * * *

"I don't know about the rest of the people here," a man yelled from somewhere in the mob of fearful and angry citizens that had formed outside the council house, "but I won't sit around idle while that *thing* lurks in the woods, waiting to pounce. I have a wife and children I aim to protect the best I can from that monstrosity. Maybe all you high and mighty Councilors think differently than me. But if you won't defend this city, we'll defend it for you. Try to stop us if you want. I'm sure the eighteen of you will pose a deadly threat to the hundreds of us."

"If you wish to die at the hands of that beast, I for one will not inhibit you," another angry man shouted from the front of the crowd. "In fact, I'll encourage it. Maybe if we throw you over the walls, you'll satisfy its bloodlust enough to appease its wrath. What do you have to say to that?"

"Please, listen to us!" Taran tried for at least the tenth time to quiet the mob, but was unsuccessful.

"Don't worry, it was just your imagination," a mocking voice jeered. "I'm sure that there's not a big bad beast out there waiting to devour you when it gets the opportunity. You'll be fine." The deceptively soft voice, like someone trying to soothe a frightened child, suddenly became harsh. "You can try to try to convince us that there's no monster lurking out there. Do your best. But I heard that sound with my own ears, and I trust my senses. Do you not?"

The mob had assailed the meeting house just after Lianna, Taran, Kedrin, and Lesric arrived. Taran, Mathalin, Ildug, and several of the other councilors had tried to calm them, but the wild horde would not be pacified. Lianna stood behind the platform from which the councilors were attempting to speak, along with Kedrin, Lesric, and several other members of the Council.

Taran looked back at them. "Lesric, see if they will listen to you," he said, a hopeless expression in his eyes. "This morning, you were a hero for warning them that this was coming. They may still respect you enough to listen."

Lesric ascended the steps to the platform, and Lianna remembered a similar scene several months previously. Then, the councilors had been trying to stop Lesric from speaking, and the mob had been threatening them if they did so. Now, the tables were turned.

As he ascended the steps, a wave of murmurs ran through the crowd. Lianna couldn't see what was going on, but something seemed to have changed. She felt a thin sliver of hope as Lesric started to speak.

"People of Pruglin! Please, listen to me. You all know me. I've seen more of the Lentours than anyone else in this city, and yesterday I returned from observing the approaching army. While I was there, I saw the creature that you justifiably fear.

"Two months ago, if someone had told me about this beast, I would have called it a mythical animal from a children's fairy tale. Seeing it myself was terrifying. But," he hurried to clarify as the voices grew in number and volume, "it was small, nowhere near big enough to do the damage the monster did to Forsid. We were there to glean information, and one thing we learned was that this was a gonadaw, a lizard-like creature, that, although it could destroy a farm, wouldn't stand a chance against a city."

"I saw Forsid burn, and I heard that monster. I tell you, this is the same thing!" One voice rose above the others.

"I'm not through!" Lesric fought to regain control of the situation. "That was not all we learned. A gonadaw has a larger relative, called a kingalor. This is the creature that wreaked such devastation on Forsid City. Their sounds are nearly identical, and, aside from their size, their appearance is similar. But we know for a fact that no kingalors traveled with the army from Lentour. There are several gonadaws, but remember what I said earlier. Their appearance is frightening, but we are inside a walled city that they cannot enter. Remember that. When that creature emerges from the forest, remember that it cannot hurt you. What can hurt you are the men, and you need to ignore the beast, as terrifying as it is, and do your duty to stop the soldiers from breaking into the city and giving the gonadaws access to you. Do you hear me?"

Another ripple of sound ran through the crowd, all voices in the affirmative.

"So, do I have your word that you won't let your fear overwhelm you, and that you will do your best to keep this city intact?"

A chorus of yeses filled the air. A minute later, someone shouted, "Three cheers for Lesric, the man who saved Pruglin!"

As cheers filled the air, Lianna turned to Kedrin. "That," she said in his ear, "was truly remarkable."

CHAPTER 21

"Lesric," Mathalin said when everyone was seated in the meeting room. "That was astounding."

Lesric seemed uncomfortable with the praise. "I've just been in the right places at the right times. It's amazing how easy it is to win people's loyalties when you are captured as a slave, escape, and run for your life to the only place where you'll be safe."

Mathalin laughed. "What we all just witnessed outside was a very close call. And the fact that a gonadaw is somewhere in the area worries me. The Lentours are supposed to be on their way to Brodalith."

"I may have an explanation for that, Councilor," Lesric said. "We were still a good distance from the army when we heard a gonadaw for the first time. Their calls can travel extraordinary distances. This could have just been a gonadaw traveling behind the army. It's certainly not definite, but there is a chance that there's no reason to be alarmed."

"If we could know for sure that were the case, it would put me considerably more at ease," Mathalin said.

"We need to make a decision, and we need to make it fast," Ildug spoke. "If there is one gonadaw lurking around the city, there may be more, and we want to keep our gates sealed, no one going in or out. However, it's possible that there are none, and we could be sending help to Brodalith, which will fall without our support. What should we do?"

"With all due respect, Brodalith will not be without support in either case." The speaker was a councilor unfamiliar to Lianna. "Etneog and Qatran know what's going on. They're closer than we are anyway, and they will reinforce the city even if we can't."

"I have a solution," Lesric said.

All eyes turned toward him. "We're listening," Taran encouraged.

"The answer is simple. Kedrin, Lianna, and I will go on a gonadaw hunt. If we find the gonadaw, we kill it. If it fails to show, we'll know it wasn't there to begin with."

I just got back yesterday! Lianna had halfway expected something like this, and she wasn't thrilled about the plan.

"I say no," Taran said. "This is far too risky. I would rather let a gonadaw roam the forest unhindered than send the three of you in a mission that, if our hypothesis is wrong, will likely end in your deaths. It's foolish."

"I agree," Mathalin said firmly. "Lesric, this would be signing your own death sentences."

"I know the Lentours," Lesric said. "Oslir excluded, I have spent more time among them than anyone else in Risclan. I'm far from helpless. If the force is too strong for us to defeat, we simply won't engage. We'll come back to Pruglin for reinforcement. If we're confident we can defeat them, we will. It's no more dangerous than the mission you sent us on yesterday."

"It's not the same thing," said Ildug. "This is foolish. We can't allow it. If there is a gonadaw out there, we'll know soon enough without you risking your life like this. I think it's better to act like we never heard the gonadaw and move on with our preparations as before. I'm sorry, Lesric."

Lesric stood up and tried to protest, but was quickly silenced. He sat down again with a look on his face that Lianna couldn't interpret. It wasn't anger. Was it was hurt that his plan had been so quickly dismissed, or determination to do better in the future? Or was it something else entirely?

Kedrin looked at him compassionately from across the table, but Lianna thought she could detect more than just sympathy. She almost thought that Kedrin agreed with Lesric.

The discussion ended with a decision to wait to see if the gonadaw showed itself again. If it didn't, they would continue their preparations to leave for Brodalith. If the gonadaw appeared, they would decide what to do from there.

When they left the building, Lesric's shoulders slumped in an expression of defeat. Lianna felt sorry for him, but she was glad that they weren't departing on a hunt for one of the deadliest creatures ever to set foot in the valley.

* * * * *

Lianna, along with every other person in Pruglin City, was on edge all afternoon, but no more was heard of the gonadaw. *Maybe we were right, and the gonadaw was just trailing behind the main army,* she thought. But she didn't want to be too sure.

When nothing more had been heard by the next morning, she decided that the gonadaw must have left the area.

Ildug prepared to leave the city with a small army to reinforce Brodalith, and Kedrin and Lesric volunteered to accompany him. Lianna worried about the fact that her brother would more than likely participate in a battle, but there was no changing his mind. Had there been any way to convince Kedrin to stay, Rilan would have found it.

Kedrin left tomorrow, and when he went up to his room to pack everything he would need, Lianna followed him.

"So, you decided not to stay and wait around for that apple pie?" she teased, recalling her mother's reminder that Kedrin would miss the first apple pie of the year.

Kedrin appeared to be resisting the urge to laugh. "No, I prefer helping to save innocent lives from sure death over staying home and eating pie. Tell Mother I asked you to eat my piece for me. Maybe that will satisfy her."

"Somehow, I don't think having an extra piece of pie is the problem."

"You're probably right. I'm just relieved the gonadaw is gone. I wouldn't like to be ambushed by that thing."

"I'm just glad we're not hunting it right now," she said. "I don't care what Lesric said, that was a bad idea."

Taran burst into the room. "A farm was just sacked by the gonadaw. Ildug has sent a team to investigate."

"So much for that," Lianna said under her breath.

Kedrin shook his head. "That was too much of a coincidence. What makes you think it was a gonadaw?" he asked Taran.

"The only survivor was a girl, eight or nine years old. She hid until the creature left and then ran to a nearby farm. When they heard her story, they fled with the girl to the city, and she told us what she saw. It sounds like a giant lizard standing on two legs came out of the forest and attacked the farm. The rest of her family didn't make it. She was hysterical, and we couldn't understand a lot of what she was saying, but it seems…" he trailed off in mid-sentence.

"Seems what?" Kedrin asked.

"The farm was burned to the ground. By the gonadaw. It breathes fire."

CHAPTER 22

"It what?" Lianna asked. "Did I just hear you right?"

"You did," Taran nodded. "Gonadaws can breathe fire, at least if the girl's account was true."

"Is Ildug still leaving tomorrow morning?" Kedrin inquired. "And were there soldiers with the gonadaw?"

"I don't know the answers to either of those questions. I'm sorry."

Suddenly, Kedrin froze.

"What is it?" Taran asked, looking worried.

"Does Lesric know? About any of this?"

"I'm not sure. I didn't tell him, but he could have heard it from someone else."

Kedrin quickly left the room, his mouth set in a thin line. He returned a moment later.

"Lesric's things are gone," he said, with something in his voice that almost sounded like desperation. "I have to go after him."

"No!" Rilan said quietly. All eyes turned to her. Lianna hadn't heard her enter the room, and neither, apparently, had Taran or Kedrin. "You can't leave this city until that monster is gone."

"Rilan, he's right. It may be dangerous out there, but we can't just let Lesric go to his death. I don't know why he's so determined to kill that thing, but he is, and

Kedrin needs to follow him. Lesric can't have gone far. If Kedrin leaves now, he can be back before nightfall."

"How could Lesric even get out of the city?" Rilan asked. "The gates are all closed."

"So Kedrin might not even have to leave the city," Taran said.

"I'm going, too," Lianna broke in.

"I thought you didn't want to go on a gonadaw hunt," Kedrin said.

"It's not a gonadaw hunt anymore. If you run into the Lentours, you're going to need some help. And if you end up having to rescue Lesric from them, you won't be able to do it on your own. You're not going to help anyone if they catch you, too."

"We leave in five minutes," Kedrin said.

Lianna nodded and started for the door.

"Do you want me to meet you at the gate?" Taran asked.

Kedrin shook his head. "I want to follow the route Lesric would have taken, in case he's still in the city. It'd be a pity to go to all the work of getting out there and searching for him if he never even left."

"As long as you're sure," Taran said.

Kedrin nodded. "Let's go, Lianna!"

She hurried to her room and grabbed her sword, bow and arrows. She hadn't unpacked her things from their last mission, and was beginning to think she shouldn't unpack at all if she was going to keep on leaving at a moment's notice like this.

Five minutes later, they were walking quickly down the lane towards the main road. Kedrin broke into a trot when they reached the road, and Lianna matched his pace.

"Which way do you think he went?" she asked.

"Father said the farm was across the river. I think that we should head for the River Gate and go from there."

"They won't let us out," Lianna said.

"No, they won't. We'll have to scale the walls."

"Kedrin, I don't like this. What if someone sees us and thinks we're spies? We'll get shot!"

"We'll be fine!" Kedrin insisted.

She was too out of breath to argue any further, so she just followed him.

About a block from the city wall, Kedrin slowed to a walk and, looking up and down the street to ensure that no one was watching, slipped into an alley. Lianna followed him.

Taking back roads, they covered the remaining distance to the wall. When they came to where the alley entered the busy road that paralleled the city wall, Kedrin stopped at the corner and motioned for her to do the same. He cautiously peered out into the street, then ducked back quickly and signaled for Lianna to be quiet. They blended into the shadows and waited as two horses clip-clopped past on the cobblestone street, pulling a wagon behind them.

Lianna stood impatiently, studying the dim alley. She saw something white lying on the ground, and as a sneaking suspicion crossed her mind, she picked it up. Her intuition proved correct. It was a piece of parchment, containing familiar handwriting. "Lesric," she breathed, showing Kedrin the paper. On it were quickly scribbled notes that Lianna recognized as the ones Lesric had taken while they were imprisoned in the Lentour camp. "He must have dropped it," she said.

Kedrin nodded. "Now we know we're on the right track." He peeked around the corner again. "Coast is clear." Quickly he crossed the street, Lianna at his heels. They dashed into the narrow opening between two houses. "Now for the tricky part," Kedrin said, walking to the end of the opening.

The space in which they stood between the houses was only about three feet wide, and Kedrin placed his left hand and foot on the wall of one house and right hand and foot on the other. With his back against the city wall and applying enough pressure with his hands and feet to hold himself up, he ascended until his head poked above the roofs. Lianna watched nervously from the ground.

Holding himself up with his feet, Kedrin gripped the roof to his left with both hands. Then he pulled himself up, until he sat, panting for breath, on the roof.

"I can't do that!" Lianna exclaimed.

"You don't have to." Kedrin pulled a rope from his pack. Crawling higher up the incline, he reached the place where a chimney poked through the roof. He tested it to make sure it would hold, then tied the rope around and threw the end down to Lianna.

She still had her doubts, but she grabbed hold of the rope with both hands and used stones that projected from the rough stone wall of the city as footholds. Within minutes, she crouched beside him on the steep incline of the roof.

"Now what?" she asked. Kedrin had thought of everything so far, and she assumed he had decided the next step in the plan. At least she hoped so.

"This is where the plan gets a little sketchy. I'm not exactly sure. We need to get from here," tapping the shingles on the roof, "to there," pointing to the battlements high above them. "The rope is plenty long, I'm just not sure where and how to attach it."

"Maybe this is where I can help," Lianna suggested, pulling an arrow from her quiver. "Do you have any string?" He did, and she tied one end of the twenty foot spool of string to the end of the rope. Then she untied the rope from around the stovepipe. "We need to coil this up neatly so that it doesn't get tangled when I shoot. If we do it right, it should unwind smoothly." As Kedrin followed her instructions, she dug through her pack, shaking her head when she didn't find anything. "Do you have some sort of anchor, or hook, that I can attach to this?"

Kedrin produced a metal grappling hook with four prongs bending back so that however it landed, at least one prong would catch hold of whatever they were trying to hook it onto. Lianna placed the grappling hook at the splice between the string and rope. "Where'd you get a grappling hook?" she asked.

"Father gave it to me. He thought we might need it to scale the wall, and I guess he was right."

"Here goes. You'd better hope this works," she said. She placed the arrow on the string, took her aim, and released the projectile.

The lighter weight of the string allowed the arrow to barely clear the wall. With momentum carrying the arrow forward, once the string ran out, the rope quickly uncoiled at Lianna's feet, until the string disappeared from view over the wall. When it finally stopped, Lianna tugged on the rope, pulling it back towards her. The grappling hook caught on the wall, and she tugged hard to be sure it would hold.

"Wait," Kedrin said. "I weigh more than you." He

grabbed onto the rope with both hands and lifted his feet off the roof, swinging with his whole weight. He dropped back to the roof, nodding in satisfaction. "That'll work." He took a deep breath, deciding on a plan. "When I get to the top, I'll signal if it's safe, and you follow. See that gap between those two turrets? I'll hide there and wait for you, in case anyone happens to look our way."

She nodded. "All right. Go ahead. You'd better hurry though; Lesric is getting farther and farther away."

Kedrin gripped the rope with both hands and launched himself up as far as he could. For an instant, he swung free, a couple feet above the roof, his feet scrabbling against the wall for a foothold. Lianna caught her breath, but then his foot found a stone projecting out from the wall slightly farther than the rest.

His ascent took nearly ten minutes. When he finally reached the top, he gingerly pulled himself onto the walkway that ran the length of the wall. Once he was safely on the wall, he moved to the crevice he planned to hide in, staying low as he did so. She saw him scan the wall in both directions carefully, then beckon to her.

Taking a deep breath, she grabbed hold of the rope and jumped as high as she could, shifting her grip on the cable to a higher hold. For a terrifying instant she swung out over the gap between the houses where they'd stood a few minutes before. The difference was that this time she was fifteen feet in the air. Her feet searched frantically for a foothold, and when she finally found one, she breathed a sigh of relief. Then she began to pull herself up, hand over hand, finding footing as she went. Her arms burned with the exertion, and each time she looked down, her stomach churned. She did her best to keep her eyes up, but that only showed her how painfully slow her progress was.

Her climb took considerably longer than Kedrin's. When she finally reached the top, he grabbed her wrists and hauled her onto the walkway, where she sat down and panted for breath, completely worn out.

"I'll go first and give you a chance to get your breath back," Kedrin said, rearranging the rope as he spoke. "We're almost there."

"I don't know if I can do this, Kedrin," Lianna said, gasping for breath.

"You can do it, Lianna," Kedrin said. "You've already done the hardest part. This time, you'll almost be able to slide."

"Kedrin..." Lianna was still uncertain.

He didn't give her time to argue. He had been rearranging the rope while they talked, and now he climbed to the top of the ramparts and dropped out of sight over the wall.

Lianna anxiously watched his descent. When he reached the bottom, she took hold of the rope and began to lower herself down cautiously. He was right; her brief rest had renewed her strength–and her resolve. She carefully kept her gaze on the section of wall in front of her as she began to descend.

Ten minutes later, she was standing on firm ground once again. As soon as she released the rope, Kedrin tugged on a string he'd been holding. The rope fell to the ground.

"How'd you do that?" she asked.

"I wrapped the string around the battlements so that when I pull on it, the grappling hook comes away from the wall. I thought a rope might come in handy later on."

He quickly coiled the rope and stuffed it into his pack. "Let's go. We've got to find Lesric before the Lentours do."

They set off towards the Pruglin River. Once they reached the river, they followed it upstream to the bridge. From there they planned to follow the road toward the farm, which was where they guessed Lesric would head.

"Look!" Kedrin said, as they reached the far side of the river.

"What is it?"

"These footprints were made within the last hour or two. The city is closed up, and no one's been out here for days, so unless it was a farmer or someone who didn't take refuge in Pruglin, I think we've found our man."

"They're pointing in the general direction of the farm, but straight through the woods, instead of following the road." Lianna bent over. "What's this?" For the second time, she picked up a slip of paper. This time, instead of a whole sheet of parchment, it was just a scrap torn off.

In Lesric's handwriting, it read: *To the lizard trackers: Meet me at the farm.*

"What's that supposed to mean?" she asked.

"He obviously knew we would follow him. I don't know why he didn't tell us he was going, though; it sure would have saved time and effort. We're the lizard trackers, I guess, although we're really tracking Lesric, not the gonadaw."

"We'd better hurry," Lianna said. "We don't want Lesric to get there too far ahead of us."

They followed the same path Lesric had taken. It wasn't hard to find. He seemed to have taken care to leave a trail that was easy to follow. Branches were broken off, and Lesric seemed to have purposefully walked through every place wet enough to leave footprints.

"A five year old could follow this trail," Kedrin said. "He sure doesn't seem to worry about the wrong person, or creature, finding it."

"I hope that he doesn't have to worry," Lianna said nervously. "I don't like this. Why is he making everything so obvious?"

"I don't have a clue. Of course, it's not like there are a lot of people around here, but the ones who are are the people he doesn't want to find him. Aside from us, of course. All I know is that he'd left a trail a blind man could follow, and we're supposed to take it."

They continued for an hour. The wind shifted so that it blew in their faces, and Lianna caught a scent of smoke. "I think we're getting close."

"I think you're right. At least, I hope you're right. I'm getting worried about Lesric. The sooner we find him, the better I'll feel."

Lianna thought she smelled another odor, this one repugnant and foul. "Do you smell something like a rotting carcass?"

Kedrin nodded slowly. They looked at each other without moving.

"I think we're real close," Lianna said in a whisper, remembering the smell that had accompanied the gonadaw when they were Calsym's prisoners.

A screech split the air.

CHAPTER 23

Lianna instinctively grabbed her bow and placed an arrow on the string. Kedrin drew his sword. They looked around in either direction, but saw nothing. The screech, the same as the one from the Lentour camp, sounded again.

A branch cracked.

"Kedrin!" she hissed between clenched teeth.

"Shh! It probably already knows where we are, but we don't want to give it any help."

They waited for several minutes, but heard nothing else.

"Forget your bow and use your sword," Kedrin breathed. "The undergrowth is so thick, we might not see it until it's on top of us and it's too late for shooting."

She slung her bow over her shoulder and tucked the arrow back into the quiver, then drew her sword. They stood back to back, scanning the surrounding forest.

Nothing.

"Let's advance, carefully," Kedrin said. "We've got to find Lesric. He's in big trouble if the gonadaw is here."

They continued to follow Lesric's trail, moving slowly, but steadily. They heard and saw nothing else.

Twenty minutes later, the path ended. They had reached their destination. The charred and smoldering remains of a house and barn crowned the top of a small rise in the ground.

Keeping a firm grip on her sword, Lianna emerged into the clearing, examining the clearing for enemies.

Reptilian tracks identical to the ones they'd seen at Forsid, except on a much smaller scale, crisscrossed the clearing. But there were other tracks too, the tracks of men. It was impossible to tell exactly how many men there had been but Lianna guessed there were at least twenty, far too many for the two of them to take on alone.

"Well, now what?" she asked. "I don't see any sign of Lesric."

"I'm not sure. I guess we should..."

A shriek split the air behind Lianna. She spun around to face the threat. Looking carefully at the trees, she saw nothing. "Kedrin..." She trailed off into silence.

"I don't like being stalked by an invisible hunter."

"Now I know how a squirrel feels when it can hear a hawk in the air above him and doesn't know when it will strike."

Kedrin moved so that they again stood back to back, and they slowly rotated in a circle, scrutinizing every inch of the forest.

"Drop your weapons!" A harsh voice spoke from where the last shriek had been.

Lianna's heart thudded in her chest. "Kedrin!"

"Wait," he whispered. Then talking out loud, he said, "Who are you?"

A silhouette emerged from the trees. Lianna recognized the shape of a gonadaw. A gonadaw with a man on its back.

It emerged into the daylight, and Lianna saw that

the speaker rode on a saddle of some sort fastened on the creature's shoulders. The man, who would have been tall on the ground, was decked in a full suit of armor. Though the gonadaw carried an immense weight, it walked as if it bore nothing. The beast pranced around them with a cruel look in its eyes, and although the man wore his helmet visor down, Lianna could perceive his arrogant, superior air without seeing his face.

The gonadaw let out a shriek that split the air. It turned its head to one side and eyed them maliciously. A serpentine tongue flicked out of its mouth.

"Do I need to repeat myself? Drop your weapons!" The gonadaw hissed as if to emphasize the man's words.

Lianna stared at him for a second or two, then glanced over at Kedrin questioningly. He looked indecisive.

"It appears I will have to take more drastic measures." The Lentour raised a hand.

From the trees a hundred feet to the left of the man, four men emerged. Three of them were armed soldiers. The fourth was a figure they recognized.

"Lesric!" they exclaimed in unison.

"You know him," the man said. "Now, are you going to make this difficult, or will you yield peacefully? I'd prefer to avoid bloodshed, but if you give me no other choice, I won't hesitate to kill."

Lianna's sword clanged to the ground an instant after Kedrin's.

"Good! I see we've come to an agreement. Now you will kindly drop all other weapons in your possession."

Lesric was gagged, but he shook his head in a nearly imperceptible movement. He glanced down at their swords, then at them. Kedrin hesitated. Lesric's guards stepped nearer to him, swords drawn menacingly.

"Drop your weapons! And don't pretend you don't have any. I see your bow, Lianna, daughter of Taran, PruglinCouncilor. And I know you hold a dagger, Kedrin, Taran's son." He laughed at the shock on their faces. "The information your friend here gave us was correct. I'm glad to know we weren't deceived. Now, do as I say, or he dies."

"How could Lesric have told him about us?" Lianna hissed.

"They must have tricked him into it. Lesric would never give us away."

"What's it to be, Kedrin, Lianna? Does your friend die?"

Lesric's eyes pleaded with them, but it wasn't to surrender. He was begging them to fight. Kedrin seemed to be battling inside himself. Looking at Lesric with his hand down at his side, he held out four fingers. Lesric shook his head.

Lianna understood that Kedrin was trying to discern if they were seeing all the soldiers or if others hid in the trees, probably wondering if fighting was even an option.

Kedrin mouthed something that looked like *more*, and Lesric nodded almost imperceptibly.

"My patience is wearing thin, Kedrin, Lianna. Make your decision."

"He wants us alive, or he'd have killed us long ago," Kedrin whispered. "He knows Lesric is too important to kill, either. Since Father is on the Council, he probably wants to use us as hostages to get him to surrender the city."

"Do we fight?"

"Sergeant!"

"Yes sir?" One of the men guarding Lesric answered, tightening his grip on his sword.

In answer to the question Lianna had just asked as well as the one that was sure to follow, Kedrin hissed, "Now!"

With a speed derived from years of practice, Lianna drew her bow, placed an arrow on the string, aimed, and shot. She struck the sergeant in the chest, and he fell over backwards. Kedrin had already recovered his sword and was sprinting towards Lesric, who was grappling with his captors in an attempt to free himself.

One soldier raised his sword over his head, preparing to bring it down in a deathblow upon Lesric. Lianna sent another arrow hurtling towards him, and a second later, the last soldier fell from her third projectile.

Lesric knelt down and used one of the blades on the ground to cut the rope that bound his wrists. Then he grabbed the sword and ran to join Kedrin. Lianna picked up her sword, and with her bow still in hand, raced towards them.

"There are dozens of them in the forest," Lesric gasped. "We'll be overrun in no time."

"They want us alive," Kedrin said. "They won't kill us unless there's no alternative. We need to make all speed for Pruglin and hope someone sees us coming and lets us into the city. Also, when we have more time, we need to talk about running off like that. That was a very bad idea."

"Sorry," Lesric said simply. "I..."

"Save your apologies. Right now we need to worry about that," Lianna interrupted, pointing.

The gonadaw was racing toward them at full speed.

"Good point," Lesric said, following her finger. "Being charged by a mythical creature that would like to rip you apart limb by limb, while you're still alive, I might add, is more exciting anyway."

As the gonadaw quickly approached, they spread out, swords at the ready, to oppose it more effectively.

The man on its back was a skilled swordsman, and combined with the gonadaw's razor claws and muscular tail, they faced a formidable enemy.

Kedrin attacked the man directly, while Lesric focused on repelling the gonadaw. Lianna, with the least amount of sword experience, did what damage she could.

At the sound of shouts, she looked over and saw men pouring from the forest about two hundred yards away. "We've got company!" she called.

The man atop the gonadaw seemed to gain strength at the sight of reinforcements, and he attacked with renewed vigor. Lianna knew that they had to defeat this adversary and leave before the other soldiers reached them, or they wouldn't stand a chance.

She slashed at the gondaw's chest, but the beast knocked the sword aside and she staggered backwards. On the other side of the beast, Lesric was also engaging it, and Lianna tried to draw its attention so that Lesric could more easily attack. When the gonadaw shrieked in agony, she assumed that Lesric had used the opportunity to wound it. The injury wasn't enough, though, and the gonadaw kept up a relentless attack while its rider rained devastating blows down on Kedrin, who was still the focus of his attention.

Lianna glanced up at the soldiers and knew that the gonadaw had to be dead within the next few seconds. If they left the gonadaw alive, it would easily outrun them, and with the help of the soldiers would make quick work of them. It was imperative that they kill the beast before the soldiers reached them. Looking up, Lianna almost despaired.

"Lesric, do they have horses?" she shouted, using her sword to just barely deflect a slash from the gonadaw's razor sharp claws.

"No," Lesric replied, attacking with renewed vigor as the men-at-arms drew ever closer.

Lianna wasn't sure if that was good or bad. If they were able to get their hands on two or three horses, they could easily escape, but only if they were able to turn the remaining horses loose. On the other hand, if they couldn't get horses, it would be easy for the soldiers to capture them. She decided that she would rather no one had horses than face the possibility that their enemies had them and they did not.

The gonadaw staggered as she slashed it across the leg. At the same instant, Kedrin managed to get past the man's defenses and embedded his sword in the man's shoulder. He screamed, and Kedrin withdrew his blade. An instant later, the man went silent as Kedrin delivered the final blow.

All three turned their attention to the gonadaw, but Lianna realized they were literally down to seconds. The men were nearly upon them.

The creature hesitated for a second, and seeing the opportunity she needed, Lianna plunged her sword into its chest. It shrieked, and then, as if in slow motion, toppled over.

They looked at each other and then at the approaching host, now less than twenty yards away. They were in trouble.

Turning, they fled the oncoming men. Lianna gasped for breath, but didn't slow down. If the soldiers caught up to them, they would be captured and probably killed.

As they raced into the treeline, Lianna realized something was wrong. The only sounds were their own ragged breathing and the snapping of twigs and rustling of leaves beneath their feet. She didn't hear the soldiers.

She finally risked a look back, even though she knew that it could cost her precious time. Their pursuers had halted at the bodies of the man and gonadaw.

"Hurry!" Kedrin said. "They've stopped!"

"If we can just manage to hide in the forest..." Lesric mumbled, glancing back at the soldiers.

Dodging between trees, they hurried onward, running for nearly a mile. They paused to catch their breath.

"Lesric," Kedrin panted, hands on his knees and gasping for breath. "If you ever do that again, I'll have to roast you alive. We're going to have to have a serious talk about this when we get back. And did you really tell them that we were coming after you?"

Lesric smirked. "I suppose that you became the head of the Pruglin Council while I was gone, or maybe it was king of Pruglin, and now it's your duty to lecture me on my misbehavior. And no, I didn't give you away. I'm not that evil. They had spies." He stopped, listening. "But we've got bigger problems. I don't know why they stopped, but I'm sure they're still looking for us. We need to get out of here. Quietly."

Kedrin nodded. "I'm ready when you are."

"Lianna?" Lesric asked.

She took a deep breath. "I'm ready."

Lesric turned and looked in the direction of the farm. Satisfied that for the present they had lost their pursuers, he set off, quickly but silently, through the forest. Lianna followed, wincing every time a twig snapped beneath her feet and marveling at Lesric's ability to move so quietly. Although she knew he had grown up in the woods in the north of the Risclan Valley, he was still more than an ordinary woodsman.

After twenty minutes, there was still no sign of pursuit. Lianna was on edge, and every time a bird flew out of the undergrowth or a stick snapped, she jumped. When something screeched, her hand flew to her sword before she realized it was only a hawk far above them.

But the forest was quiet. Too quiet. Something was wrong.

CHAPTER 24

"Lesric!" Kedrin finally slowed to a standstill. "Either the soldiers completely lost us and are going in a totally different direction, or they gave up, or they have some other plan that we don't know about. I'm fairly certain that it's the last possibility."

"You're right. It's too quiet. We should hear something. They could easily have caught us when we first ran, but they stopped instead. They must have set a trap."

"They're expecting us to go to Pruglin," Kedrin said.

"Yes," Lesric said. "Where else would we go?"

"So that's where their trap will be."

"Yes. But there's nothing we can do except proceed with caution."

"But that's just walking right into their trap," Kedrin protested. "We need to do what they don't expect."

"Which is?"

"Not go to Pruglin."

"And where else do you want to go? Your father will be worried sick about us. If we hurry, we might be able to reach the city before they can set their ambush. If we don't go now, we might be stuck outside the city for days."

"We could always go towards Brodalith and harass

any scouting parties the army sends out."

"I thought Lesric was the one with the crazy ideas. It turns out my own brother is the real culprit," Lianna said.

"I'm not quite sure about that idea, but we might be able to circumvent their trap," Lesric mused.

Lianna pulled out a stack of papers from her pack. She hadn't taken anything out since they got back from spying on the army. She quickly scanned through them until she found the one she was looking for: a map of the Risclan Valley. It showed the valley in detail, and she looked intently at Pruglin and the surrounding areas. "We're here," she said, pointing at the map, "and Pruglin is here. The trap, assuming there is one, is likely in this area." She circled with her hand.

"Why don't we go towards Linstown, south of Pruglin, and from there circle up back to the city?" Lesric suggested.

"Linstown is just a village with a hundred or so people in it. Why would we go there?" Kedrin asked. "It doesn't benefit us, and we still have the problem of getting back to the city."

"Because I have a friend in Linstown who might be able to help us get back to the city, assuming he hasn't already evacuated the town."

"Why didn't you think of that before?" Kedrin asked.

Lesric hesitated. "I did, it's just..." he broke off.

"We need to hurry," Lianna interrupted. "If we were wrong and just haven't heard them following us, the soldiers could catch up at any minute. We don't want that to happen."

"You're right. We should keep moving."

They set off again, altering their direction to take them toward the village of Linstown instead of toward Pruglin. Lianna hoped it was enough to evade their pursuers, but she couldn't ignore her own anxiety. Something just wasn't right.

Half an hour later, they stopped and surveyed the scene in front of them.

They were on the bank of the Pruglin River, overlooking the rushing current. At this point, the river was only slightly over a hundred yards wide, but the white water writhed and swirled its way downstream.

"And how are we supposed to cross this?" she asked Lesric.

"Have any suggestions?"

"You're not being serious, are you?" Lianna asked. "There's a ford about a mile upstream. That's too close to Pruglin, though, and it's probably watched, at least, assuming there is a trap. Then there's a ferry ten miles downstream, but that's too far away."

Lesric nodded. "I know. But I didn't grow up in Pruglin, and I was hoping you knew another way, a shortcut locals use or something."

Lianna shook her head, and Kedrin groaned. "Lesric, you're drawn to trouble like bees to honey. Why do you have to get us into these messes? If you had just stayed in Pruglin, we wouldn't be in this mess, now would we?"

"If neither of you can think of anything, I do have an idea," Lesric said, acting like he hadn't even heard Kedrin. "Someone came up with the idea of building a crossing here, some type of bridge or something. He was half crazy, and as you can imagine, it didn't work, but there still is, or should I say still *was* last time I was here, a pulley across the river, that he used to get materials, and even workers, across the river." He paused to think.

"Actually, now that I think of it, he stopped working on the bridge when one of the workers fell in and drowned. All that to say, if we can find the pulley, we can use it to get across, just like he transported workers."

"You'd better have a saner idea, because there is no way that I'm going to be suspended above that river," Lianna said.

"It's perfectly safe!" When Lesric saw her unconvinced expression, he looked helplessly at Kedrin. "You tell her."

"And you say this after you tell me that this man stopped working on the bridge when someone drowned in the river, crossing on the same pulley system you are telling us we need to use." Lianna shook her head. "There is no way I'm getting on that thing."

Lesric ignored her. "Aha, here it is. Still intact." He pointed to a weathered pulley that spanned the river. He quickly dug a rope from his pack and fashioned a type of seat attached to the rope. He made a loop to sit on, one for the back of the seat, and a safety harness connected to the seat to keep the rider from falling out.

"Who wants to go first?" Lesric asked. Without giving them time to respond, he said, "All right, Kedrin, go ahead."

Kedrin tugged on the rope pulley, then on the harness. Satisfied that it would hold his weight, he carefully stepped into the harness, tightened it around himself, and sat down in the makeshift chair. Lesric gripped the windlass that moved the pulley and began to turn it. In a few seconds, Kedrin was suspended above the raging water. The rope jerked, and Kedrin slipped. He caught himself, and Lianna let out her breath. Lesric continued to carefully haul him across the river. Five minutes later, Kedrin reached the far side of the river. He slipped the harness over his head and set his feet back on solid ground. Lesric wheeled the pulley back towards them. It went much faster this time since Lesric wasn't worried about making sure no one fell out, and soon the harness was back on their side of the river.

"Your turn, Lianna," Lesric said, offering the contraption to her.

"I told you already, there is no way I'm doing that. I'll wait for the soldiers to find us, or for another gonadaw to sniff us out, but I am not getting on that thing. I'm sorry."

"How serious are you being?" Lesric said, looking over her shoulder.

"Very. Why?" She turned and followed his gaze. Emerging from the forest some ways down the river was a group of men, and another, larger shape she had learned to recognize. They didn't appear to have spotted the trio at the river yet, but were heading in their direction.

"You still want to stay?"

Lianna pulled the harness over her head and quickly fastened the loops, then held on tight. Lesric began to turn the windlass again, and the ground beneath gave way to the turbulent water. She was moving faster than Kedrin had, but it was still taking an agonizingly long time to cross. The contraption swayed in the wind, and she felt lightheaded. She was afraid she would be sick. Looking back, she saw Lesric turning the windlass as quickly as he could, beads of sweat on his face. The exertion was taking its toll on him, and her speed began to slow. The men were closer, and a gonadaw trotted at their lead.

On the other side of the river, Kedrin had found another windlass. He began to turn it, and Lianna's speed nearly doubled. She was in the middle of the river now, fully exposed to whatever soldier looked her way. She was still out of arrow range, but it wouldn't be long before they were close enough that a good archer could hit her.

Finally, Lianna reached the other side. She frantically pulled the harness off, and as soon as she was free of the rope, Lesric began pulling it back towards himself.

One of the soldiers pointed.

Kedrin turned the windlass again, and the seat was halfway across the river. Soon only fifty feet were left, then thirty, then ten. Lesric secured himself in the harness and swung out over the river. Kedrin worked furiously, and Lianna gripped the end of the windlass and added her efforts to his.

The soldiers were running now, and Lesric was only a third of the way across the river. Lianna's heartbeat raced as they neared, and she knew from her own experience that a good archer could probably hit him. But the men seemed more concerned with getting closer than with stopping and taking a shot. Lianna released the windlass and drew an arrow from her quiver, preparing to shoot anyone who appeared to be a threat.

Lesric had loosened the knot that attached the harness to the pulley rope, and was pulling himself hand over hand to add to his momentum. He was past the halfway point, but Lianna knew that he was now well within the range of most archers.

"Hurry up, Kedrin," she said through clenched teeth, selecting her first target and preparing to fire.

He glanced up at the approaching soldiers and then returned his concentration to getting Lesric across the river, turning the pulley with renewed vigor. The gap between them continued to narrow until Lesric was only fifty yards away.

The soldiers had reached the tree.

One of them motioned, and a soldier stepped forward towards the rope, drawing his sword as he did so. Lianna realized what he was about to do and released her arrow, sending the missile hurtling into his chest. He collapsed, and another man took his place. She plucked another arrow from her quiver and downed the next man.

Lesric was almost there. He had drawn his knife and was ready to cut the harness and run as soon as he reached solid ground.

Lianna shot the fifth man to attempt cutting the rope and the Lentours seemed to realize they weren't getting anywhere and needed to rethink their strategy. They were almost out of time; Lesric would be at the other side in less than twenty seconds.

Then a man stepped out of the throng of soldiers. He had been hiding behind them so that Lianna could not see his bow in hand, ready to shoot. He took aim and released the string.

A fraction of a second later, Lianna had sent a missile hurtling towards the archer, but the damage was done. With a gasp Kedrin fell and rolled on the ground, clutching at his shoulder.

Lianna screamed, dropped her bow, and ran to her brother.

"Lianna, the rope! You need to get Lesric across," Kedrin said through clenched teeth.

She gripped the windlass with both hands and

began to turn. She wasn't as strong as Kedrin, and Lesric's progress slowed dramatically, but he was still moving.

"Forget me! They're going to shoot again!" Lesric shouted and pointed at the men.

She dropped the windlass, grabbed her bow, and fired. An arrow whizzed dangerously close past her head and embedded itself with a *thunk* in a nearby tree. Lesric was almost here now, but with Kedrin injured, she wasn't sure how they were going to make their escape. She forced herself to concentrate solely on the soldiers and let Lesric come up with the plan. He'd proven himself skilled in that respect before, and she hoped he'd live up to his reputation in this instance when the result would be the difference between life or death.

Lesric pulled himself hand over hand the last ten feet, and with a quick stroke of his knife, severed the harness. In one smooth motion, he dropped to the ground and swung Kedrin's pack over his shoulder. "Lianna, cut the rope! I don't want them crossing."

"I don't think they need the rope. Look!" Fear gripped her as she saw the gonadaw, rider on its back, step into the gushing torrent.

"Cut it anyway! The other men can use it!"

She obeyed, her gaze not leaving the scaly monster coming closer with each step. Behind her, Lesric dragged Kedrin away from the riverbank.

"Lianna, see if you can slow that lizard down!"

She took a deep breath, aimed, and fired. The arrow hit the creature's hide at an angle and glanced off.

"This isn't working, Lesric!"

"If you can, slow it down. Otherwise, forget it. Don't waste your arrows."

She decided to try again. This time she aimed for

the eye, because even though it was a smaller target, she figured it was her best chance of doing any real damage. The arrow hit the bony socket surrounding the orb, bounced off and disappeared into the water. She groaned and drew another arrow, noting with dismay that she only had a dozen or so left.

"Lesric, hurry up! We've got to get out of here!"

"I'm going as fast as I can, but unless you want your brother to bleed to death, I've got to take care of this."

Lianna determined to try one last time, reasoning that any more than that would be a waste of her few remaining arrows. She took careful aim and let fly. The creature bucked its head as she released the arrow, and she knew that she'd missed. She looked down in defeat.

The gonadaw let out the bone chilling scream she had learned to recognize—and dread.

She looked up in surprise. The arrow had found its mark in the beast's right nostril. It screeched again and thrashed about. Lianna smiled with satisfaction.

She turned towards Lesric and Kedrin slowly, not wanting to see how bad the injury was. Lesric had torn aside Kedrin's shirt and was examining the wound. "Lianna, I need to pull this arrow out. As soon as I do, it's going to start bleeding. You need to put pressure on the wound until I can bandage it up."

"All right." She had carefully avoided looking at Kedrin's shoulder, but now she forced herself to inspect it. She felt sick at the sight of the bloody and torn tissue. The shaft of the arrow protruded from the wound.

"First, I need to break off the tip of the arrow. Can you lift him off the ground?"

"I can try." Lianna wasn't overly confident of her ability, but she didn't have time to think about it.

"Ready?" When he nodded, she heaved up with all her might. Kedrin moaned as Lesric snapped off the arrowhead. Lianna set him down again as gently as she could.

"All right, now I need to pull out the arrow. You have to stop the bleeding as best as you can." Lesric placed a wad of fabric under Kedrin's shoulder to stop the blood at the back of his arm. Lianna took the strip of fabric he offered her.

Kedrin's cry joined the screeches of the gonadaw as Lesric yanked the arrow from his flesh. Lianna packed the fabric into the wound, causing Kedrin to grimace in agony. Lesric wrapped the wound several times as tightly as he could in a makeshift bandage, then tied it off and stood up.

"Done."

Kedrin sighed in relief.

"Are you strong enough to walk?"

"I...think so." Kedrin sat up.

"You can lean on me. But we need to go. Those soldiers are probably on their way to the nearest crossing."

"Are we still going to Linstown?" Lianna asked.

"Yes. Kedrin needs rest and a doctor to examine his wound. I took care of it as best as I could, but I'm not an expert, and it still needs attention."

"Let's go." Kedrin stood up with Lesric's help, and with his good arm wrapped around him, took a cautious step forward.

Lianna fell into step behind him and they began their painfully slow journey to Linstown. Kedrin wasn't able to move faster than a slow walk, and they took frequent breaks.

Two hours later they stumbled into Linstown.

The streets were empty. Lianna hoped against hope that the villagers were just hiding in their houses because of the nearby soldiers.

"Hello!" Lesric called, his voice echoing in the lonely streets. No one responded.

Lianna groaned. The town was deserted.

CHAPTER 25

"It looks like we should have gone to Pruglin," Kedrin said, looking up and down the empty streets.

"It looks like you're right," Lesric said. "Let's go to my friend's house anyway. Even if he's not there, we can get some things to better bind up Kedrin's shoulder. I'll pay him back later."

"Where does this friend of yours live? I can't go much farther."

Although he hadn't complained, Lianna knew that her brother was at the end of his strength. His face was pale, and he was more tired looking than she ever remembered seeing him.

"It's just a little farther. I haven't been here for a long time, so I might not be able to find it immediately. Why don't you wait here while I see if he left with everyone else?"

"I'm not sure about that. Do we really want to split up, with Lentours and gonadaws in the area?" Lianna didn't want to be solely responsible for defending her brother, who would be helpless if they were attacked.

"We'll be fine," Kedrin said.

"If I'm not back in an hour, then I'm dead or captured and you're on your own," Lesric said, turning to leave.

"Thank you for the encouraging last words," Lianna said, trying to force a smile.

"You're welcome," Lesric said without turning around as he walked down the empty street.

"Kedrin, why don't we go into that house over there? I'd feel better if we weren't in the open."

He stumbled into the house, collapsing in a heap once in the door. Lianna went back outside in time to see Lesric turn a corner and disappear. She stood there a few moments, staring at nothing in particular, then sighed and made her way back to Kedrin. He sat motionless, a grimace crossing his face as another wave of pain shot through his arm.

She looked around, and saw that dust had gathered on the furniture. The occupants had left days previous, before Pruglin's gates were closed. A withered plant sat in the corner, giving more proof to her hypothesis.

She sat down on the floor and waited. The minutes stretched on like hours. Finally, in the unnerving silence, she was acutely aware of the sound of approaching footsteps and stood up, about to call out. Something stopped her. She quietly moved to the window and peeked out. No one was in sight, but the steps were nearer. She realized that they belonged to several people, so unless Lesric was returning with his friend, it was someone else.

When the men finally came into view, she ducked out of sight behind the window frame. A trio of soldiers marched down the road, getting nearer to them with every passing second. She tensed and waited.

After what seemed like forever, the footsteps

passed the house and finally faded into the distance. She let out her breath, which she'd been holding unknowingly.

"What's wrong?" Kedrin asked, groaning as he shifted and his shoulder screamed in protest.

"Kedrin, we have to find Lesric. He should be back by now, and three soldiers just walked past."

"All right. Let's go!" Kedrin sat upright, then moaned. "Ow, my shoulder!"

Lianna watched him with sympathy, but she had to be firm. "Kedrin, we need to go. Come on."

He grabbed a chair for support and pulled upright. "Be patient with your poor old brother. You've never been shot before."

"Yes, but when you're not injured, you're faster and stronger than me, so being shot should even us out."

"You underestimate the agony of such a wound, dear sister," Kedrin said, with a look of anguish that was only slightly exaggerated. "If you had undergone such a grievous injury, you would have more sympathy for me."

Lianna slung her pack over her shoulder, and picked up Kedrin's as well. "We need to go. Any idea where Lesric was headed?"

"He didn't know."

"True. What do you suggest doing? If we don't find him, the soldiers might."

"While you figure it out, I think I'll just take a nap. Wake me up when it's time to leave."

"Kedrin, this is serious. We...let me go!" He clapped a hand over her mouth and motioned for her to be quiet. She pushed his hand aside and whispered angrily. "What do you think you're doing?"

"Shh! I heard something." He listened for several

minutes, then began to crawl deeper into the house, using only his good arm.

Lianna followed her brother, dragging the packs. He stopped in the small kitchen. "I think that we were followed to Linstown. The soldiers you saw are probably searching for us."

"We need to find Lesric immediately. I knew we shouldn't have split up."

"We're going to have to find him, staying off the streets and keeping as quiet as possible. Any ideas?"

The front door swung open with a creak. "Right now, run," she said as she slipped out the back door. After Kedrin was out, she closed it gently. They jogged through the overgrown garden. A six foot fence enclosed the area.

"I can't climb that with one arm!" Kedrin exclaimed.

Lianna's eyes darted back and forth. "This way!" She hurried over to where a rain barrel stood in the corner. Kedrin climbed up and slipped over the fence. Lianna followed right behind him. They were in a long, narrow alley. "Lesric went this way," she said.

"Lead on."

They hurried down the alley, stopping occasionally to get their bearings. The streets seemed deserted, but they couldn't be too sure.

"Kedrin, we need to leave the alley if we're going to find Lesric."

"I know. I feel safer here, though. I don't want to leave until we have to."

"Why, oh why, did we split up?"

A shriek split the air.

"I think our friend the gonadaw is here," Kedrin said. "Now Lesric knows there are enemies in the area.

We don't have to worry about him walking into a trap. All we have to do is find him."

"Which will be harder now because he will be trying to stay out of sight," Lianna pointed out. "Why didn't we agree on a rendezvous?"

"We didn't think we'd need it."

"Shh!" Lianna froze.

From a distance came a crashing sound, like all the pots and pans falling out of the cupboard at home.

"What in the world was that?" Kedrin asked in a low voice.

"I don't know." Lianna's voice was equally quiet.

From the same direction, they heard the distinct sound of swords clashing.

"I think we found our man. Let's go."

"Kedrin, you're in no condition to fight. You need to stay away from the conflict."

"All right, all right. But you'd better hurry up before that noise draws all the Lentours in the area."

Lianna hurried towards the sound of the conflict, bow in hand. As she exited the alley, she saw the unmistakable figure of Lesric. Two soldiers faced him, and three more were running up the street. With an arrow ready, she stood still and surveyed the situation, then dropped one of the soldiers engaging Lesric, evening out the fight. She selected the nearest of the three soldiers for her next target, and by the time she had shot a third man, Lesric had finished off his opponent. He quickly dispatched the final soldier.

"Lesric, we need to get out of here. Hurry!"

"You don't need to give me a second invitation. I'm just glad that I found you."

"You found us!" Kedrin exclaimed as they reached

him. "We risk our lives to find you, and when we save your life, you don't even bother to thank us, but state how glad you are that you found us! Unbelievable."

A shriek pierced the air.

"Uh, Lesric, any ideas? I can't run away from that thing, or fight if it catches us," Kedrin said with an abrupt change of tone.

"I'm about out of tricks up my sleeve. Lianna?"

"You didn't find your friend?"

He shook his head. "It's been so long since I was here, I don't even know exactly where to look. I could have missed him, but I doubt it."

"I have nothing," she said. "And I'm almost out of arrows, too."

They were out of the village now, ducking under branches and around trees, moving as fast as Kedrin could go.

Another screech sounded, closer this time. Lianna's heart pounded in her chest. She knew that the soldiers and the gonadaw would catch them any minute, and once they did they were as good as dead. She almost bumped into Kedrin when he abruptly stopped. She could see why. They stood on the bank of the river.

"We're almost out of places to go." Lesric said. He turned to go back the way they'd come and froze. "Omit the almost. We are out."

Lianna twisted around to see what had caught his attention. She felt panic rising as she realized he was right.

CHAPTER 26

A creature Lianna recognized as a siladis emerged from the treeline. She'd seen its like only twice before, both times on the way to Cortim Castle. They had still been in the Risclan Valley when they were attacked by the first siladis, and in the Syntor the second time, and she didn't want to repeat either experience.

But the siladis wasn't what really caught her attention. What she stared at was the man who sat on its back.

His clothes were ragged, and his hair was matted and so dirty that Lianna couldn't discern its color. He had a wild look about him, and the fact that he was riding on a siladis did nothing to soften her impression of him. Then he spoke.

"Lesric? Is that you?"

"Pardil?" Lesric asked, bewildered.

"Yes, it's me. What are you doing here?" A gonadaw shrieked off in the distance, and Pardil stiffened. "No time. We'll talk later. Right now, we need to get out of here. Follow me."

"Pardil, wait. My friend is wounded."

Pardil flicked his eyes back and forth nervously, scanning the trees. "We'll go as fast as he can keep up. But hurry! We can't let them trap us against the river."

The siladis turned and headed back into the trees. They had no choice but to follow.

Kedrin staggered on as quickly as he could, but he was even paler than before, and his bandage was soaked through with blood. He couldn't keep moving at this pace much longer. Lesric saw that Kedrin was barely able to keep up, and moved over to support him. Still, his strength was failing, and it was clear Kedrin couldn't go much farther.

"Pardil, how much farther?" Lesric called out.

"Not far now!" Pardil responded cheerfully. "We'll be there in time for supper."

"Very helpful," Lesric said under his breath.

Ten minutes later, they stopped at the edge of a thicket. The interlaced branches would be impossible to navigate, but Pardil didn't seem concerned. He looked behind them into the forest, then back at the thicket, as if judging something. Then he grabbed a protruding branch and pulled on it. By some hidden mechanism, a network of branches lifted up, forming a doorway big enough for the siladis to pass through.

He rode in and looked back. When they hesitated, he urged, "Hurry! The soldiers will be here soon."

Lesric stepped forward first, still supporting Kedrin. Lianna followed. Once they were inside, Pardil pulled another branch, and the doorway closed. A bend twenty feet down the path obscured Lianna's vision, but it appeared to wind its way deep into the thicket. Pardil and the siladis moved forward, and Lianna followed behind her brother and Lesric. They followed the twisting path for what must have been nearly a quarter of a mile, then found themselves in a sort of room. Branches and vines had interwoven to form a ceiling ten feet above

THE SWORD OF TORRAC

their heads, through which the sunlight filtered. The room was twenty feet across and roughly circular. At the far side was another path, but this one was more like a tunnel, covered by the same ceiling of intertwined branches.

Leaving the beast behind, Pardil dismounted the siladis and walked toward the tunnel, and the others followed. As they entered it, Lianna saw that it was a sort of hallway lined with doorways. Pardil turned into the first door to the right. They followed him and found themselves in a large open area. This room was different from the others in that no light seeped through the leafy ceiling. Instead, on the walls, holes like windows angled down from the top of the thicket to allow sunlight in. Lianna guessed that the thicker overhead canopy offered better protection from rain.

A fire crackled in the stone fireplace, the first thing Lianna had seen there made of something other than vines and branches. In the center of the room stood a table, and around it were four rough wooden chairs. Along the walls were other items whose purpose she couldn't identify.

"Welcome to my castle," Pardil said. "My home is yours, Lesric, and your friends' as well."

"Thank you," Lesric replied. "Kedrin here is injured and needs help," he added.

"Sit down," Pardil said to Kedrin.

Kedrin nodded and collapsed gratefully into one of the chairs. As Pardil began to pull away the bandage to examine the wound, though, Kedrin started to tremble uncontrollably. Pardil looked at him worriedly, then removed the bandage the rest of the way. Lianna gasped.

A bluish substance oozing from the wound had

formed a crust around its edges. Although the bandage was soaked with old blood, little came from the injury now. The entire area surrounding the injury was red and inflamed.

Pardil shook his head. "Oh dear. Not good, not good at all. The arrow was poisoned. A scratch from an arrow with this poison on it is fatal, if not treated properly and in a timely fashion. When did this happen?"

Lesric thought for a moment. "Maybe four hours ago."

"Not good, not good. I'll do what I can. Kedrin, we need to get you in bed. All the exertion since you were injured just speeds up the poison. We're going to have to work quickly. Lesric, there's a bedroom straight across the hall. Take him there and get him in bed. I'll be there as soon as I get my equipment."

Lianna followed as Lesric half carried, half dragged Kedrin to the room. Once he lay, they went back to see if they could help Pardil.

He was rummaging through cupboards that, until he opened a door hidden in the tangle of vines, were all but invisible. From them he grabbed different herbs and small cylinders, mumbling to himself as he did.

"Pardil, do you need help?" Lesric asked.

"No, no, no help. I can do it. It's just been too long. I'm not quite sure about the ratio of deathberries to Dolpe's nettle..." and he drifted off into a string of words meaningless to Lianna. "Ah, here it is. Slug slime. Perfect."

Lianna and Lesric exchanged a confused glance.

"Well, what are you waiting for? Let's get to work. If you grab that bowl, we can start."

Pardil walked across the hall into Kedrin's room.

When he was out of earshot, Lianna whispered, "Is he crazy?"

"Something happened to him when his wife died. He changed, mostly kept to himself. Yes, a lot of people call him crazy. He is a doctor, though. Or he was, five or ten years ago. He knows what he's doing." Lesric hesitated. "I hope."

Lianna picked up the bowl and followed Pardil, not feeling overly confident in their host's abilities to save her brother's life.

When she entered the room, Kedrin was tossing and turning. He mumbled incoherently. "He's got a high fever," Pardil said. "If we don't hurry, he'll enter the coma, and it will be too late."

"You've treated patients with this poison before?" Lianna asked. "And what is the poison exactly?"

"Yes, I've treated them before." Pardil looked off into the distance. "Do you mean you don't know what the poison is?"

"No, I don't."

"Well, let me enlighten you." Pardil acted as if he were about to divulge something of great importance. "The deadly substance pumping through your brother's veins is saliva from a gonadaw."

CHAPTER 27

"A gonadaw?" Lianna asked, bewildered.

"Yes, a gonadaw. You know, the lizards with the cruel claws and crueler teeth." Pardil shivered. "Gonadaw saliva has long been considered one of the most effective poisons for use on arrows. Like I said, the smallest amount in the smallest wound will prove fatal. Of course, it doesn't help when an entire arrow that has been soaked in the poison passes completely through you."

As he spoke, Pardil added the ingredients he'd collected to a glass container. "After several hours, even up to a day and a half after the injury, victims fall into a coma, from which they may or may not wake. If they do, it's only for a short amount of time, and they often hallucinate. Once they have entered the coma, though, it's too late."

Lianna winced as she saw him add the contents of the cylinder labeled 'Slug Slime' to a second container. She didn't know what Pardil planned to use the concoction for, and she didn't really want to find out. He added several more things to the second container, then mashed the ingredients of the separate dishes to form two pastes.

Taking the first paste, he walked to Kedrin's bedside and carefully smeared the stuff into the wound. He then took a bandage and wrapped it tightly around Kedrin's shoulder.

Finally, he cleaned up the mess, set aside the second paste to use later, and said, "Now that that's done, I can start supper. If we're lucky, he might even survive."

"Thank you, Pardil," Lesric said sincerely. "I can't tell you how much I appreciate your help."

"You're welcome," Pardil said, turning to leave. "I'm going to start supper. You can do whatever you want, but don't be too loud. Kedrin needs quiet right now. He should stop thrashing soon, and once his fever breaks, I can add the second salve."

After he was gone, Lianna turned to Lesric. She spoke in a voice just above a whisper. "I think it's time I learn exactly who our host is and how you know him. Also, he'd better know what he's doing, taking care of Kedrin. I'm not so sure about some of the ingredients he used in those so-called miraculous cures."

"Pardil and my father knew each other growing up. They were good friends. Pardil was a merchant, and even though he lived far away, we saw him often. Then his wife died." He paused, thoughtful.

"I'm not exactly sure what happened, but he went half mad and started wandering the valley. Every so often he would pass through our town. He stayed with us sometimes when I was young, and I always liked him. Then several years went by, and he didn't visit. We were worried about him, until my father heard that he had settled down in Linstown and become a doctor. That was years ago, though, and we hadn't heard from him since then. Until today, that is."

"He was your friend in Linstown, then?" Lianna asked.

"Yes."

"And you took us there, not knowing whether or not he even lived there still? We're lucky he found us, or we'd all be dead right now." Lianna looked at Kedrin's still form and thought about how close to death, even now, her brother was. For some reason she couldn't explain, she was angry.

"It was our only option. I realize you think it was my fault Kedrin got hurt, and maybe you're right. But you don't understand that I'm as upset about it as you are. Kedrin is like a brother to me, and I couldn't forgive myself if something happened to him." He looked off into nothingness.

"You say that, but the whole reason we're here and not safe in Pruglin is because you decided to go on a crazy mission against all advice to try to get yourself killed by a gonadaw. Of course, Kedrin and I weren't going to let that happen, so we followed you, and Kedrin nearly lost his life for it. He still could. I don't think you understand."

"Lianna," Lesric said, and Lianna saw that there were tears in his eyes. "I do understand. I told you my family moved to the mountains of Etneog when I was seven. Did I tell you why?

"I had a brother, once. He was two years older than me, and he was my hero. We did everything together, and he didn't care that I slowed him down and couldn't do everything he could. We ran together, swam together, climbed trees, played war games, everything two boys of six and eight do. And we loved the outdoors. We couldn't stand the weeks in the winter when the snow was so deep and the air so cold that we were confined to the house.

"Then I got sick. I almost died. Wilmen was beside himself and didn't know what to do. I think he wanted to die with me. He stayed by my bedside for six weeks while I hovered in the balance between life and death. When I passed the crisis and the doctor said I was going to recover, Wilmen couldn't contain his joy. Mother and Father were finally able to convince him to spend some time outside, something I don't believe he had done once while I was sick, and if you knew Wilmen, you would understand what a sacrifice that was. Mother told him he needed to build up his strength again so that when I recovered we could play together, so he started visiting all our favorite haunts, making sure they were ready for when I was ready to join him. That was what did it. If he hadn't wandered so far from the house alone..." Lesric trailed off, shaking his head.

"Around the same time, a band of marauders, thieving lawbreakers who were running from the law and had settled in our mountains, traveled around the countryside where we lived, getting their revenge by killing and stealing. Occasionally, they would kidnap a child and hold him for ransom. Even after the ransom was paid, the child almost never returned. Sometimes the parents would find his body, or sometimes they just wouldn't hear from him again.

"It was a spring day. The flowers were open and the birds were singing. Wilmen left to play outside." Lesric paused and stared blankly at the opposite wall again. When he spoke again, his voice was husky. "He never came back. The marauders stole him. My parents sold everything they could to pay the ransom. Once they had the money, the marauders disappeared. We never heard from them again." Tears ran down Lesric's cheeks. "I had a relapse, and my parents thought they would lose us both. Everything reminded us of Wilmen's death, and my parents were afraid for my safety. The pain was too great. We tried to escape it; we left our home and made a fresh start. I was lost without Wilmen. I was only six years old, but I never fully recovered from that blow. Then I came to Pruglin and met your family. Over the past few months, Kedrin has become a better friend than I've had for two decades. He came as close to filling the role of brother as anyone could." He looked away.

"I'm sorry, Lesric. I didn't know."

Kedrin stirred. "Lianna?"

"I'm here, Kedrin," Lianna said, hurrying to Kedrin's side.

Lesric hurried to fetch Pardil.

"My shoulder hurts. What happened? And where am I?"

"You were shot by one of Torrac's men while we were crossing the river. And we're at Lesric's friend, Pardil's, house," she explained.

At that moment, Pardil entered the room. "I see your fever has broken, Kedrin. It's good to see you doing better. Let me check your arm."

The bandage fell away, and the transformation was amazing. Almost none of the blue substance remained, and a scab was forming. Taking a fresh bandage, Pardil applied the second concoction, and bound the wound tightly once again. Lianna winced, remembering the ingredients of the paste.

"Supper is ready for you, Lesric and Lianna. Kedrin, you shouldn't eat yet. Your body is still recovering from the shock of the injury. I'll bring you some of my stew in a little while."

Kedrin leaned back in bed and closed his eyes. Lianna followed Lesric and Pardil to the dining room, where Pardil spooned steaming stew into three bowls.

As they were finishing the meal, a shriek pierced the still air. It was slightly muffled by the thicket, but Lianna had heard it enough times to recognize it easily.

"That would be your friend the gonadaw," Pardil said. "You remember him?"

"It would be hard not to," Lesric said. "We were nearly eaten by his brothers on numerous occasions."

"Oh." A look of anger and grief flashed across Pardil's face, so fast Lianna almost thought she'd imagined it. "I see."

Lianna stood up. "I'm going to check on Kedrin." She left the room.

Kedrin was asleep, and aside from the bandage around his shoulder, he looked perfectly well. She sat down on the floor next to the bed and wished they were safe at home in Pruglin, not in the home of a man wild enough to ride a siladis like a horse, but who had somehow been able to save Kedrin's life. Yet here they were, hiding from Lentour patrols that wanted them dead. *If Lesric had just stayed in Pruglin, like everyone told him to, none of this would have happened. Instead, he had to nearly get himself killed, and after we saved him, he still nearly managed to get Kedrin killed.* It was hard to believe that six months ago they thought Torrac was long dead and had never heard of Lesric. She almost wished it had stayed that way.

Looking at Kedrin's still form, she had to struggle to contain the anger that threatened to overwhelm her. This was the cost of this war. And while Kedrin had been lucky enough to survive, many hadn't. Others had paid terrible prices, and would carry the scars, both physical and mental, of their encounters with the Lentours for the rest of their lives.

She determined to do her best to help stop this war and the carnage that followed in its wake.

CHAPTER 28

"I tell you, give me a day to recuperate and I can do it!" Kedrin insisted.

It was the next morning, and they were trying to decide what to do next.

"No, no, and no again." Lesric was firm. "You aren't strong enough yet. What if we were attacked? You can't even hold a sword, let alone fight, and we can't fight and defend you at the same time. Think reasonably, Kedrin. You know you can't do it. Wait three days and we can leave."

"Lianna, help me talk sense into him. You know what Father will do when we're not home on time. He'll talk to Ildug and the Council, and they will end up sending a rescue team, which is exactly what we don't want. If even the Lentours couldn't find us here, of course they won't either, and when they return empty handed, Father will probably send out the army! The sooner we get back, the better."

"Three days will be plenty soon. And I don't think you're thinking clearly. Father would have to have much more reason to send out the army than that we're a few days late coming back. We're always late, Kedrin. He probably expects it."

"Whatever!" Kedrin was exasperated. "Listen to me! Lianna, you know Father is worried, and you know..."

"And I know he would much rather you stay here where it's perfectly safe, even if it means he's worried about you, than try to get home while you're still recovering, and get killed. We're not going to let you leave. Sorry, Kedrin."

Pardil entered the room. "What is going on? My patient needs rest and quiet, and you're in here squawking like a flock of angry crows! Also, in case you forgot, your hunters are outside in the near vicinity, and screeching at each other is as good a way as any to alert them to your whereabouts."

"Sorry," Lesric said.

"Sorry, my foot. If he's not kept here for the next couple days resting in quiet, he might never recover."

Lesric and Lianna looked at Kedrin.

"I appreciate the concern, but I'm not as weak as you seem to think. I really can..."

"No, you can't. Trust me. I know." A faraway look entered Pardil's face. "I know," he said softly. "I know how you feel. You've passed the crisis, you're well into the healing process, and you're stronger by the hour. But you're not well. This is the most dangerous time, Kedrin, when you are overconfident. You overestimate your strength."

"Pardil, please!"

"No! I know what you want to do. You want to go home. You think you can do it. So did she. I let her, and what happened? Dead. She's dead." He trailed off.

"What are you talking about?" Lesric asked.

Pardil shook his head sadly.

"Pardil, when you...left, you never told us exactly what happened. That was fifteen years ago. I think I have a right to know."

"Those brutes!" Pardil exclaimed.

"What brutes?"

"Lentours." Pardil spat out the word. "They attacked my caravan. They killed almost everyone. While Insal and I were fleeing, they shot her with a poisoned arrow. We hid in a cave in the mountains. I was able to stop the poison, and she started to recover." He stopped, the memory brutally painful.

"But they were searching for us," he continued. "She was still weak, and I knew that she shouldn't be moved, but I also knew we would be found if we stayed. She knew the danger, and insisted that we leave. When the searching parties drew nearer, I agreed. It was too much for her. She died two days later."

"I'm sorry, Pardil. Why didn't you tell us? No one knew what happened to you, and we were worried sick about you. And if you knew about the Lentours, why didn't you tell anyone in fifteen years?"

Pardil shook his head. "I didn't recognize them for who they were until Forsid was destroyed. Then I realized they were the same brutes who killed her. Before that, I thought they were just a band of marauders who knew the secret of making deadly poisoned arrows. I've barely made contact with anyone since then. I couldn't, Lesric. No one could understand my grief, not even your family."

"Why was your wife with you on that trip? She never accompanied you when you passed through our area. I never even met her."

"It was the only time she ever went," Pardil said. "I'll never forgive myself for asking her to come along."

"Pardil, it's not your fault."

"We can avoid the same ending this time, though. Kedrin will stay in bed until there is not the slightest risk." Pardil left the room.

"I can..." Kedrin began several seconds after Pardil was gone.

"Sorry, Kedrin. Doctor's orders." Lianna grinned, but she felt for Pardil and the weight of guilt that had plagued him for years.

Her brother glared at her. "Fine. Not tomorrow but the next day. And don't try to argue."

* * * * *

That night, Lianna, Lesric, and Pardil sat at the table eating something Pardil had roasted over the fire. Lianna didn't know what it was and was afraid to ask after seeing a sample of what Pardil kept in his cupboards. The food had a rubbery consistency, but the taste wasn't terrible.

Only faint twilight seeped through the slanted windows, and the remainder of the light was shed by lanterns casting a soft glow about the room.

Lianna was chewing a particularly tough bite when Pardil stiffened. He turned in the direction of the room where the siladis lived and appeared to be listening.

"What is it?" she asked.

"Shh!" Pardil rose to his feet slowly. He circled around the table, his eyes never leaving the direction of the passage to the outdoors. Eyes alert and muscles tense, he slowly made his way to the door, picking up a spear-like weapon leaning against the wall on his way.

Lianna stared at the weapon, something she hadn't noticed before. It was a heavy staff of some kind with a stone blade on the end. Although it was obviously homemade, it was an impressive weapon that somehow fit Pardil's rugged appearance.

He disappeared around the corner. Lianna and Lesric stood up, and Lesric hurried to the doorway. Lianna followed right behind him.

"Lianna, Lesric, what's going..." Kedrin, still not allowed out of bed, began as they passed.

"Shh!" Lesric put a finger to his lips and hurried after Pardil.

Lianna emerged into the dusk of the courtyard that was the home of the siladis. Pardil was staring down the passageway, listening. The siladis crouched, ready to spring, hackles raised. A low growl came from its throat.

"What's going on?" Lianna whispered.

"They found us," Pardil answered just as quietly. "I don't know how they did it, but they found us." He turned. "You need to hide."

"Pardil, what about Kedrin?"

Pardil ignored him and touched the siladis lightly on the shoulder. The beast turned and looked at him with large, knowing eyes. "You keep us safe. You hear me? Keep us safe!"

The siladis looked at Pardil a moment longer, then turned and looked again towards the passageway.

"We need to hurry. If you're right and they're in the passage, we only have a few minutes."

"Lesric! You get Kedrin, then follow me. Lianna, grab the packs."

A change seemed to have come over Pardil. He no longer carried his crushed look. He seemed energetic, and was doing everything he could to ensure their escape.

Lesric left the room with Kedrin behind him.

"Lesric! Let Kedrin lean on you. He shouldn't be walking around by himself."

"I'm perfectly capable..."

"Do as I say."

Lianna slung the last pack over her shoulder. "How far are we going, Pardil? I thought one pack was heavy, three are significantly more so."

"Just keep up for a little farther and we'll rethink things."

The four quickly made their way deeper into the thicket. Several minutes later the sound of fighting broke out behind them.

"Pardil!" Lesric looked back nervously. "I hope you have a plan."

"I do."

"I hope it's a good one."

"We're almost there."

Pardil led them through a doorway on the right of the passageway and they emerged into a small room. He hurried over to the fireplace and stuck his head inside. Lianna saw that there were no ashes in the fireplace, and although the walls had been blackened by soot, it didn't look like a fire had been lit for years.

Pardil reached into the back of the fireplace and pulled on a hidden latch. The bottom of the fireplace swung outward, revealing a ladder descending into darkness.

"Lesric, you go first. It's about eight feet down." Lesric nodded and began his descent. "Hurry!" Pardil said, looking nervously at the doorway. When Lesric reached the bottom, Lianna dropped the packs to him and then followed into the darkness below. Kedrin was next. Using only his good arm, he carefully made his way down the ladder.

Pardil was last, and as his head dropped beneath the level of the floor, he pulled the grate closed after them. In the weak light cast by his lantern, Lianna saw him pull a lever. Then he jumped and landed crouching like a cat ready to pounce.

Holding a finger to his lips, he pointed above. A moment later, Lianna tensed as she heard men enter the room and circle the area directly above their heads, inspecting it.

"You know that fireplace has no ashes in it and obviously hasn't been used in years. Aren't they going to be suspicious?" Lesric whispered.

"No, they won't. The lever I pulled released a bag of ashes onto the grate. I knew this day would come, and I've been preparing an escape route for years."

For the first time, Lianna took a good look around the room. It was about twelve feet square, the walls and ceiling reinforced by slabs of wood that ran the length of the room.

"Escape route?" Kedrin asked skeptically.

"Yes." Pardil pulled one of the planks of wood aside and revealed a hidden door. "My hope was that even if someone happened to find the room, they'd think this is all there is to it."

The sounds of footsteps clumped towards the doorway of the small room above them, then faded into the distance. Lianna breathed a sigh of relief.

"Now," Pardil said. "Get some rest and we can move in the morning. The passage will take us to the edge of the thicket underground, and then we can go to Pruglin. But first we need to sleep."

Lianna was amazed at the change in Pardil. Ever

since he had told them the full story about the death of his wife, he seemed a different man. The change was a welcome one.

Kedrin was asleep almost instantly, and Lianna wished she could do the same. She lay awake for what seemed like hours before finally drifting off into a restless sleep.

CHAPTER 29

T aran didn't know what to do. Lianna and Kedrin should have been back long ago. He had told Ildug, but his friend had reminded him that Lianna and Kedrin were rarely home from such expeditions when they were expected. "They seem to have an uncanny ability to not only find trouble but also to escape it," Ildug had said, and insisted that they give more time before sending out a search party.

When the missing three had failed to show after another day, Taran had brought his concern before the Pruglin Council. They had all been sympathetic, but had agreed almost unanimously that it was too risky to send out a search party. Another farm had been leveled, several gonadaws were sighted, and everyone was more concerned with stopping the creatures than finding three people who had slipped out of the city contrary to all instructions and advice.

Rilan was beside herself. It was all Taran could do to convince her that Lianna and Kedrin were not dead and would return soon. But now he was becoming nervous and found it difficult to control his rising apprehension.

Finally, when they had been gone for two nights, he decided that he had to take action. He couldn't wait around idly any longer.

Taran was preparing to call another Council meeting, but Ildug beat him to it. A messenger pounded furiously on the door, and when the maid escorted him into Taran's office, his face was pale.

"Councilor Taran, sir," he said, fear in his voice. "Councilor Ildug has summoned an emergency meeting. It's the Lentours. They're coming."

"What do you mean? I thought they already bypassed us."

"I don't know the details. All I know is that Councilor Ildug says that we have a few hours at the most. And Councilor?"

"Yes?"

"You remember the messenger from Forsid?"

"I do. He died almost as soon as he returned from some kind of poison."

"The man who brought the news has the same thing. He fell into a coma almost as soon as he returned. Dr. Jedur is doing his best, but he's losing him rapidly. I don't know what happened to him, but if the Lentours can use that against us, we don't stand a chance."

"That's not true," Taran said. "We do stand a chance, and I don't want you to tell anyone else what you just told me. We want to be boosting the men's morale, not destroying it. The better chance they think we have of winning, the better we'll do. If they give up, we will be crushed. Do you hear me?"

"Yes, sir."

"You may go."

Taran followed the messenger out of the room, nearly bumping into Rilan in the hallway. "Ildug called an emergency meeting."

"What is it now?"

He hesitated, wondering if it was a good time to break the news to her or not. "The Lentours are coming."

"I thought they passed us!"

"They did. It must have been some sort of trick. I need to hurry, though. I don't want to keep the Council waiting."

Taran rushed out of the house, swung onto his horse, and galloped towards the city square.

Reaching his destination, he hastily dismounted and tied his horse to a post near the door. Many of the Council members were already assembled. Ildug, as head of military operations and the one who had called the meeting, stood in Mathalin's usual place at the head of the table, his mouth a grim line and a hint of pallor to his face.

When the last councilor entered, Ildug began. "Thank you all for coming at such a short notice. I know you've had a lot of that lately, and I apologize. We don't have much time, so I'll get right to the point." He took a breath, then continued.

"When the Lentour army passed Pruglin, we assumed we were safe and commenced preparations to aid Brodalith in their defense if necessary. But we were wrong. It was a trick, and we're lucky we hadn't left for Brodalith yet, or the city would have been defenseless.

"There are not one but two armies. The first appeared to be heading for Brodalith. In reality, they are camped a short distance in that direction. A second army marched several miles behind them. It seems they are trying to trap us between the two armies. They will be here in a few short hours." He paused and cleared his throat, then hesitated.

"But there's more. The second army is not alone.

There's a monster with it. According to Lesric's report, it is called a kingalor."

Gasps of dismay filled the room. Taran's head spun. His son and daughter had told him of the destruction that had been wreaked on Forsid and the mammoth footprints they had seen around the ruins of the city. The thought that the beast was coming to Pruglin was terrifying.

"You don't mean..." the Council member trailed off, but everyone knew what he meant.

"This beast is the same as the kind that decimated Forsid." Someone started to speak, but Ildug held up a hand for silence. "There's more. Some of you may know that the messenger from Forsid seemed to have contracted some mysterious illness. We now know that he was poisoned. Today's messenger has the same symptoms. As yet, we're not certain, but Dr. Jedur believes the Lentours use poisoned arrows. A scratch from one of them can prove fatal, at least in theory."

"What you're trying to tell us is that by this time tomorrow, we'll all be dead," someone concluded.

"No!" Ildug spoke loudly. "If we believe that, we don't stand a chance. We need to give the men hope. We need to let them know that there is a chance, and we can survive. Then and only then can we conquer this enemy. Fear is our foe, and we cannot let it overcome us. If we lose our courage, our people will too, and we will be dead men.

"Now, we need to put all our efforts into our defenses. Weldon, you marshal the archers and prepare them. Gaflen, you lead the crew fortifying the River Gate. Taran, you will help me lead the men from the walls. Farcoy, you..."

Taran listened impatiently as Ildug assigned each man a job. When they were finally dismissed, he walked over to Ildug.

"Taran? What can I do for you?"

"My children are out there, Ildug. They will die if they're not inside the city before the army arrives."

"Taran, it pains me to say this, but the city is at stake. As much as I care about your children, I must prepare the city. I'm sorry. There's nothing I can do right now."

"I know, and that's not what I wanted."

"What is it?"

"I'm needed here too. I can't leave to look for them. All I ask is that you give me ten men to send after them."

"Taran, I need every man I can get."

"Ten men. If they can't find Kedrin and Lianna, they can still come back and fight."

"And if your children and Lesric have been captured and my men are killed?"

"Ildug, please. You have a family. You know what I feel like right now."

"I can't spare anyone, Taran. I'm sorry."

Taran turned away. He understood. But he didn't know how he would break the news to Rilan. He couldn't forgive himself for not insisting that the search party left earlier.

* * * * *

When Taran reached home, Rilan was waiting. She stiffened as Taran told her the details of the approaching danger, then of Ildug's refusal to lend him the men.

Tears formed in her eyes. "How can he?"

Taran shook his head. "It's my fault. I should have

ABIGAIL CLEEK

sent a team yesterday."

A ray of hope lit Rilan's eyes. "You say Ildug can't spare one man?"

"That's what he says."

"I know two people who might be able to get out."

"Who?" Taran asked, hope forming in his heart.

CHAPTER 30

Where am I? Lianna was lying on a hard dirt floor. It was completely dark, giving her no hints as to where they were. Then she remembered. They were in Pardil's secret passage.

She lay still until Pardil lit the lantern. She groaned and stretched her cramped muscles as the light illuminated the small room. Rising to a sitting position, she looked at Kedrin, who was awake and looking stronger than he'd been since his injury.

"I'm in a bit of a dilemma." Pardil said. "We can't stay here, but I'm still not convinced that Kedrin is ready to travel."

"It's not that far to Pruglin. I'm perfectly able to walk that distance."

"No, you're not. You are most certainly not walking that distance. I'm worried that you're not strong enough to ride that distance."

Kedrin put on an insulted air. "I don't know what you're planning on having me ride, but it takes no physical strain to ride to Pruglin. You insult me by saying I'm not capable of anything but lying in bed. I appreciate the concern, but I don't need to be treated like an invalid."

"Kedrin, don't make this any harder than it has to be."

"Pardil, I don't think we have a choice," Lesric

said. "I have an odd feeling that something is wrong and we need to be back as soon as possible."

"I agree," Kedrin said. "If we aren't back soon, Father will send the army after us. Maybe not something quite so drastic, but I know that Mother won't let him rest until he insists that Idlug send a search party."

"It's something bigger than that," Lesric said. "Something's not right."

"Fine. We eat some food and we leave," Pardil said. "But Kedrin, if you have the slightest appearance of needing rest, we are stopping right there and making camp, even if it's in the middle of the Pruglin River. Agreed?"

"What if it's in the middle of a battle, or with a gonadaw in mid-leap, about to pounce on us?"

Pardil scowled. "This isn't funny."

Kedrin wasn't paying attention. He crammed his mouth full of a sticky glazed cinnamon raisin bun. Even on dangerous missions, Rilan always managed to spoil them with treats that probably weren't the ideally nutritious meals to be consumed on a trip where energy was crucial. Lianna was glad she did, though, because they had enabled her to decline some of Pardil's less appetizing meals.

She took some food from her own knapsack, amazed that the bread Rilan had packed still tasted fresh and soft after she'd been packing it around for several days.

After breakfast, Pardil stood up. "If we're going to do this, we might as well not put it off anymore. Let's go."

"Uh, Pardil, what was the ride you mentioned?" Kedrin asked slowly.

Pardil didn't look up from where he was prying open the secret door he'd shown them the night before.

"I'm hoping she's still alive after last night. If she is, then you'll see her at the end of the tunnel."

Lianna had a nagging suspicion, but she was too tired to voice it. Time would tell if she was right or not.

The door swung inward and hit the wall with a thud as Pardil managed to pry it open. It was only four feet tall, but as wide as an average doorway. He beckoned to Kedrin, standing closest to the entrance to the passage, and stooping nearly double, Kedrin disappeared through the small door. Lianna waited for Lesric to go through, but he stepped back. "Ladies first."

She ducked low enough for her pack to clear the doorway. Once inside, she found that the ceiling was high enough to easily stand up. The dim lantern Pardil held illuminated a dusty passageway with stone walls for a yard or two past where she stood, and then all was darkness.

Pardil followed Lesric through the door, and then pulled it closed behind him. A dull thud echoed through the chamber.

Then they set off down the winding passage, on their way back to Pruglin.

* * * * *

The wind caught the door and slammed it shut behind Taran. He mounted the steps to the second floor two at a time. Rilan heard him coming and hurried to meet him.

"Well? What did they say?"

"I need to be at the gate in an hour so the gatekeeper will let them out."

"Thank goodness!" Rilan said, relief on her face.

"Lianna and Kedrin should be home within a day. Don't worry about them."

Inwardly, Taran hoped they were home sooner than that, because if they weren't, they weren't coming home until the battle was over. And after that, there was a good possibility that they wouldn't have a home to come back to.

But the look on Rilan's face as she anticipated Kedrin and Lianna's imminent return was enough to make him keep his reflections to himself.

CHAPTER 31

S everal minutes later, Pardil reached the tunnel and climbed up a rickety old ladder, shouldering open the heavy wooden trapdoor at the top and climbing out. The sunlight stung Lianna's eyes after being underground since the night before. She squinted and blinked rapidly.

They emerged on the edge of the thicket opposite that from which they'd entered. Birds sang in the trees. Lianna breathed in the fresh air deeply.

Then she looked down. Two yards in front of her was an indentation in the ground, nearly an inch deep and in the shape of a lizard's foot. She froze.

Pardil bent down and examined the print. "It's no more than an hour old." When he stood up, his eyes said more than his words. A fierce anger burned in them, and Lianna knew he was determined to be revenged for the death of his wife.

The bushes rustled in front of them, and two figures with swords drawn emerged from them.

In an instant, Lianna had an arrow aimed for the heart of the nearest one. Behind her, three swords slid from their sheaths. She realized that Kedrin must have drawn his sword with his left hand.

"Thank goodness! We found you!" The voice was familiar.

Lianna looked at the face of her target and gasped in astonishment, lowering her bow. "Alssa? What are you doing here?"

"Looking for you," her cousin said.

Lesric looked at Kedrin. "Quite the army he sent after us."

"Why you? I mean, why just the two of you?" Lianna realized that the other person was Elariam, Alssa's older sister.

"Because Ildug won't let a single man out of the city. He says he needs everyone to defend it, and your father couldn't convince him otherwise. But we need to hurry. It took us longer to find you than we'd expected, and we may be out of time."

"Defend the city from what?" Lesric asked impatiently. Lianna swallowed hard. The knot of apprehension in her throat was growing.

"The Lentours are coming. It was a trick, bypassing the city, and there was a second army behind the first. The city is trapped between the two armies, and the second one has..." Alssa hesitated.

"Has what?" Lianna demanded, although she was pretty sure she knew.

"A kingalor," Alssa said, fear in her voice. "They're coming with a kingalor."

"No!" Lesric exclaimed. "They could never have gotten a kingalor that close to the city without our knowing."

"It's true," Elariam confirmed. "We need to go. If we're not back by the time the Lentours arrive, we won't be able to get back into the city."

"Well, what are we waiting for? Let's go." Kedrin set off at a brisk pace.

"Hold up there, my young patient. You're moving far too fast. Slow down, or we're going back to the thicket and waiting this battle out."

"You just want to stand around and let the owner of that footprint find us? Going to Pruglin sounds much safer in my opinion."

Pardil pursed his lips. "If she survived last night, it won't be a problem. Otherwise, we're going to have to move very slowly. We'll just have to wait and see if she finds us. I hope for your sake and for mine that she does."

"She," Lianna said. "Does she happen to be the siladis?"

"Yes," he said evenly. "She does."

"You have a siladis?" Alssa asked skeptically.

"I do." Pardil started walking at nearly the same pace Kedrin had been earlier.

"And you want Kedrin to ride it?"

Pardil ignored her.

Alssa fell into step beside Lianna. "Who is he, and what happened to Kedrin?" she asked quietly.

"The Lentours were chasing us and shot Kedrin with a poisoned arrow. We got away from them, but they followed and almost caught us. Pardil found us and saved Kedrin's life. He's Lesric's friend, or else he probably would have killed us himself."

"Oh," Alssa said. Suddenly she stopped. "A poisoned arrow?"

"Yes. Why?"

"What were the symptoms? A blue substance oozing from his wound? A coma?"

"Yes, although Pardil stopped the poison before the coma. Once the victim enters the coma, it's too late."

"Elariam, come here."

Elariam hurried to join them. "Yes?"

"Kedrin was poisoned by the same thing as the messenger. Pardil," she said, motioning in his direction, "saved him."

"What? Is that possible?"

"What's going on?" Lianna asked. "Why is this so incredible?"

"Did your father never tell you what happened to the messenger who brought the news that Forsid was gone?"

"No. Why?"

"He had the exact same symptoms. Dr. Jedur did everything he could to save him, but he died. People forgot about it until the same thing happened to the messenger who warned us that the Lentours were coming. The first victim had only been scratched by whatever hurt him, but it was still fatal."

"If he can really do that, Pardil has to get there before the army does," Elariam said. "He could save hundreds of lives."

Lianna quickened her pace to catch up with Lesric and Pardil at the head of the procession and passed on the information.

"I have something better, though," Pardil said, smiling with satisfaction.

"What?"

"There's an antidote for the poison, that, if taken before the poison enters the bloodstream, will render it harmless."

"And you can make enough of this for the army?"

"Most of them, yes."

They emerged from the treeline on the banks of the river. A hundred yards downstream stood the bridge, and just a little farther yet was Pruglin.

Above the roaring of the river, Lianna heard a crashing sound. Before she had a chance to search for its source, a beast burst out of the trees. Pardil's reaction was faster than anyone else's, and he ran to the siladis and threw his arms around it. "I was worried you didn't make it!" he exclaimed, burying his head in the creature's fur.

Lianna reconsidered her verdict on the change she had seen in him over the past eighteen hours. Pardil still wasn't normal. There was no denying that he had improved significantly since he told them the story of his wife's death, but there was still something in there that would probably never go away.

After Pardil had embraced the monster, he turned to Kedrin. "Climb on."

Kedrin stared at him.

"I said, get on."

"I'm not riding that thing." Kedrin spoke quietly but firmly.

"Yes, you are. Now get on before I'm sorry I let you come. We could have waited out the battle in my home."

"You know that's not safe anymore. I'm perfectly capable of this. The city is in sight. And I know what those beasts do. I'm not riding that."

Pardil's face reflected hurt and shock. "Kedrin, please."

"Look!" Lesric pointed. A flock of crows flew above the city. "They know what's coming. We do too, and we need to be in that city before it strikes."

A deafening bellow reverberated through the air. It was nearly identical to the shrieks Lianna had heard so many times from the throats of the gonadaws, but so much deeper and on such a larger scale that it shocked her. She clapped her hands over her ears.

"We're not going to make it," Kedrin whispered beside her.

Lesric took control. "Pardil, get on the siladis and ride to Pruglin. They need you there. We'll find somewhere to hide until this is over."

"No! Kedrin might die without me! And they won't let me into the city either."

"Yes, they will. Kedrin will go too. That is, if the siladis can carry you both and still make it in time."

Pardil nodded.

"Good. They will let Kedrin in. Now go." When Pardil still hesitated, he shouted. "Go!"

"Wait!" Elariam said. "We still might make it."

Lesric shook his head. "They're too close. The four of us will have to wait it out."

"No, listen! There's another way," Alssa said. "Taran said that if we were too late to get through the gate, there's another way in. A secret passage. It starts by the fishing dock and goes into the city." She paused.

"What's the catch?" Lianna asked.

"Since they're so close, we don't want to be on that side of the river until we have to. Taran said we need to cross at the fishing dock. We'll be exposed on the water."

"Are you sure?" Lesric asked. "If you're wrong, or if we can't find the passage, we'll likely be caught."

They both nodded.

"All right. We'll try it. We'd better hurry, though. I don't want to be caught in the middle of the river when they reach that side of the city. But in case we don't make it, Pardil and Kedrin should still leave on the siladis."

"I'm not just going to abandon you," Pardil argued,

still not convinced.

"Hundreds are going to die if you don't. Go!"

Pardil mounted the siladis.

"Kedrin, get on."

"Don't make me do this, Lesric."

"You know he's right. They won't let him in without you. You're injured, and if we have to fight, you're just going to hinder us."

"Lesric, please!"

"Kedrin, go!"

Kedrin swung onto the siladis behind Pardil. Pardil whispered something in the creature's ear, and the siladis leapt forward, streaked across the bridge, and then was gone.

"Now," Lesric said. "Where's that passage?"

CHAPTER 32

T hey set off at a brisk pace, heading toward the city. The roar of the kingalor sounded once again, and Lianna resisted the urge to turn and run. The sound was terrible, but at the same time possessed an eerie, almost beautiful quality. She remembered her father saying that a man who had been in the vicinity of Forsid City when it was destroyed had been drawn to the sound, couldn't escape it, and she almost understood why. It had a more majestic tone than that of a gonadaw, something of regal dignity. But it was still the cry of a deadly predator, wired to kill, and she was glad that for the present they were out of its reach.

Within the forest directly above the ferry, they stopped. Lianna stood still, listening for anything that would indicate that soldiers were in the area. Hearing nothing, she was about to emerge from the cover of the trees when Lesric held up a hand. He put his finger to his lips and pointed south.

She looked where he pointed, frozen in place as she looked for whatever had drawn his attention. But she didn't see anything.

Then she heard it. A faint cracking, snapping sound, like twigs breaking, only much louder and farther away. There were also resounding crashes, as if large objects were falling to the forest floor.

"What is that?" she mouthed, still not making a sound.

Lesric read her expression as much as her lips. He responded in a low voice. "Kingalor."

"That close?" Elariam whispered.

"That's the only thing I can think of that would snap trees like twigs. We need to cross the river, now."

"Can we make it in time?" Lianna was doubtful.

"We don't have a choice. We have to run for it." Lesric broke cover, racing for the water, with the three girls right behind. Lianna stopped short in horror when the ferry came into full view. The rope had been slashed to pieces and the ferry was gone, washed downstream.

"What do we do?" Alssa's empty voice echoed Lianna's despair.

Lianna's eyes searched their surroundings. They had no way to cross and the Lentours were getting nearer with every passing second. They were running out of options fast.

Then she saw something. It took her a second to realize that it was a rowboat, hidden in the weeds growing close to the water's edge. She ran to it, and the others followed her. Two oars lay in the bottom of the small boat. While it appeared watertight, it was tiny.

Lesric looked it over. "It will hold two of us."

Lianna looked around, but didn't see anything else they could use to their advantage.

"Who destroyed the ferry?" Elariam asked.

"Who knows? It could have been the Lentours, or the Council could have had it done so the Lentours couldn't cross the river here. Regardless, we're in trouble if we don't cross within the next couple minutes."

Alssa dug in her pack. "I brought a rope. Two of us

can cross and take the rope with us, leaving one end here. The other two can pull the boat back to them."

Lesric looked at it and nodded. "It's our only option. Alssa, Elariam, you go first. You know where to look for the passage. Find it while we're crossing."

He looked at them closely. "If we don't make it, don't wait for us. It's vital that you two continue to the city."

Alssa nodded in understanding. "Let's do this."

Tying one end of the rope to the boat, she handed the other to Lesric. She stepped in, and Elariam was right behind her. Lianna pushed the boat as far as she could into the current of the river, and the two girls began to paddle for the far side.

It seemed to take an eternity for them to make their way across the river. As soon as they were close enough to wade the rest of the way to shore, Alssa and Elariam jumped out, hurrying to the fishing docks. Lesric pulled the boat back across the river, hand over hand.

When it reached them again, Lianna climbed in. While Lesric began rowing, Lianna kept an eye out for any sign of danger. Being so close to the city and the approaching Lentours made her nervous, and she couldn't take her eyes off the trees on the other side of the river.

They were twenty yards out when Alssa and Elariam seemed to find what they were looking for. Elariam crawled underneath the dock and moments later, disappeared into the side of the hill. Alssa followed her, only to emerge an instant later. She was about to shout to Lianna and Lesric, but something caught her eye. She pointed frantically to the belt of trees that separated the river from the city, then disappeared back into the passageway.

Lianna looked where her cousin had pointed. "Lesric, look!"

A group of soldiers had emerged from the trees and was pointing at them.

"Hold them off with your bow," Lesric said, rowing furiously.

"I only have seven arrows!"

"I see ten soldiers. If you can hit seven, that should do enough damage to their ranks for us to make it across."

Lianna nodded and took an arrow from her quiver. The boat was rocking too much for her usual accuracy, and her arrow struck low. The man let out a scream as it pierced his leg, but in a life or death situation, Lianna knew that he would still be able to put up a fight.

She took another arrow and selected a new target. This time her aim was true, and the next man fell soundlessly to the ground. By now the remaining men had taken their bows and were preparing to fight back. One man had been quicker to react than his fellows, and as he drew back the string, Lianna released her arrow. She was just in time to stop his missile.

The seven soldiers who remained uninjured sent a volley of arrows towards the small boat. Anticipating the action, Lianna and Lesric ducked and the arrows passed harmlessly over and around them.

Lianna hurried to get a shot before the soldiers released another barrage of arrows. She continued to pick them off between volleys until, by the time they reached shore, four soldiers remained on their feet. Lianna fingered the end of her last arrow.

"Save it," Lesric said. "You may need it later."

He drew his sword and rushed the soldiers. Lianna pulled hers from its sheath and followed with less enthusiasm. Her father had taught her well, but hand-to-hand combat still wasn't her forte, and she knew she was facing trained men. She was far more comfortable keeping her distance and using arrows to hold off her opponents.

Lesric's sword flew, and by the time she reached the conflict, only two soldiers remained. Lesric had already engaged one of them, and Lianna attacked the other. At first she flailed her sword around frantically, forgetting her father's instructions. Slowly her thrusts grew more accurate, and just when she was beginning to think she would win the fight, a sword sprouted from the man's chest. He fell to the ground, and Lesric stood behind him. He looked around, confirming that there were no more soldiers in the immediate vicinity.

"Now what? We can't use the passage. If there are soldiers around and they see us, the city is doomed."

"It's probably doomed anyway, but you're right." He appeared to be thinking.

In the frenzy of the fight with the soldiers, Lianna had forgotten about the quickly approaching army. Now she thought she could make out the distant sounds of men marching, and officers calling out commands.

When the ground seemed to vibrate under her feet, she supposed she was more tired than she realized.

But then Lesric met her eyes. "Did you feel that?"

As if in answer, the ground shook again, and a thud reverberated through the earth.

"What is going o..." She was cut short as another thud sent vibrations through the ground.

A thunderous roar split the air, and she dropped her sword and covered her ears.

When the sound faded away, she bent to retrieve her sword. She looked at Lesric questioningly. "Now what?" She wondered if he could hear her pounding heart.

"I don't know." Lesric stared into the forest from where the kingalor's bellow had come. Then, he started walking forward.

"Lesric! Are you crazy?"

"No. I'm not. Come on."

"Are you trying to get caught? I thought you changed your mind about that theory." Lianna remembered how, when they were captured by General Calsym, Lesric had stated that being captured by the Lentours had enabled them to learn more than they ever could have by observing from a distance. She also remembered him deciding, after they had barely escaped with their lives only to be caught again by the Glinsieran scouts, that the risk involved in that strategy outweighed the benefits.

"It worked twice."

"Yes, and only because we had the help of another army, this one who happened to be on our side. You'd better not be serious."

He stopped and turned. "About getting captured? I'm not. But we can't just stay here. And I want to see what's going on. We might be able to find a place to hide."

"Or we might not."

"Lianna, if you want to accompany me, you are more than welcome. Otherwise, you can find your own place to hide." He turned back and continued walking.

Lianna didn't know what to do. Walking into the jaws of the waiting army was lunacy. But then, maybe staying alone was too. At least she had a better chance with Lesric.

I don't know why I'm doing this, and I'm probably

going to get myself killed, she thought as she started forward. By now, Lesric was out of sight, and she hurried to catch up. As she neared the edge of the trees, she bent over double, not wanting to be spotted.

She found Lesric crouching behind a bush, looking around to be sure no enemies were in sight.

"What's the plan?" she whispered.

"Glad you asked. The plan is, well, the plan is that I don't have a plan."

"You'd better be kidding."

"No. But we need a place to hide, so I thought we might as well hide where we can watch the action."

"If you mean behind this bush, I'm going to be forced to disagree."

"You can spare yourself the trouble. I was considering that tree."

"You want to hide in a tree?" Lianna was incredulous. "And if one of our soldier friends happen to look up?"

"They won't," he said. "From up in a tree, we'll be able to see the army and know exactly what's going on. I doubt any soldiers will even be over here, in a thicket, when there's a huge open clearing just over there."

She was still skeptical. "You had better know what you're doing. My father isn't going to like it if he goes to the trouble to get a search party out of the city to find us and we still end up getting killed."

"I'll do my best to avoid that. Don't worry. I'm going to make a dash for that tree. When I signal that it's safe, follow." He gave her no time to argue, keeping low and moving as fast as possible. The lowest branch was over seven feet off the ground, and he had to jump to grab hold of it. He hauled himself up, looked around, and beckoned to Lianna.

Staying low to the ground, she raced to the tree. Lesric reached down and grabbed her hand, pulling her up. Once she was in the tree, Lesric began to climb higher, not stopping until he was nearly twenty feet above her. She took a deep breath and followed. When she was nearly level with him, she stopped and took a deep breath. Then she parted the leafy branches and peered out in the direction of the clearing where the Lentours were assembling.

Lianna gasped.

CHAPTER 33

Ranks of men stood in perfect order, facing the city without moving a muscle. The hundreds of still forms were one of the more ominous sights Lianna had seen, but she would have been able to handle it if it weren't for the monstrosity that stood in their midst.

The kingalor was bigger than Lianna had ever imagined. She could well see how, defenseless and unaided, Forsid had been crushed.

Pruglin didn't stand a chance.

"A little bigger than I'd imagined," Lesric laughed nervously.

"Uh-huh." Lianna trailed off into silence. "Was the one at Forsid really that big?"

"I have a feeling they're one and the same."

"I hope so. Maybe they're hard to come by, and once we kill this one, we won't have to worry about any more."

"You want to?" He looked down at her.

"Want to what?"

"Kill it."

Lianna stared at him. "That was *we* as in the Pruglin army, not *we* as in the two of us. We can't kill that thing!"

"The Lentours don't have enough men to conquer

the city. Their whole plan is based on the kingalor. Once it dies, this becomes a whole different situation."

"Sure," Lianna said sarcastically. "And how do you suggest going about the slaying of that behemoth?"

"It's big, but it can't be invincible. Maybe a sword in the eye, or something like that."

Lianna studied the beast, looking for a weakness. It stood a good forty feet tall. Two rows of spikes ran down its back, shorter at the base of the skull and the tip of the tail, and growing to six feet tall in the middle of its back. Unlike a gonadaw, it stood on all four legs, although Lianna guessed by looking at it that it could rise on its hind legs like a bear and stand, at least for short periods of time. A frill similar to that of a gonadaw encircled its neck. Massive fangs protruded from its mouth like a crocodile's, and each foot boasted four grisly claws. Its skin was scaly, like a lizard's, and reddish brown. As she watched, a serpentine tongue flicked from its mouth.

She shuddered.

A man separated from the main body and walked boldly toward the gate of Pruglin. Figures moved on the wall, but at this distance Lianna couldn't recognize them. She guessed that her father was among them.

The herald started talking. He had a thick accent, and was far enough away that it was difficult to hear what he said. She strained to hear and made out a few words.

"Pruglin... gracious king, Torrac... chance to surrender..."

"I don't think they made that offer to Forsid," Lianna said.

"If they did, Forsid obviously wasn't interested."

"And Pruglin won't be either. I know my father, and I know Mathalin, Ildug, and many of the other councilors. They won't even consider it."

Someone stepped forward to answer the herald. Lianna guessed it was Mathalin. Behind him stood two other men, and although she couldn't be sure, she thought the nearer of the two was her father.

Mathalin's voice echoed across the clearing. "Tell Torrac it will take more than that to defeat us, Lentour. You and your pathetic lizard are going to have to fight for this city, and we're going to make it a fight you'll remember. Now back off, before I let my archers fire."

The man took Mathalin for his word and backed off quickly, obviously nervous. At a safe distance, he spoke again. This time, Lianna was able to make out his words. "You shall regret your insolent words, Councilor. The mighty army of the Lentours will destroy Pruglin as easily as it has so many others. Forsid, Medfe, Yndua, none could stand against the Lentours, and you shall be no different. Your rash words have sealed your fate." He turned and hurried back to the army.

"I wasn't aware that Medfe was actually conquered by the Lentours," Lesric said. "And I've never heard of Yndua."

"Torrac must have been busy during the past fifty years."

"Yes. To change the subject, any ideas about killing that monster? We're running out of time. Once they decide to use that living, breathing weapon of theirs, it's over. And I don't think that time is very far away."

"You're being serious about this?" Lianna asked. When he nodded, she took a deep breath. "All right. I don't think we'll be able to penetrate its hide, and even if we can, unless we can hit vitals, it won't do much good. Slashing at its legs isn't going to do anything but make it mad, so we're going to have to somehow get up high enough to attack it." She shook her head. "This is a pretty impossible mission you thought up." Lianna didn't have any idea of how to go about killing something like the monster she was looking at, and she was pretty sure that if they tried to, they would just get themselves killed. She didn't like Lesric's idea.

"Notice anything strange about that army?"

"No. Why?"

"The army that passed us on its way to Brodalith isn't there. There are only a few hundred men here. The other army had several thousand."

"Didn't Alssa and Elariam say that it came back?"

"Yes, they did. It's probably waiting on the other side of the city to divide our forces once the battle starts."

"The only real threat here is the kingalor."

"True. Which is why we have to destroy it before it goes from threatening to attacking."

The kingalor lifted its head and bellowed into the air. Lianna shivered. "And the plan is?"

* * * * *

When Kedrin and a wild man with a shaggy mane of hair raced up to the front door on a siladis, Taran wasn't sure what to think. Kedrin assured him and Rilan that Lianna was safe and would be home soon. Then he explained Pardil's ability to treat patients poisoned with gonadaw saliva. Taran hadn't waited for any more, and escorted them straight to Dr. Jedur's headquarters.

The doctor had set up a makeshift hospital for injured soldiers, and together with several doctors working under him was preparing for the wounded men who would soon flood the hospital.

"You can save someone poisoned by...well, whatever you said that stuff is?" Jedur's eyes grew wider and wider as Pardil explained his discovery.

"Gonadaw saliva. Yes, I can. But I can do something better than that."

"What?"

Taran smiled. Jedur seemed unable to believe that anything was better than a cure for the deadly poison.

"I can make it so the poison is completely harmless. The victim won't even need to be treated."

Jedur's jaw dropped and he gave a squeal of delight. Taran's smile grew wider, and he strongly suspected that Kedrin was fighting the urge to laugh.

An instant later, the doctor sobered, fearing it was some cruel joke. "That's not possible."

"It is," Pardil said. "Kedrin is living proof. He should have been dead twenty-four hours ago."

"What is this miraculous treatment?"

Pardil smiled with the eager anticipation of one about to divulge a tremendous secret. "The main ingredient happens to be one of my favorite dishes. Snails."

It was Taran's turn to stare in disbelief.

CHAPTER 34

As the Lentours prepared to march on the city, Lianna racked her brain for some way to kill the great beast.

"That's an awfully big lizard," she said, staring at the kingalor through the leaves she had parted. "You sure you want to do this?"

"It's our only hope," Lesric said, not taking his eyes off the beast. "Cheer up. Something that big will be able to squash us into jelly so fast, there'll be no pain whatsoever."

"That's encouraging."

"It is, isn't it?" He seemed pleased with himself. "And if we're lucky enough to get past its stomping feet with claws that will impale us to the ground, we can always get shredded into ribbons by its monstrous teeth. A delightful meal for the crows. And best of all," he snapped his fingers, "in any of the above, it will all be over, just like that. You won't feel a thing."

"You're making me feel really good about this whole plan."

"It's nice to be appreciated." He looked at the kingalor again, then back at Lianna. "I'm getting an idea."

"As long as it's safe and not just some foolhardy attempt to get killed, I'm all for it."

"Oh, it's not safe. I don't suppose there's any way

something like this could be safe. But I would say it has a fifty percent chance of success."

* * * * *

Taran didn't know what to say when he learned that Alssa and Elariam were back, but that they'd been attacked and Lianna and Lesric were still outside the city. He knew it wasn't their fault, but he couldn't help but be angry that after all his efforts to get Lianna back before the battle, she was locked outside with the Lentour army and a kingalor. He was disgusted with himself, even though he knew there was nothing else he could have done.

He stood on the wall with Mathalin now, looking over the army. Ildug said there were no more than three hundred soldiers, probably less. But those three hundred soldiers weren't alone.

He'd heard about the size of kingalors from the team he'd sent to Forsid after it was destroyed, from Kedrin, Lianna, Oslir, and Lesric, who had seen the ruins of the city, and from a woodcutter who witnessed the destruction of Forsid. But nothing had prepared him for the monster that stood at the gates.

Nevertheless, when a herald rode up from the army and offered them a chance to surrender, he wanted to laugh out loud. Torrac couldn't believe that they would be fool enough for that. Mathalin had been just as incredulous. After scorning the offer, he, Taran, and Ildug held a quick discussion before scattering to prepare for the coming battle.

"The fight will begin shortly," Ildug said, looking over Taran's shoulder towards the army. "I suspect that the first army, the one that bypassed us, will attack from the north. I have men stationed there, ready to defend against any such attempt."

"What about the kingalor?" Mathalin asked.

"We're going to have to hope that thing doesn't attack. I don't think we can stop it if it does."

"Somehow I don't think they want to obliterate Pruglin like they did to Forsid. The way they are going about this seems like they want the city in one piece, or at least in as few pieces as possible." Taran spoke his thoughts.

"Maybe," Ildug said. "Let's hope so."

"Ildug, I'm no tactician, and I won't be any good commanding. Tell me what I can do, though, and I'll do my best," Mathalin said.

"I want you to help Jedur distribute the vaccine against the gonadaw poison throughout the army. Without it, those poisoned arrows could wreak havoc."

Mathalin set off.

"Ildug, I know you need to command your soldiers on the north end of the city. I doubt I'll succeed in entirely stopping it, but I think I can at least hold off that kingalor and buy you some more time."

"Are you sure, Taran? Anyone in the way when that thing charges won't last long."

"Someone has to do it," Taran said, forcing a smile.

Ildug was reluctant. "I suppose you're right." He looked at Taran sadly and clapped him on the back. "Good luck, my friend."

And then he was gone.

Taran looked out over the battlements as the Lentours assembled for war. The clearing to the south of the city was just large enough that the army, including the kingalor could fit in it. He shuddered as he looked at it, fervently hoping his daughter had found a good place to hide.

"Pardil told me to give this to all the men on this section of the wall."

He turned at the voice. Kedrin stood before him, holding a bowl of some greenish brown substance in one hand and offering Taran a spoon of the stuff with the other.

"What's that?" Taran asked, eying the slime suspiciously.

"It's the antidote to the poison."

Taran took the spoon. "But what's in it?"

"I don't think you want to know."

Taran stared at it, then reluctantly swallowed the paste. He gagged. "What was that?"

"Are you sure you want to know?" Kedrin asked. When Taran nodded, he said, "Snails. It's a base of mashed snails. And that's the best part. It gets worse from there."

Taran resisted the urge to vomit. "Are you serious?"

"Pardil swears that it completely neutralizes the poison."

"Thanks. I guess." Taran looked over the battlements. "Are you sure that stuff is safe to eat?"

"No. I'm just hoping it is, because otherwise Pruglin is going to have no army when the Lentours attack." Kedrin followed his father's gaze. "Don't worry. She'll be fine. She's with Lesric, after all. He knows how to escape the Lentours better than anyone."

"Maybe."

"Don't worry!" Kedrin said. "They're safer than we are! They'll just hide out somewhere until this is all over. They're probably miles away by now."

"I hope so," Taran sighed.

The look on Kedrin's face said that he hoped so, too.

CHAPTER 35

"Ready?" Lesric asked.

Lianna nodded. "As ready as I'll ever be."

"Here goes. Let's hope this works."

Lianna's hands were tied behind her back, and she fought the urge to slip them from the loosely knotted rope as Lesric pushed her into the sunny field—and into full view of the Lentours. She tried to appear frightened, which wasn't too hard, since she was terrified that they were going to be discovered.

Walking behind and slightly to the left of her, Lesric was dressed in a Lentour uniform he'd scavenged from the body of one of the soldiers they'd killed. Lianna's bow was slung over his shoulder, and he carried her sword in addition to his own.

A Lentour soldier came to meet them. "What are you doing with a prisoner? Commander won't be pleased. You know we're supposed to kill all the miserable peasants we find."

"I thought this one would be a treat for the kingalor before the battle." At first startled by Lesric's surprisingly good Lentour accent, Lianna then recalled he had lived as a slave in their midst for two years.

"You'd better hope the Commander thinks so too," the man growled. "He doesn't take fondly to rules being broken."

Lianna felt her heart's steady rate start accelerating. Maybe their disguise wasn't going to work after all.

"But," the man continued, "the kingalor hasn't had any human flesh for a while, so maybe he'll pardon you."

They walked through the ranks of soldiers, getting closer and closer to the monstrous beast. Lianna's heart beat faster with each step she took. She didn't have to fake terror as they hurried on.

One wrong move, one wrong word, and they would be dead in an instant. Or worse, they might really be fed to the kingalor. She shuddered as they drew nearer and nearer to the beast, acutely aware of the many eyes boring into her.

When they were about fifty yards away, Lesric whispered just loud enough for her to hear, his lips not moving. "We're going around to the back, just like we planned. You ready?"

She gave an almost imperceptible nod.

As they approached closer, the kingalor turned its head to look at them with one eye that, though small in comparison to the rest of the body, was still massive. Seeing a thin tendril of smoke escape its nostrils, Lianna remembered Taran's warning that gonadaws could breathe fire. Could kingalors too? Its crocodile teeth tapered to sharp points, and its tongue flicked from its mouth, tasting the air. She shivered.

Clustered behind the monster stood a small knot of men. One who appeared to be in charge issued orders. As they watched, two men carrying a leather contraption between them walked up the kingalor's tail, between the rows of spikes, to the beast's back. When they reached the point where the spikes were still four feet tall, they fastened the object between two spines.

"Is that..." Lianna stopped, remembering she wasn't supposed to talk.

"A saddle," Lesric whispered under his breath. "Someone's going to ride that beast!"

The two men made their way down and reached the ground.

"Ready?" Lesric asked as they stopped twenty feet from the kingalor's tail. When she nodded, he began to count down. "Three." Lianna's heart pounded, knowing that failure would mean death. Even success carried no promise of safety. "Two." She shifted her wrists in preparation to rip off the loose ropes. "One." She felt her muscles tense as they prepared to run. "Now!"

Lianna yanked her wrists from the ropes, grabbed her sword and bow from Lesric, and sprinted towards the kingalor's tail. She leaped onto the muscular limb, slipped, caught her footing, and hurried on, climbing the beast's tail. The kingalor twisted its massive neck around and looked at them, then flicked its tail in irritation.

She stumbled and caught herself, hesitating an instant to be sure of her balance, then kept going at a slower pace.

"Lianna, slow down," Lesric admonished. "We don't want to make this thing mad any sooner than we have to."

Lianna obeyed, noting with apprehension that the soldiers below had seen them and were taking action. She had to reach the kingalor's head before they were stopped.

By the time she reached the spines tall enough to hide her from the Lentours below, archers were aiming for them. She knew that for the present they were relatively safe; the beast's nervous movements and their own constant motion made them a difficult target at best. Once they were no longer within the spikes, however, they would be much easier to hit.

The spines grew shorter, and as first her head, then her shoulders were visible above them, she became increasingly uneasy. Then she spotted the first flaw in their plan. The frill around the kingalor's neck flared out, and she realized that it was taller than she was. From the trees a quarter mile away, they had underestimated its size.

"Lesric! What now?" She couldn't get over the barrier.

"This is where things could get exciting. Stay low and hold on to whatever you can," Lesric called as he pushed around her, sword raised over his head, and brought the weapon down on the frill. The sword clove the thin membrane in two, bouncing off the hard scales on the creature's head. Lesric didn't hesitate, slipping through the slit in the membrane. The gap closed like a curtain behind him.

Lianna took a deep breath and followed. Hot blood spurted from the wound and covered her as she passed. Nauseated by it, she cringed and dropped to her hands and knees.

She was just in time. The creature bucked its head and bellowed. She fell on her face, sprawled out on the beast's massive head. She wondered how much it would hurt to fall forty feet. Assuming she survived the fall, of course.

The only good thing about the kingalor's frenzied actions was that the humans below could do nothing to interfere. No archer could hit them with the kingalor bucking like it was, and no one else could follow them up the creature's back.

It was a meager consolation.

The world spun and she grew dizzy as the kingalor bellowed again. Then a bright light filled her vision and she felt heat. She had the sensation of rising, but with the head thrashing about like it was, it was impossible to tell. She closed her eyes and pressed herself flat on the lizard's head, clinging to the scaly hide as best as she could.

She didn't have to be told that she was about to die.

CHAPTER 36

T aran looked up, startled, as the kingalor let out a ear-splitting bellow. It sounded like it was in pain. He hurried to the ramparts and saw that the frill around the beast's neck was flared out. What surprised him even more was the fact that two figures stood precariously on the head of the kingalor. It was too far to tell who they were, but he had a nagging, uneasy suspicion.

The figures sank to their hands and knees just as the kingalor began to toss its head about. Then a stream of fire burst from its mouth, and bellowing in anger, the beast rose to stand on its back legs. A fiery spiral writhed and twisted around its skull as the beast continued to fling its head around.

On hind legs, the kingalor stood nearly eighty feet high. Taran watched in fascination and horror as the monster wrought devastation on the Lentour troops, knocking dozens of soldiers to the ground with its tail, and crushing others beneath its feet. Terrified, the soldiers scattered. Taran smiled.

The creature sank to all fours again, but its head was still enveloped in a swirling, deadly inferno. Taran held his breath, wondering if there was any way whoever was perched on the kingalor's head could survive.

The commanders appeared to be trying to establish order, but the panicked men continued to flee in all directions.

As he watched, Taran felt his spirits rising. Maybe they had a chance after all.

* * * * *

Lianna remained with her eyes closed and face pressed to the scaly hide of the kingalor for what seemed like an eternity. She felt like she was falling, but the scales of the kingalor still felt rough beneath her. Her position relative to the monster hadn't changed. The heat that had surrounded her suddenly vanished, and after a few moments, when the beast seemed to have calmed, she raised her head cautiously and looked around.

The kingalor was standing nearly still, just shifting uneasily every few moments. She guessed that it would take very little to provoke it to the wild frenzy it had just left, and she didn't want to be in this position if its wrath was once again incurred.

Several feet away from her, Lesric surveyed the situation. "Are you okay?" he asked quietly.

She nodded.

"Don't move," he said. "It would be dangerous right now with this monster so nervous, and the soldiers can't see us if we keep low. It's to our advantage if they think us dead."

She nodded. She was content to stay where she was until the kingalor's rage subsided.

Several minutes later, when the creature was as calm as it was going to get, Lesric spoke again. "I'm going to move, slowly. Hang on and stay where you are for now. Things could get wild again."

"You don't have to tell me twice," she said.

Lesric slowly began to slither farther down the kingalor's head. Lianna watched anxiously, desperately hoping the kingalor didn't react violently to his movement.

"Lianna, we're back to plan A. Stay low and move slowly. When you're in position, let me know, and I'll signal when to make your move."

"All right." Lianna began to edge her way cautiously down the right side of the scaly snout. On the left side, Lesric continued to move into the agreed upon position.

When Lianna finally lay directly behind the kingalor's right nostril, she signalled to Lesric, at the same time sliding her sword from its sheath.

"Here goes," he said. He rose to his hands and knees slowly, then waited to see if the kingalor reacted. When it didn't, he cautiously rose to his feet. Still nothing. Inch by inch he drew his sword.

"If this doesn't work, that last wild ride is going to be a breeze compared to this. Get as far away from the edge as you can and hold on for dear life."

"I'll do that," Lianna said, rising to her knees and waiting for his word.

"Three...two...one..." Lesric plunged his sword into the kingalor's left eye. At the same time, Lianna thrust hers in the creature's right nostril. When only four inches of the blade protruded from the surface, she dropped to her stomach and held on to the hilt. If the kingalor went wild, it would serve as a handhold to keep her from plunging to her death.

The kingalor bellowed and bucked its head. Lianna was precariously close to the edge of the beast's snout, and she clung desperately to the hilt of the sword.

Out of the corner of her eye, she saw Lesric withdraw his sword and drive it into the beast's eye a second time. Another roar emanated from the creature, and Lesric withdrew his sword only to plunge it in a third time.

Lianna knew that if the sword could penetrate to the brain directly behind the eye, the beast would die. They had based their entire strategy on that knowledge, and had placed all hope on Lesric's ability to do that. The problem was, if the sword only hit bone, they would just succeed in half blinding and completely infuriating the creature. And if they didn't kill it, they would die. It was the kingalor's life or theirs.

For the fourth time, Lesric stabbed his sword into the eye. This time, though, something was different. Rather than striking some immovable object and stopping there, the sword sunk deep into the kingalor's eye. It continued until first the guard and then the hilt of the sword vanished into the eyeball. Only the pommel now protruded.

Instantly, Lianna felt the difference. The beast froze. And then, so slowly that she almost thought she was imagining it, the kingalor began to topple to the right. Lianna held onto the hilt of her sword and repositioned her body so that she crouched on the edge of its jaw, ready to jump when the kingalor was close to hitting the ground.

As the kingalor fell, it gained momentum until she wondered if she would be able to jump in time. When it neared the ground, Lianna released the sword and jumped off the monster's snout. She landed awkwardly, the jarring impact even worse than she had imagined. The shock sent pain throughout her whole body ached, and the fall had winded her. She didn't want to move, but she knew that remaining where she was was not an option. She gave herself ten seconds to gather her strength, then slowly rose to her feet. Looking over, she saw that Lesric had landed fifteen feet away from her and a few seconds later.

As she hurried back to the body of the kingalor, she discovered to her dismay that her jump was not without a price. Her left knee was injured, and though she could still hobble, each step sent a wave of pain through her leg. Her left wrist was screaming in pain, and she thought she might have broken it in her fall.

Reaching the now stilled body of the monster, Lianna grasped the hilt of her sword and tugged hard. The sword didn't budge. She pulled harder, but there was still no movement. She looked around for anything else she could use as a weapon. Many men had been killed by the kingalor, both in its violent thrashing and in its actual fall. She wearily limped to one of the bodies, acutely aware she was running out of time, and grabbed the sword.

Lianna glanced over her shoulder to see if Lesric was on his feet yet. Instead of Lesric, she saw a blade arcing towards her. Knowing she didn't have time block the sword or duck to either side, Lianna dove towards her attacker, passing under his sword. She caught the man by surprise, and within seconds the fight was over.

But she wasn't out of danger yet. Enraged men, determined to avenge the death of their monster, ran towards her with swords drawn. She looked around desperately for Lesric, but he was nowhere to be seen. She knew she wouldn't last long without him. At best, her swordsmanship wasn't expert, and right now she was injured and exhausted. She doubted she could hold her own against an average swordsman in a one-on-one fight, much less engage an army and come out alive.

Lianna backed towards the body of the kingalor, to prevent soldiers from attacking her from behind.

Her only hope was if Lesric joined her, and even then, they didn't stand much of a chance. Unless...there was always the possibility that men from Pruglin would come to their aid. But she pushed the possibility out of her head, refusing to get her hopes up.

She knew that they had saved the city. But victory couldn't come without some cost, and the price she was going to pay was her life. It had been worth it, but now she was going to die.

The first soldier engaged her. Struggling to stay calm and remember the hours of training with her father, Lianna downed the man. Her next two opponents engaged simultaneously. Lianna blocked a blow from the first one, but the second man thrust for her as soon as she was out of position. She knew she couldn't recover in time. She did her best to deflect the blow, but it wasn't enough.

The cold steel sliced through the flesh just above her knee and she screamed and collapsed to the ground, unable to support her weight. Her sword clattered from her hand as she fell, landing somewhere on the periphery of her vision. The Lentour advanced and raised his sword for another blow. Unarmed, Lianna tried to crawl away, but the effort was too great. She made it less than a yard before collapsing, defeated, onto the ground. The blade descended, and Lianna knew she had no way to save herself. *So this is how it ends,* she thought, closing her eyes and waiting for the blow to land.

But it never did.

CHAPTER 37

"Sir!" one of the soldiers called to Taran, trying to get his attention.

But Taran was already watching. As the man standing on the kingalor's head plunged his sword into its eye, and at the same time the woman stabbed the beast in the nostril, Taran knew. Knew without a doubt that his daughter was in the middle of the Lentour army, standing on top of the creature that was about to destroy the city, and that she would die if he didn't do something.

"Sergeant!" Taran began to bark orders as a bellow sounded from the kingalor. He didn't have much time.

"Yes sir?"

"Get a team together immediately, as many soldiers as we can spare from the wall. Meet me at the gate."

"Yes, sir." The sergeant hurried off to do as Taran had said.

Taran looked around for the messenger Ildug had left with him. He finally spotted the boy twenty yards down the wall. "You!" he said, trying to get the boy's attention.

"Me, sir?"

"Yes, you. Can you take a message to Ildug for me?"

"Yes, sir!" Taran had his full attention now.

"Tell Ildug that Lesric and Lianna are attacking the kingalor and are in grave danger, and that I am leaving

269

with a group of men to help them. If he can spare them, have him send thirty men to help defend this wall."

"Is that all, sir?"

Taran nodded. "Go!"

The boy took off running, and Taran set off to find his second in command, Captain Rynd.

"Rynd!"

"Yes, sir?"

"I'm taking a team out there. Take charge here while I'm gone."

"But sir, that's suicide! You can't go out there!"

"My daughter is risking her life to kill that kingalor. Successful or not, she needs help, and she needs it now!"

"But sir, is it worth risking the lives of all those men for just one person? I mean, I understand that she's your daughter, but still..."

"Lesric is there too. They are both risking their lives for us. And even if that weren't the case, I am in charge here, and I expect to be obeyed. Do you understand?"

"Yes, sir! Sorry, sir. By all means, rescue Lesric. We can't let him die."

It still amazed Taran to see how much respect the people had for Lesric.

Taran looked back towards the kingalor just in time to see Lesric thrust his sword into the creature's eye again. The beast stiffened, then slowly began to topple.

Taran broke into a run. He might be too late already, but he was determined to do his best.

He reached the gate where the team of men waited. Giving the sergeant a look of grateful approval, he nodded to the gatekeeper.

As the gate swung open, Taran and his men raced out. When the last man was outside, the gate closed behind them with a resounding bang. Taran knew that they were sealed out of the city and fully committed to this mission.

As they raced toward the enemy, Taran hoped they were in time to rescue more than the heroes' dead bodies. They engaged the first wave of enemies and fought their way toward the massive body of the kingalor, Taran constantly scanning the area for any sign of Lianna. Nothing. Apprehension mounting, he searched desperately, but there was no sign of her.

When he finally spotted her, his worst fears seemed realized.

Lianna lay on her back, arms thrown up in a vain attempt to defend herself from the sword that was descending to finish her off.

Men moved between them, cutting off his view, and Taran broke into a run. He knew he would never make it in time.

He was too late.

* * * * *

The blow didn't land, and instead, Lianna heard the metallic clang of steel on steel. She opened her eyes, startled. Another sword had intercepted the one that was about to end her life. She followed the sword to the man who yielded it and was even more bewildered to see that her deliverer was another Lentour.

The man dispatched her would-be killer, then stood over her protectively, defending her from the advancing soldiers. The Lentours hung back, confused that one of their own was defending the one who had just destroyed their monster, and with it, the hope of winning the battle. Lianna was as confused as they were.

The man bent down, watching the soldiers out of the corner of his eye. "Lianna! Lianna, answer me!"

She thought she recognized the voice, but everything was growing foggy, and she couldn't place it with a name. "Lesric?" she whispered, barely able to keep her eyes open. She was so tired. She just wanted to close her eyes, wanted to forget this nightmare. Maybe it was all just a bad dream, the whole past five months. Maybe she would wake up to the life she had known before Torrac and the Lentours came back from the dead.

"It's me," he said. "Thank goodness, you're still alive!" He paused, turning to look at the soldiers, then looked at her again. "Your father is coming. We're going to make it."

Lesric stood up again and faced the soldiers now surging forward to finish the fight.

As if in a dream, Lianna heard the faraway sounds of swords clashing and men shouting. She heard her name called, but she was too exhausted to answer. She wanted to let her tired eyes fall closed, but refusing to give up now, she struggled to maintain consciousness.

The pain in her leg faded to a dull throb. Losing all track of time, she lay there only half aware of her surroundings.

Suddenly, everything became clear. A man slipped around Lesric and aimed a slice at Lianna. Lesric turned on him, but the maneuver left his back unguarded. As the first man fell to the ground, another soldier swung his sword at Lesric's exposed back. Lesric turned to face him, but he was too late. The sword sliced into his side as he spun around to engage the Lentour. Lesric retaliated by bringing his sword across in a lightning-quick motion and killing the man. But the damage was done. Lesric staggered, nearly falling over, fighting to maintain his footing and attack the next soldier.

The man swung his sword. Lesric was able to deflect the attack enough to save his life, but not enough to escape completely unscathed. The blade tore his helmet off, and Lianna heard it clatter to the ground. The next thing she heard was a sword clanging as it hit the earth. She knew it was Lesric's.

"I know you!" the Lentour exclaimed in surprise, looking closer at Lesric. "You're the slave who escaped from Cortim, what was it, six months, a year ago? Lesric, I believe it was. Do you regret your decision now? Torrac liked what he saw in you. He might have promoted you, might have made you great. But you rebelled, and now you will die as a result of your folly."

Through the haze in her mind, Lianna wondered how the man still remembered Lesric. It was eight months since Lesric had been a slave at Cortim Castle, and it seemed strange that the soldier would recognize a slave gone so long.

"I would never have helped him," Lesric gasped. "You slaughter innocent people and pillage their homes. A path of destruction follows in your wake. I refuse to be a part of that." In a swift movement, Lesric dove for his sword.

"You will regret your words, slave." The man raised his sword over his head. It began to descend in seemingly slow motion, but Lianna knew that Lesric couldn't block the blow before it landed.

"No!" Lianna heard herself screaming with the last of her strength.

Then everything went black.

CHAPTER 38

W here am I? The fog in Lianna's mind was lifting, and she opened her eyes. Shapes blurred together, but she could make out the faint outline of someone bending over her. She was in bed, although she didn't know how she got there.

Then a voice broke the stillness, seeming harsh and loud after the silence. "Go tell Taran she's awake."

Her brain was sending her one message from every part of her body: pain. Lianna struggled to sit up. Agony shot through her body. She collapsed back on the bed, trying to remember what had happened. Like a flash, everything came back to her. The kingalor. The soldiers. Lesric. And then blackness.

Her vision grew clearer, and she realized she was in her own bedroom and that her mother was standing over her.

"Lianna?" Rilan wrapped Lianna in a loose hug, tears streaming down her face to land on Lianna's. Lianna weakly returned her embrace, and a moment later Taran entered her field of vision.

She had never seen her father cry, but his eyes were shimmering, and one tear rolled down his cheek. Taran and Rilan both seemed unable to believe she was all right.

"I was sure you were dead," Taran said, looking

down at her. "I came as fast as I could, but I would have been too late if Lesric hadn't been there." Suddenly, he stopped and looked away.

"Lesric," Lianna said. "What happened to Lesric?"

Taran shook his head. "I was too late. I barely made it in time to save you. The last time I saw him, the Lentour had disarmed him and..." he stopped. "Men got between us and I couldn't see any more until I reached you. Lesric wasn't there."

Lianna remembered how Lesric had saved her life and in her mind saw the sword of the Lentour descending again. Tears blurred her vision. Over the last few months, Lesric had been her brother's friend, or the leader of their various spying missions. But she realized that something had changed back at Pardil's hideout, as Kedrin hovered between life and death. Lesric had become her friend, too, almost a kind of second brother. He had saved her life, and he had died for it. It wasn't right.

Then Kedrin entered the room. His eyes, too, were watery. "I thought we lost you too," he said. "You saved the city, Lianna. After the kingalor was dead, the Lentours didn't have any fight left in them."

"It wasn't me," Lianna said. "It was Lesric. He came up with the plan, and he was the one who actually killed it."

"Still, I doubt that he could have done it alone," Taran said.

"And the people don't think so either," Kedrin said. "You're a hero, Lianna. You wouldn't believe how many of them have come asking how you're doing. It got to the point we had to ban everyone from the property, and even then there were so many trespassers that Father had to set a guard. Now there's just a crowd on the road, waiting for a glimpse of the kingalor killer."

"You had better be joking, Kedrin," Lianna said, looking at him closely.

"He's not," Taran said, holding back a smile. They all knew how much Lianna hated being the center of attention.

"It's awful," Kedrin said. "Every time I step outside the house, I'm surrounded by a hundred people, all asking a million questions and wanting to know exactly how you're doing. It's rather annoying. You may want to consider wearing a disguise once you're well enough to go outside again."

"You're not making me feel any better," Lianna said.

"Actually, maybe having a sister who is the most famous person in the city isn't so bad after all. Imagine all the speeches I'll get to watch you make! It will be amazing. In fact..."

"Kedrin! Stop it!"

"As you wish, Lady Kingalor Killer."

"Leave the poor girl alone, Kedrin," Rilan said. "She finally wakes up after being unconscious for four days and you immediately start teasing her. You should be ashamed of yourself."

Kedrin started to apologize, but Lianna interrupted. "Four days? It's been four days?"

Rilan nodded.

Lianna was shocked. She couldn't believe that it had been that long.

"I'm sorry, Lianna. I'm sure you want to rest." Rilan turned and was about to leave, but Lianna stopped her.

"No, don't. I'm fine."

Someone knocked on the door, and Taran hurried to open it. A servant entered, carrying a bowl of soup. Rilan took it and thanked her.

"I thought that you might be ready for some food, Lianna. If you're not, you don't have to eat it."

Lianna forced a smile. "I'll take it."

* * * * *

Lianna's injuries were more severe than she thought at first, and it was two weeks before she was strong enough to leave her room. When she finally hobbled downstairs one night, Rilan and the cook prepared a feast to celebrate, and invited Alssa, Elariam, and their parents to join them. It was the first time Lianna had seen them since they were separated all those weeks before at the river.

"Well, Lianna, it's good to see you alive and well," Alssa said. "You know you're the talk of the city after what you did."

"So I've been told," Lianna sighed. "Unfortunately."

"Oh, cheer up. It's not that bad," Elariam said. "Better to be famous and have people flock to you every time you step outside than to have been killed. When we got separated at the river, we were sure we had failed and we would never see you again. And when we heard you were fighting the kingalor…" Her voice trailed off. " It–it wasn't good."

Lianna tried to smile, but couldn't. Kedrin, standing nearby, had the same faraway look in his eyes. With Lesric, they had penetrated Cortim Castle, been captured by Torrac's men, and nearly been killed a number of different times. On many of those occasions, Lesric had saved their lives. She still couldn't believe that Lesric was dead, and the knowledge he was killed protecting her filled her with guilt. If it weren't for her, Lesric would have survived.

"I'm so sorry," Alssa said. "We were as sad to learn about Lesric as you and Kedrin." She stopped to consider her words. "Well, maybe it's not quite the same. We didn't know Lesric as well as you did, but I did go to Cortim Castle, and his abilities as a leader saved our lives on a number of occasions."

"I know," Lianna said. Even she hadn't known Lesric as well as Kedrin had. Lesric had been the brother Kedrin had never had, and he was having a harder time coping with Lesric's death than anyone else.

Watching him while they ate, Lianna was worried about her brother. He seemed distant and quiet, staring off into nothingness. The others seemed to notice and tried to engage him in conversation, but Kedrin only talked when necessary. Lianna knew he was thinking about his friend.

While it was meant to be a joyful occasion, an air of sorrow hung over the room.

Life would never be quite the same again.

CHAPTER 39

Six weeks after the battle, Lianna finally left the house. She had put it off as long as possible, but it was inevitable, and even though she was still weak, she couldn't procrastinate any longer. And it was just as bad as she had expected.

A throng of people swarmed her, asking questions and expressing their gratitude to her for saving the city. Kedrin smirked as he watched her struggle to retain her composure, and she could tell he found it amusing. Although it irritated her, she was glad to see some of the old Kedrin back. This glimpse of the Kedrin from before the battle and Lesric's death gave her hope that his condition wasn't permanent.

She, Kedrin, and Rilan were going to meet Taran at the meeting house. Lianna dreaded having to endure the crowds of people as they walked to the heart of the city, but she dreaded what would happen once they arrived even more. The Council had insisted on having a ceremony in her honor. She had done everything she could to avoid it, but Taran said that the whole city was starting to complain that nothing had been done for her. Something had to be done.

She was grateful when Kedrin returned to the house, riding back and leading two horses behind him. At least she could reach the square quicker this way, and it would be easier than walking. She had improved significantly, but she was still weak and tried not to stay on her feet for too long.

When they arrived at the city square, Lianna dismounted and tied her horse to a post, then entered the meeting house. She noticed that the square was full of people, and her apprehension mounted. She followed Kedrin into the large room where the Council met, and as soon as she entered, a cheer broke out. The councilors rose to their feet as if she were royalty.

Lianna flushed with embarrassment. It was already more than enough for the citizens to treat her this way, but for the councilors to do so was a different matter entirely. She saw her father cast a sympathetic glance in her direction, and she knew that he had done his best to dissuade the rest of the Council from what they were about to do. Regardless of his efforts, she was still being cheered on, and the worst part hadn't come yet.

When the councilors finally quieted, Mathalin spoke. "Lianna, the city is in your debt for saving us from the kingalor. We know you would rather not go through with this ceremony, but the people demand it, and we hope you will bear with us."

Lianna inwardly groaned. She was desperate for a way out, but she knew there was nothing she could do to stop this.

A servant entered the room and whispered something in Mathalin's ear. Mathalin nodded, and the servant left. "It's time to go."

The councilors left their table and moved towards the door. "Lianna, wait inside the door while we go onto the platform. We'll let you know when to follow us." Then they left.

Lianna looked at her mother. "Why, oh why couldn't Father have stopped them?"

"He tried," Rilan said, "but they wouldn't listen. They understand that it's not what you want, but it's more for the people than for you. The city insisted that something be done, and this is what the councilors came up with. Your father was outvoted. I know you don't want to do this, but it's important you do."

Lianna groaned. "I didn't even do anything!"

"You may not have dealt the deathblow to the kingalor, but if it weren't for you, I doubt the city would still be here. They need someone to praise, and you're the one they have."

Lianna stopped around the corner from the open door and heard Mathalin talking. "People of Pruglin! About a month ago, a monster threatened our walls, and we had no hope against the Lentours. But when the army was about to destroy us, Lesric and Lianna attacked them first. They rode the kingalor eighty feet in the air, surrounded by flames, while it did its best to kill them. Then, when its wrath had cooled, they wounded it mortally. After the creature fell, they fought the Lentour army until help could arrive, and in the battle Lesric was killed. But Lianna survived, and today we are here to thank her for what she did." He paused, and Lianna knew it was time for her dreaded ordeal.

She took a deep breath, then stepped into the bright sunlight. A cheer erupted from the crowd, and she forced herself to mount the steps. Her father met her at the top.

"As members of the Pruglin Council, we would like to thank you for your service to the city," he told her. The crowd continued to cheer, and Lianna was grateful that her father and Mathalin were making their speeches short. Several other Council members added to what Mathalin had said, droning on for another two minutes.

She was relieved beyond measure when she finally descended the steps of the platform. Ducking out of sight of the assembled crowd, she returned to the building as quickly as possible.

"I'm proud of you," Rilan said.

Lianna attempted to smile, but was unable to muster the will. "Just don't ever make me do that again."

"If you agree not to do anything else important, and to stay away from other people doing anything important, and to not do anything helpful to other people, then you probably won't have to again. But the damage from doing it this time is already done. You're just lucky you're not queen of Pruglin." Kedrin's face was straight, but Lianna knew he was inwardly amused.

"Kedrin, stop it! Can't you just listen to me this once?"

He smirked, and Lianna sighed. The old Kedrin was back, all right. Maybe that wasn't as good as she had thought earlier.

As Lianna sat down with Kedrin and her parents, the smell of roast hog wafted through the room. Other scents permeated the air, and her mouth watered as servants began to bring out the food. She didn't remember the last time she'd eaten this well.

When the meal was over, they set off for home. Once again, citizens swarmed Lianna, eager to see the one who had killed the kingalor. It didn't matter how much Lianna insisted that she hadn't killed the monster. Everyone was convinced that she was a hero.

Lianna did her best to be polite, but as hard as she

tried, she simply couldn't come across as friendly as she would have liked. Her frustration mounting, she found it harder and harder to keep a smile on her face as the unending line of people flocked about her. She was tired, and all she wanted to do was go home, but their progress was severely hampered by the crowd.

When she finally reached the house, Lianna could barely walk. Supported by her mother, she staggered upstairs and collapsed onto her bed. Her leg was paining her more than it had for weeks, and she was sure the strain of the evening had reinjured it.

"I'm so sorry, Lianna," Rilan said. "I didn't think it would be that bad."

"If this doesn't improve, I don't know what I'll do," Lianna moaned. "I just can't do that again."

"I know," her mother said sympathetically. "Is there anything I can get for you?"

Lianna wearily shook her head. She just wanted to go to sleep.

Rilan nodded, turned, and left the room. Lianna was asleep before the door closed behind her.

* * * * *

The next morning, Lianna felt worse than she had in several weeks. Her wrist ached, the slash on her leg felt as if it had reopened, and her head throbbed nearly unbearably. She didn't know what she would do if this was what happened when she left the security of the estate for an hour and a half. At this rate, she was going to have to stay in the house until she was completely well again.

"I shouldn't have let you do it," Rilan murmured when she came to check on her. Lianna barely heard her, and was only distantly aware when her mother left the room.

An hour later, Rilan returned with Taran. Lianna forced herself to sit up as they told her what they had decided to do.

"We're going to leave the city," Rilan said. "Until you recover, we're going to stay with my sister, Kiral, in her farm on the outside borders of Pruglin District."

A wave of relief swept over Lianna. In the country, away from the people so grateful to her for something she wasn't even certain she had helped to do, she would finally be able to recover fully.

"We'll leave as soon as we can be ready," Taran continued. "Oslir will take care of the house while we're gone, and the Council will have to do without me for a few weeks. We need to get away from the city anyway, and this is as good an opportunity as any."

* * * * *

Kiral and her family welcomed them warmly, and Lianna knew as soon as they arrived that she would be able to recuperate in no time at all.

Kalindra, her cousin, was five years younger than Lianna, and they had only seen each other a few times, but Lianna liked her. After a week at the farm, Lianna was sure they could become good friends.

Kalindra and her younger brother, Tomas, eagerly plied both Lianna and Kedrin for stories of their adventures with the Lentours. Lianna became certain that their interest in gonadaws contained far too little awe for the beasts' ability to rip a full grown man to shreds. On the other hand, Kedrin, in her opinion, did a little too much to cultivate a healthy respect in them for the killing powers of the creature. She was surprised that her cousins still asked for stories after the bloody ones he managed to come up with.

Lianna appreciated that though Kalindra was always asking for stories, she still treated her normally. She seemed to sense Lianna's reluctance to be admired as a hero, and gave her just enough commendation to show approval, but not so much to make Lianna uncomfortable. The only other people capable of that were her parents, and she was grateful for Kalindra's understanding.

Lianna improved rapidly with the combination of fresh country air and relative solitude. In the peace of the farm, Lianna wanted to forget about the Lentours. About the destruction they had caused and the people they had slaughtered. About everything that had happened since Lesric showed up in Pruglin City all those months ago. She almost did. Almost, but not quite. She allowed the war to slip to a back corner of her mind, feeling safe and secure in the rural, secluded area.

Maybe now that his kingalor is dead and he's failed to defeat Pruglin, Torrac will give up. Maybe this reprieve is permanent. Maybe.... Lianna knew her reflections were unrealistic, but she wanted to believe that they were safe from Torrac and his armies.

She didn't think about the island far to the south, off the coast of Milsad Forest.

And she didn't know about the weapon the Lentours were at work on, an instrument of destruction meant to conquer Pruglin once and for all.

Or the gonadaws that stalked the forest in the former district of Forsid.

"Lianna! Why don't you come and tell us about the siladis in the Syntor Wasteland?"

"Again?" she asked, and Kedrin grinned from behind Tomas.

"It's never going to end," he said. "Killing the kingalor ensured that. You might as well just get used to being a hero, because that's your new life."

"You were there too. You can't tell them?"

"Come on, Lianna!" Tomas said eagerly.

"All right," Lianna said, trying to ignore Kedrin's *I-told-you* look. "But then I think you need to have Kedrin tell you about the time he got shot crossing the Pruglin River."

It was Kedrin's turn to scowl.

Made in the USA
San Bernardino, CA
15 December 2019